T0168122

SOMETHING LIKE A LOVESONG

SomeThing Like a LoveSong

BECCA BURTON

interlude **press** • new york

interlude ✦✦ press • new york

To everyone who has had to fight to love whom they love.

CHAPTER 1

The waiting room is drab, the chairs are too soft and the worn beige carpet has seen better days. A photograph of a bright yellow sunflower hangs on the wall next to the clock, and Dylan wonders if it's supposed to cheer him up, supposed to remind him of the vibrant beauty of life or some other ridiculous sentiment.

It doesn't.

He stares at the clock, which is bolted behind a cage of bars, as if clocks stolen from waiting rooms are in high demand. The second hand jumps as though trying to escape the bars; the hour hand strains toward the three.

Dylan closes his eyes, leans back in his chair and tries to ignore the throbbing of his arm, the pounding in his head, the aching in his throat. His hands are still shaking; his whole body vibrates with each beat of his heart. He tries to take deep breaths, the way the emergency room nurse told him to, but his chest feels tight, as if iron bands have wrapped around his ribs. He can't breathe, but he wants to scream, wants to do something,

1

anything, to escape the overwhelming emptiness of the waiting room pressing in around him; the neverending ticking of the clock, like gunshots in his ears; the flower glaring bright yellow at him.

"Mr. Nayar?" A quiet voice disturbs the empty waiting room. Dylan's eyes snap open. A nurse in dark green scrubs is looking at him. A wave of dizziness hits him when he stands, and he reaches back for the chair, misses. Then a hand is at his right elbow. It holds him steady until he can blink away the pinpoints of light at the edge of his vision.

"There you go." The nurse steadying him looks pointedly at the sling sheathing his left arm. "Feeling better?"

Dylan nods, despite the pounding in his head.

"Landon... Is he..." The words catch in his throat; his eyes are glued to the nurse's face for any hint of what she's about to tell him.

"We finished the surgery." Her voice is calm and infuriatingly even. "The doctor will come talk to you soon, but we're moving him into his room now."

"Can I... Will I..."

"Someone will come get you when he's settled," the nurse reassures him with her hand still gentle on his arm. Should he ask her name? "I know waiting is hard, but I promise you Landon is in good hands."

Dylan swallows, nods and looks at his feet. He's not sure what else he's supposed to do.

"Have you called your family?"

"No," Dylan manages, still staring at his shoes: once-white Converse, now stained with dirt and gravel and the dark brown of dried blood.

"Call someone." The nurse gives his arm a tiny squeeze. "You shouldn't be alone right now."

"Okay." Dylan looks up when the nurse steps away. She offers him a reassuring smile and exits through the doors that lead into the operating room. He falls back into his seat and fumbles with his bag until he manages to find his phone. It takes two attempts to type in his passcode, and his hands shake so much that he almost dials the wrong number before finally selecting the one he wants.

It rings, rings again, and a sudden urgency comes over him: He needs to talk to someone *now*, and he doesn't know why he waited this long to call in the first place.

A tired voice comes through, soft and hoarse with sleep. "Hello?"

"Mom?" Dylan doesn't have the energy to be embarrassed by the way his voice cracks, as it used to so often when he was a teenager.

"Dylan? Honey, what time is it?" Dylan can hear the sound of something being knocked over, the click of a lamp switch.

"I'm sorry, it's so late… I shouldn't have called." A glance up at the caged clock shows that it's nearly three-thirty in the morning.

"Nonsense." Her voice is less tired, now, and taking on the edge of panic that only late night phone calls can induce. "What's going on?"

Dylan's response catches in his throat like broken glass, and he can't do it, he can't say it.

"Dylan, you need to talk to me, okay? Are you hurt?" His mother uses the even, commanding cadence she employs during her yoga classes, and Dylan's chest loosens almost immediately.

His eyes close and he tries to imagine sitting on a mat in her studio, imagine that everything is calm around him.

"I'm okay, just…" He takes a deep breath and tries to swallow around the cutting dryness of his throat. "Just a dislocated shoulder and… " Exhale. Inhale. "A sprained wrist. But… Lan…" He can't finish. The lump in his throat is too painful.

"Are you at the hospital?" He hears the sound of rustling fabric, his dad's voice in the background.

Dylan nods, still fixated by the brown smudge on his shoe.

"They won't let me see him," he manages in a choked whisper.

"We're on our way, right now, okay? You stay right there and we'll be there as soon as we can."

Dylan can hear a door slam, a car engine rev to life.

"Thank you," he whispers and disconnects the call with numb fingers. He stares at his phone. The background is a picture of Landon from a few weeks ago sitting in the grass with a praying mantis cupped in his hands and a look of amazement on his face. Dylan told him to put it down, that he was disrupting the poor insect's life, but Landon insisted on taking a picture first. "Because it's cool," Landon said, and Dylan chided him for being twenty-six going on five, and that he was turning into one of the kids he works with at the children's hospital but took the photo anyway.

The screen goes black, and Dylan lets the phone fall onto his lap. Now Landon is somewhere in this hospital; his skull is a mess of pieces that even a surgeon can't seem to puzzle back together. Dylan has no idea if he's supposed to be screaming, or crying inconsolably, or demanding something, *anything*—if there's some code for situations like this that he doesn't know and isn't following, a convenient waiting room etiquette guide detailing what to do after your entire life has been ripped from your hands, beaten down and torn apart, leaving you with only the immeasurable horror that this is it: This is the end, and it's all your fault. It's the end and you didn't even get to say goodbye.

He focuses on the simple act of breathing, stares at the clock where it nestles in safety behind its iron bars and gears himself up for another conversation, this time with Landon's parents.

"Family of Lewin?"

Dylan blinks his eyes open, and the world slowly rights itself around him. He doesn't know when he started to drift off, or whether it was exhaustion or the inability to cope that made his eyelids so heavy. Maybe it was the pain meds floating through his system, filling his brain with cotton as they ease the pain in his arm. They seem to be making everything around him both surreal and muted, with sounds and colors running together like an old videotape.

"Excuse me, are you Landon's husband?" Dylan forces himself to look up and sees a nurse, her face full of concern. It's a different nurse, with light blonde hair and pale blue scrubs.

"Fiancé," he says, and groans when he tries to sit up straight.

"Easy, hon," the nurse says, a hand on his shoulder. She kneels in front of him, offers him a Styrofoam cup. Dylan takes it in his good hand, sips the cold water and wills his head to stop spinning.

"How are you feeling?"

"Okay." Dylan takes another sip of water. He blinks and takes in the chairs, the carpet, the bright flower picture. "Landon—how is he? Is he okay?"

"That's what I'm here for." Only the small smile on her face keeps Dylan from panicking. "We have him settled into his room, and the doctor has okayed visitors, if you'd like to see him."

"Yes, yes, of course." Dylan quickly stands, wavering as he finds his footing.

"Careful," the nurse says, with a gentle hand on his back and an expression of concern. Her nametag identifies her as "Brittany." "You need to take it easy."

"Please, I need to see him," Dylan stresses, urgency welling inside him. "He's… he's going to be okay, right? He's going to live?"

The nurse meets his eyes; her gaze is warm. "The doctor will talk to you about everything soon, but Landon is still in critical condition. Right now we're working on keeping down his brain swelling."

Dylan nods. Brittany touches his elbow and leads him out of the waiting room, to an elevator and onto another floor. The intensive care unit is huge, quiet but still bustling with activity, even this late at night. Dylan barely notices, just follows Brittany, in her baby blue scrubs, down to the end of the hall. She takes him to a room in the corner with large, sliding glass doors and a half-drawn tan curtain covering the entrance.

They pause outside the door. Brittany helps Dylan clean his good hand with sanitizer and offers him an encouraging look before leading him inside. The room is dimly lit and oddly quiet; only a gentle *whirr-click* fills the space. The walls are light tan, Dylan notes, his mind oddly distant, and there's another flower picture near the bathroom, this one a pale purple.

Landon's bed is in the center of the room, and Dylan's heart begins to pound in his chest as he takes a step forward, hesitates.

Landon looks so small, tucked into the middle of the bed, and everything about the scene is unnatural and wrong. His head is wrapped with thick bandages, for which Dylan is grateful—he isn't sure he could handle *that*. Just the thought of what's happening to Landon, to his fiancé, is enough to make his throat constrict, his chest tighten.

A ventilator tube parts Landon's lips, and his chest rises and falls in equal, rhythmic whirrs. IVs line his arms; the wires snake from under his hospital gown. His freckles stand out starkly against the unnatural pale hue of his skin, except where the deep purple of a bruise creeps from under the bandages and swells down to his left cheekbone. It seems impossible that only hours ago they were laughing in the park, holding hands and eating gyros from the small corner stand; it's like some distant memory, a fading dream. But the ache deep in Dylan's chest, the way his stomach is knotting itself, the too-clean smell of the hospital burning his nose, Landon's face, battered and bruised—Dylan can't look away—all this is too real to be a dream, no matter how badly Dylan wants to just wake up, wants all this to go away and everything to be *okay*.

"You can touch him, if you want," Brittany says, her voice soft. "We need to make sure to reduce extra stimulation, to allow his brain time to recover, but it's okay to hold his hand."

Dylan looks up at her. Her smile is kind and understanding. Then he turns back to Landon and takes a small step forward. Landon's hand is right there, resting above the covers, and Dylan doesn't know why he's so nervous; he's held Landon's hand more times than he could begin to count. But, surrounded by machines and tubes, Landon has never looked so utterly fragile, as if he could shatter at the lightest touch.

"It's okay," Brittany says from behind him, and Dylan squeezes his eyes shut, tears pricking behind his eyelids. "You won't hurt him."

Landon's skin is cold; his hand is unnaturally still. Even in sleep Landon's hand would always find Dylan's, their fingers would curl together like a reflex.

Not now.

"I'm so sorry," Dylan whispers, holding on a little tighter. "I'm so…"

His voice catches; the words bottle up in his throat, unable to escape. Landon's chest rises, falls, in, out.

In, out.

"You're so hurt, and it's my fault," Dylan manages, his voice barely audible above the machines keeping Landon alive. "It's all my fault and I'm…" He exhales slowly. "I'm so sorry."

He swipes his thumb across Landon's knuckles, over the dips and grooves, and vaguely notes that Brittany has left them alone. He sinks down into the small chair beside the bed, not letting go of Landon's hand.

"You need to fight, okay? I need you here, with me, and I can't…" There's nothing left inside him except an empty, hollow feeling and the knowledge that Landon can't hear him. Landon's engagement ring is in a dish on a table beside the bed, along with his watch, and Dylan fishes them out and tucks them into his pocket.

Sometime in the next hour, Landon's blood pressure drops; alarms sound, and a nurse takes Dylan back to another waiting room, uses big words that Dylan doesn't understand and asks him to wait while they stabilize Landon. The doctor finally makes an appearance and uses more big words that leave Dylan blinking and his mind spinning as he tries to understand. But he's too tired; exhaustion weighs into his bones, and all he wants to do is curl up on the floor and sleep until this is all over.

"Honey?" His mom's voice is soft, and Dylan raises his eyes— he doesn't have the energy to do much more—as she approaches, followed closely by his father. She's wearing a purple silk shrug over her nightgown, and her dark, curly hair is swept back in a hasty ponytail. His dad has actually changed into a semblance of normal clothing: worn jeans and a T-shirt Dylan's grandparents sent from India.

"Darling, are you okay?" his mom asks, hesitating only for a second before crouching to wrap Dylan in a hug while being cautious with the sling on his left arm. Dylan doesn't respond, just lets his head fall against his mother's shoulder, breathes in the familiar sandalwood scent of her perfume and lets himself go. For the first time since he was separated from Landon, coming off the ambulance, the tears come, hot and thick. His shoulders shake from the force of them, and he can't stop, doesn't even try to stop, as he sinks into the warmth of his mother's embrace.

"It's okay," she murmurs, as her hand lightly strokes his back. "It's going to be okay."

Dylan doesn't believe it. Nothing is going to be okay again. There's no guarantee that Landon will even make it through the night. But he doesn't argue, just closes his eyes and drifts in the familiar sound of her voice.

"Adele," his dad says, "let him breathe."

Adele draws away, her hand still resting on Dylan's shoulder.

"Dylan, what happened?" his dad asks, taking a seat in the chair beside him. Adele shoots his dad a look.

"Give him time, Sam," she says, turning back to look at Dylan, with her hand on his shoulder. "When you're ready, honey."

Dylan looks at his dad, at his face lined with concern and fear, and knows they deserve an explanation after a late night phone call that no parent wants.

"We, um…" He licks his lips and tries to hold his voice steady. The police have taken his statement, and he's had to relay everything to the doctor's and nurses, and he's not sure he can get through another retelling. "We went out for gyros, and it was so nice out, you know? Landon wanted…" He wavers, almost loses the words and looks down at his right hand, clenched into a fist in his lap. "We wanted to enjoy the weather and there's a gyro stand a few blocks away, so we decided to go for a… a walk. The, uh, the sun was starting to set and…"

He pauses, his jaw clenches at the memory: the golden sunset, long shadows starting to drift over the park, Landon whining playfully, the taste of tzatziki still on his lips.

"I insisted on taking the shortcut through the alley and Landon didn't want to, and I told him…" The painful knot is back in Dylan's throat and tears threaten to overwhelm him once again. "I told him to stop worrying so much and live a little, and…" Dylan looks up at his mom; his eyes plead with her to understand.

"We, um, kissed in the alley, and then there was this group of guys. They pulled us apart and said such… *awful* things, and I yelled at them and one of them grabbed me and Landon…"

He takes a shaky breath and tries to wipe away the tears on his cheeks, but they won't stop. Adele takes his hand and holds it in a loose grip, anchoring him. Calming him.

"Landon tried to push them away, but one of them…" His heart begins to race, his breaths come more quickly. "One of them picked up a pipe and they just… beat him. And I couldn't do anything and I… I thought he was dead. I thought he was dead."

He can barely get any air. Every inhalation is ragged and painful.

"Is he…" Sam starts. Dylan shifts in his seat and winces when his arm throbs.

"He's alive," Dylan says, his voice flat; he's utterly drained now, and his remaining energy ebbs with every word. "His skull… they said it was badly fractured. And they did surgery, but his brain is swelling too much, so they have to leave his head open and they won't let me stay with him and… and they're not sure if he's going to make it."

His parents are silent and Dylan is glad; he's so *tired*, tired of talking, tired of waiting rooms and the burning smell of hospitals, tired of the fear curling tightly inside him, and all he wants to do is sleep. He just wants to sleep.

"They won't let you see him?" Sam asks, an edge to his voice.

"It's not… a *gay* thing," Dylan says without opening his eyes. "He's just… he's so critical right now they need room to work, I guess. They said I could go back again when he's more stable."

An odd calm descends over Dylan, a strange stillness.

"What did they say his chances are?" Sam asks cautiously. Dylan's mom's grip on his hand tightens.

"If they can stop the bleeding and get the swelling down he might make it." The doctor's words are almost a distant memory. "But they said… there's so much trauma, even if he does make it, he'll be… he won't…"

11

Dylan opens his eyes. His mom is still crouched in front of him, concern on her face, and Dylan thinks of Landon, down the hall and behind those glass doors, thinks of the nurses and doctors trying their hardest to save him.

"It's all my fault, I shouldn't have..." Dylan starts. He doesn't remember when he started crying again. "It was my *stupid* idea to take that shortcut and... Landon didn't want to, but I did and then... those guys... and I yelled at them when I should have just ignored it and now Landon might die, and it's all my fault..."

"It's *not* your fault," Adele is firm despite the tears in her eyes. "No one is to blame except those men, okay?"

Dylan nods, sniffling. He doesn't believe it.

"No more of those thoughts, all right?"

Dylan just looks at her; his eyelids feel heavy, as if every blink is taking more energy that he doesn't have.

"I'm going to go see if I can talk to someone," Adele says, looking at her husband. "Stay with Dylan."

His mother rises gracefully and makes her way out of the waiting room in the direction of the nursing desk. Sam doesn't say anything; Dylan supposes there's really nothing left to say, and his dad has never been one to fill silence with meaningless words. So they wait and listen to the bustle of the intensive care unit as the night bleeds into morning, with the clock still ticking behind its cage.

Adele returns ten minutes later with Brittany. She stands to the side and lets the nurse crouch in front of Dylan, in almost the exact spot Adele had been in earlier. Brittany places a soft hand on his knee.

"Landon's as stable as he can be right now," Brittany says. Her blonde hair is pulled back but strands escape unnoticed, the evidence of a busy shift. "Go home and get some rest. We'll call you if anything happens, I promise."

"I just saw him and he's doing fine, honey," Adele adds. Her eyes are red, as if she's been crying. "We'll come back as soon as you get some sleep."

Dylan nods, and both the nurse and Adele look surprised, as if they'd been expecting him to argue with them. But he has nothing left inside of him to argue with; he feels wilted and wrung out. Sleeping sounds like the only thing he could do right now.

"Okay," he says. The nurse squeezes his knee, stands and turns to his mom.

"Call anytime for an update." Brittany looks back at Dylan. "I promise we'll take good care of him."

Adele gives the nurse a hug and thanks her for everything. Dylan wonders if he should say something, if he should make some outrageous demand or insist on staying with Landon. Instead he wants to run away, to get away from the cheerful pictures of flowers, the clocks behind cages and the smells and sounds of the hospital pressing in around him.

"Can we go home?" he asks in a whisper, looking up at his mom.

"Of course," she says, her hands under his good arm when he stands, firm and supportive against his back. "We'll take you home."

He doesn't remember leaving the hospital, barely remembers sitting in the back of his parents' car with his forehead pressed against the cool glass of the window as he watched the world pass by: the sun beginning to rise, a few runners out for early morning jogs, people walking dogs pulling eagerly at leashes. It was all so *normal*, the world going on with its business as if nothing had happened, as if two lives weren't entirely changed last night. As if nothing was wrong.

Now, back in their apartment, the air is warm; they'd left the windows open before they went out and July has been hot in a pleasant way. Landon always runs slightly cold. He loves the summer and sleeping in underwear, loves waking up to the smell of fresh air and the sounds of the city below them.

Dylan breathes in the salty tang of the Play-Doh Landon had been preparing for the kids at work, the sweet note from the cucumber reed diffuser Dylan had picked up on his last Target run, the ever-present aroma of morning coffee; the familiar scents of the apartment wash out the too-clean smell of hospital. Everything is the same as they left it: Landon's work schedule stuck to the fridge, his keys forgotten on the counter even though he'd insisted he had them when they left, his sweatshirt thrown across the back of the couch despite Dylan's constant reminders that they have a perfectly functional closet in the bedroom.

Adele and Sam are talking softly, but he doesn't pay them any attention as he picks up the sweatshirt, the material worn and thin, and drapes it over his arm. He makes his way through the small apartment to the bedroom. Everything is too quiet, too empty. Landon's absence makes everything seem off-kilter, as though this isn't the place they've called home for the past three years.

The edge of the bed dips where he sits and stares at the dried blood on his shoes, at the blood soaked into his jeans, so dark the drops could be mistaken for dirt. He remembers the overwhelming anger, the way it felt to yell at those men, the smell of alcohol on their breath, the pop his shoulder made when they grabbed him, the crack as the pipe connected with Landon's head, the way he just dropped, immediately limp, and still they kept going, kept hitting him over and over again. He remembers fighting against them, screaming. They were *killing* Landon, and there was nothing Dylan could do; they were too strong and Landon was going to die, right there in front of him.

Dylan shakes his head and tries to clear the thoughts, but they won't go. He clutches Landon's sweatshirt to his chest and buries his face in it. He remembers the shout down the alley when someone finally approached, the way the men scattered, the way the pavement jarred his knees when they let him go. He remembers crawling over to Landon, remembers the man, a cop, calling in for help, remembers the fear sinking into him that Landon was dead. He remembers hovering over Landon, unsure where to touch him with Landon's blood soaking into his own pants, his shoes.

"He's not dead," Dylan whispers into the sweatshirt. "He's not dead."

He puts the sweatshirt down and pulls off his clothes—awkward, with only one working arm—and then buries them in the hamper, hidden, forgotten. It's too warm, but he slips the sweatshirt on anyway. He can almost pretend Landon is there, brushing his teeth and getting ready to curl into bed beside him.

He crawls into bed alone and pulls Landon's pillow against his chest. Someone enters the room and sits on the bed next to him. A hand rests gently on his shoulder, but he doesn't open his eyes; he's already beginning to drift into sleep.

Chapter 2

It happens in the library.

Dylan glances down at the scrap of paper in his hand and reads the call number of the book he's looking for, scribbled in the handwriting of the librarian at the front desk.

"HB," he murmurs, glancing up at the rows of bookshelves. He feels as though he's trying to find his way through a maze, trying to find one specific book in a sea of thousands. This part of the library is surprisingly void of students, tucked away in the back, and one of the overhead lights keeps flickering.

Dylan locates the shelf and runs his finger along the spines of the books until he finds the one he's looking for: The Global Economic Crisis and Potential Implications for Foreign Policy and National Security, *a book that hasn't been touched in years, if the layer of dust he brushes from it is any indication. He breathes a sigh of relief; he can finally finish that ten-page paper he has to write for history class, the paper on a topic so weirdly specific he can't finish it without this book.*

Tucking the book against his chest, he turns to make his way back to the front desk and runs into something solid. Something solid and warm and breathing.

"I'm sorry," Dylan says, taking a quick step back.

"It's okay, I snuck up on you," the boy says, offering Dylan a smile. Dylan pauses and an embarrassed blush creeps across his cheeks, though he's not sure why. The boy is cute, with auburn hair that could probably use a good brushing and freckles that dust his face and throat. He's wearing the baggy sweatshirt and wrinkled jeans combo that's so common on college students this late in the semester, but he somehow manages to make it look good. Dylan's blush deepens at these thoughts.

"Is that…" The boy looks down at the slip clutched in his hand. The handwriting on his note is the same as the one in Dylan's hand. "I think you have the book I'm looking for."

Dylan blinks and forces himself to look away from the cute upturn of this stranger's nose and down at the book he is holding.

"This one?" Dylan holds out the book he so desperately needs for his paper.

The stranger laughs. It's a smooth, gentle laugh. "That's exactly the book. What are the odds?"

"I don't think this book has been touched in five years." Dylan brushes off more dust.

"I just… I have a stupid paper for my economics class, and I really need that book."

"Oh." Dylan thinks about his own paper and the document open on his laptop, waiting for him to return with this ridiculously specific book so he can finish. "I don't really need it."

"Really?" The cute stranger's eyes meet Dylan's.

"Really." Dylan holds the book out. This is stupid, *he tells himself*, just take the book and go. You got here first, you deserve the book and your paper is still due tomorrow night. Cute strangers in the library are not an excuse for a bad grade.

"Wow." *Cute Stranger reaches out almost hesitantly to take the book.* "You're saving my life. I always tell myself not to put things off until the night before, but I still do. Every time."

"I know how that goes," *Dylan says, and Cute Stranger glances at him.*

"Are you sure you don't need it?"

Dylan feels himself shake his head. What is happening to him?

"Nope."

"Thank you." *A mirror of Dylan, Cute Stranger clutches the book to his own chest.* "I, um…" *He looks as if he wants to say something more, but shakes his head.* "Thanks."

"Looks like a thrilling read," *Dylan says, and immediately bites his lip to keep himself from saying anything else idiotic.*

"It'll probably keep me up all night." *This time Dylan doesn't imagine the blush on Cute Stranger's cheeks. It makes his freckles stand out.* "That was stupid."

Dylan laughs, and Cute Stranger glances up at him one last time, his hazel eyes wide and warm.

"Thanks again," *Cute Stranger says, and Dylan's pretty sure the unintelligible mess that falls from his own lips is* "Sure," *or* "No problem," *or* "Good luck," *or maybe even an embarrassing* "You're really cute, do you want to get a drink sometime?" *But Cute Stranger is already walking away, stopping at the end of the row to shoot a quick glance back. His cheeks redden when he realizes Dylan is still watching him, and he quickly scurries away.*

"Shit," Dylan says to the empty row of books. He sits on the hard, carpeted floor and leans back against the shelves. His stomach sinks; there's no way he can finish his paper now that he just acted like a complete idiot and sabotaged himself over a cute boy that he'll probably never see again.

But when he closes his eyes, he sees freckles and messy auburn hair. And he smiles.

Dylan wakes to the sound of banging in the kitchen. Is Landon making coffee? Landon doesn't function in the morning without at least twelve ounces of coffee in his veins, and he has usually finished half the pot before Dylan rolls out of bed.

The throbbing in his head and the ache in his arm remind him otherwise. Landon isn't here.

Light, warm and bright, filters between the gaps in the curtains. Dylan glances at the clock beside their bed and blinks. It's nearly eleven in the morning. He can't remember the last time he slept this late. He slips out of bed, notices that someone has taken the laundry and makes his way from the bedroom into the kitchen. Adele is fiddling with the coffee maker. Landon's younger sister stands beside her. She has the same red-brown hair as Landon, the same splash of freckles across her nose and cheeks, the same way of scrunching her eyebrows together when she's deep in thought.

"Hi, Lana," Dylan says, shuffling into the kitchen. Lana looks up, and Dylan can tell she's been crying. Her eyes are red and puffy.

"Hi," she says back and tries to smile.

19

"How are you feeling, sweetie?" Adele asks, looking up at him as she pours some coffee into a mug. Lana rests against a counter and crosses her arms over her stomach.

"I'm okay."

His mom's eyes flicker to the sling.

"Take these," Adele says. She shakes two pills from an orange bottle on the counter and slides a cup of coffee over to Dylan. "They're for pain."

He takes them without protest. The coffee is bitter on his tongue, unlike the coffee Landon makes. Used to make.

"I called the hospital," Adele says. Dylan tightens his grip around the mug. "Not many changes, but they said he's more stable now."

"Okay." Dylan pushes his coffee away as he stands up. "I'm going to shower and then I'd like to go back to the hospital. Even if we can't be in there for long, I... I just want to be there."

"Of course," Adele says with a nod. Dylan turns toward the bathroom, but stops at the sound of Lana's voice.

"Dylan, wait." He turns back. Lana steps forward, hesitating only a second before wrapping her arms around his waist in a gentle hug.

"I'm glad you're okay," she says into his shoulder. Dylan thinks of Landon, of the machines and doctors and nurses keeping him alive, of how unsure everything is, and doesn't know what to say.

"My parents are already at the hospital," Lana says when she lets go. She shuffles back toward the counter. "So he's not alone."

Helen and John left to make the four-hour drive from Madison to St. Paul after Dylan talked to them last night, and Dylan should feel glad to know Landon has someone with him, but his emotions have stopped working properly and he's not sure how he feels about anything. Only when the hot water is beating down on him, steam curling up around him and fogging the mirror, does he let himself break down; his salty tears mix with water and wash down the drain.

On the ride to the hospital Lana watches Dylan's face reflected in the rearview mirror. He's staring out the window, but his eyes are unfocused, his gaze is uncomfortably blank. A bruise purples the edge of his jaw, an echo of the night before. He shifts slightly and winces as the sling slips on his shoulder.

His eyes are shadowed by his dark hair, which flops over them, unkempt and wavy, in a way Lana's never seen. It's a contrast from how put together Dylan normally looks, with his shoulders held high and hair styled. She's always teased Landon about how he managed to snag such an attractive boyfriend, with the warm brown skin of his father's Indian heritage and his wide, dark eyes framed by long eyelashes. She's always been jealous of those eyelashes, and had made the fact known well enough that Dylan had jokingly gotten her Latisse for Christmas a few years ago. He'd kissed her cheek when she opened it, and Landon had laughed so hard he cried.

A weight forms in her stomach at the memory. She'd woken up this morning to four missed calls and frantic voice messages giving her only the most basic information: *There was an incident. Landon's been hurt.* Her parents hadn't answered her call; her mom had texted her that they were still talking with the doctor. So she'd called Dylan, and Adele had answered, updated her and, when Lana started to panic on the phone, insisted she come with them. She hadn't cried until she'd seen Dylan's mom standing there in the kitchen and sunk into her warm, comforting arms.

Even then it hadn't seemed real, as if Landon would emerge from the bedroom at any moment, or walk in the door with his hair still wet from an early morning swim.

But now, watching Dylan in the car, seeing how absolutely defeated he looks, she knows.

This is real.

Dylan closes his eyes and leans his head against the window, and Lana looks away. She stares out her own window, watching as the hospital approaches. Her nerves build as they park and make their way inside. Adele leads them to the elevator, up to the fourth floor and into the intensive care unit. They check in at the front desk. A nurse smiles kindly at them and leads them to a room in the corner. Her parents are already inside; her mom's face is drawn and pale, and her dad looks uncomfortable and stiff, standing off in the corner of the room. A nurse is beside the bed, looking through the medication hanging from the IV pole, then writing something down on a wrinkled piece of paper.

This is all so much worse than she imagined. The sight of Landon in the bed is too much; she can't take it. She starts to cry, sinks down into the seat beside the bed and buries her face in her hands. Landon used to tease her when they were little about how she should be an actress, because she could cry at anything. Landon might never be able to tease her about anything, ever again, and the reality of that only makes her cry harder.

She feels a hand on her shoulder and hears a voice in her ear, but she doesn't listen. No words can make this better; no words can change what's already happened; no words can heal something like this. So she cries, and they let her.

Dylan leaves the room when Lana starts to cry, and leans against the wall in the hallway. He doesn't want to intrude on Landon's family; they need time together, and he doesn't fit in there, not now. Not when it's his fault that this happened, his fault that Lana might lose her brother, that John and Helen might lose their son.

When he might lose his fiancé.

Someone leans on the wall beside him. The distinctive scent of his mother's perfume drifts over him.

"I remember the day you first met Landon," Adele says, her voice soft. "It was during finals your first semester of college, and you had some paper you were writing… the history of something or other."

"The History of the Economic Effects of World War I on Oppressed Nations," Dylan fills in. He opens his eyes to look at his mom.

She laughs. "That's right. Forgive me for not remembering." Dylan chuckles at her comment and looks at the floor, at tan tiles speckled with brown. "You were so stressed out about it, and you called me that night nearly in tears because there was one book you needed, and you had gone to the library to find it and another boy needed that same book and you gave it to him."

Dylan smiles at the memory and scuffs the floor with his toe.

"You could have taken the book for yourself, but you saw Landon, and I think something in you knew that he was special, and you gave him the book. And then you called me on the verge of a breakdown because you didn't have the book you needed for your research paper, but you'd just met the most amazing boy."

Adele turns to face Dylan and brushes his arm with her hand.

"Landon found you the next day to give you that book back, because he knew you needed it."

Dylan nods and makes a noise somewhere between a laugh and a sob.

Adele smiles. "Even from the day you met, you've always known what he needs, and he's always been there for you. And I know that things haven't always been easy, but you've always been there for each other. I'm not going to tell you that everything is going to be all right, because I don't believe in false hope, but I do believe you two were meant to find each other."

Dylan closes his eyes again and lets his head fall back against the wall.

"I know you think I'm crazy when I talk about these things," Adele continues. She sounds worn, tired. "But you and Landon were meant to be in each other's lives, ever since that first day in the library."

"Then why did this have to happen?" Dylan asks, his voice thin. "What's the point?"

"Sometimes bad things happen," Adele says. Dylan hears her lean back against the wall. "And there are no answers. But I know Landon is lucky to have someone who loves him as much as you do. And I know Landon loves you so much, and he's not going to give that up without a fight."

He doesn't have a choice, Dylan wants to say, but he doesn't trust himself to speak.

"You're not going to be alone."

Dylan digs his fingernails into his palm, looking for some way to channel the hurt building inside of him. He slides down the wall, his knees hunched before him, until the cold tile floor meets his body. Adele runs a hand through his hair and he lets her hold him, the way she used to when he scraped his knees playing in the trees outside their house. "I promise. You're not going to be alone."

Landon's brain is still swelling, the doctor tells them later, when the crying has calmed and the sun has lowered in the sky. They're giving him medication to draw the extra fluid off of his brain. A piece of his skull is still missing, embedded in his abdomen for safekeeping. His blood pressure has been mostly stabilized with more medication, and they're keeping him sedated so he can rest. He won't feel any pain.

Is that supposed to make them feel better, knowing that Landon isn't in any pain? Dylan concentrates on Landon while the doctor is talking. He sees the man he's supposed to marry, the man who was so vibrant, so energetic that Dylan used to insist there was more coffee than blood in his veins. He watches the rhythm of Landon's chest as it rises and falls with each whirr of the ventilator and the way he lies so unnaturally still, showing not even the slightest change in expression or the smallest twitch of his fingers when Dylan takes his hand. It's so wrong, the opposite of everything that Landon is, and there's nothing the doctor can say to make this better.

Someone asks questions. *Helen*, Dylan thinks. How long until they can expect changes? How long until they know what his prognosis is? What are his chances?

Dylan focuses on the hand in his, the freckled skin still showing the remnants of a tan from the summer sun. He's always prided himself in being logical, on knowing numbers and statistics and organizing everything into neat categories, but he can't bring himself to do that now. He doesn't want to know what chance Landon has of surviving, because then he'll know what chance he doesn't have. There's no way to calculate or figure his way out of this situation, to try to force things to make sense. He has no control, and it scares him.

He pretends to listen while the doctor rattles off terms he doesn't understand, answers questions he's too afraid to ask and gives reassurances he doesn't want to hear. He likes facts and truths and automatically distrusts anyone duplicitous, anyone who misleads and sugarcoats and manipulates. So he mentally lists the things he knows, marking each truth with a line in the starched white hospital blanket.

Landon is in the hospital.

Landon's brain is swelling.

Landon's skull is in his abdomen.

Landon's blood pressure isn't regulating itself as it should.

Landon can't even breathe on his own.

Landon might die.

The doctors have no real answers.

Adele watches her son while the doctor speaks. He stares at the blanket covering Landon, and his knuckles are tense where he grips Landon's hand, as if he's afraid to let go. The bruise on his jaw is turning a deeper purple, fading into the tan of his skin, and the tired shadows under his eyes are darker than they were this morning. Dylan has never reacted well to stressful situations; even when he was little, he could never make a decision without weighing every possible outcome and considering every detail.

There is guilt in Dylan's eyes and tension in his jaw, and he jabs lines into the blanket instead of listening. Adele has never been one for regrets, has never dwelled on the what-ifs and what-could-have-beens in life; she is a firm believer in accepting the past and moving on with the future. But now, more than anything, she wishes that she could take all this away: Rip the seams, tear it from their lives, and then mend everything, put it back together just as it was before.

She tried that once, with a hole in one of Dylan's shirts, and no matter how careful she was, the fabric still scrunched and pulled and never looked as perfect as it once had. *Some things can't be mended,* Adele thinks. *Sometimes you just have to put things back together as carefully as you can and be satisfied knowing you did the best that you could. Dylan needs strength, he needs gentle words and an encouraging presence, and he needs to know he's capable of getting through this.*

The doctor finishes talking. Landon's mother, Helen, thanks him with tears in her eyes and clasps her hands. They're shaking. Her face drawn, Helen looks at Landon, at the hand that Dylan holds.

"I think I need some coffee," Helen says, suddenly. She pauses, and then nods as if assuring herself of her decision and strides out of the room. Landon's father closes his eyes for only a second before following his wife into the hall.

Adele steps forward until she's next to Landon's bed, across from Dylan. She lets the backs of her fingers brush Landon's cheek, lets her thumb graze the line of his jaw. She remembers the first time she met Landon, how overdue it seemed after months of listening to Dylan talk about him over the phone. Landon had been shy and very nervous, bouncing on his heels with energy that seemed to have no outlet. Dylan hadn't stopped smiling at him all night, and it had been so long since she'd seen her son smile like that, she had pretended not to see the way they brushed hands under the dinner table, and lacked the heart to point out that Landon had tucked his shirt through his pants' zipper.

She'd never worried about them. Though she had seen the occasional story on TV and various headlines in the newspaper about intolerant and prejudiced people hurting others just because they didn't understand them, she never thought it would happen—not to them. When you're surrounded by so much love, it's easy to forget that the world is a cruel place, and that, for some people, love isn't enough. It hits her now, how close she came to losing Dylan last night, how close she came to losing her son. And Landon... she loves him as much as any of her family, and it hurts to see him here, fighting for his life.

All because of whom he loves.

"He's strong," Adele says, her fingers touching the worn fabric of Landon's hospital gown. "He's always been strong."

Lana sniffs beside her and wipes her nose with a tissue clutched tightly in her hand.

"I can't believe this is happening," Lana says quietly, glancing up at Adele. "I keep expecting to wake up and have this all be a dream."

"We all do, honey," Adele says, resting a reassuring hand on Lana's shoulder.

"I just want him to be okay," Lana whispers. She looks to Dylan, as if he's the only one who could reassure her. Dylan lets go of Landon's hand and leans back in his chair, looking utterly exhausted.

"Me too," he says, his eyes glued to Landon's face.

Adele wants to make this better, to make this easier, to take away the pain of it all. But she doesn't know how.

Later that night, sitting at their small dining room table with his mom across from him, Dylan stares at a sandwich he doesn't want to eat. "I need to call work."

"I'll call them on Monday," Adele says.

Dylan blinks and looks up at the calendar on the wall. It's only Saturday. Only one day since Landon begged Dylan to go get gyros with him in the park, since Landon was here beside him, smiling and happy. It feels like forever, and time no longer seems to work in any way that makes sense.

"I had… there was a big project." Dylan runs a finger along the table and thumbs at the indent left where they ran into the door with it as they were moving in. They'd broken into overtired laughing fits; they had been so giddy then, moving in together, fresh out of college and ready to take on the world.

Adele covers Dylan's hand and stops him from scratching the table. "They won't blame you."

"It was *my* project." Dylan looks up at her. "They were letting me do the designs. I don't…"

"There will be more designs. There will be more projects. *After* you heal."

Dylan nods. He can't bring himself to argue.

"Get some sleep, sweetie." Adele stands and Dylan follows suit, gazing wistfully around the apartment.

"And Landon's work," Dylan adds, his eyes lingering on the reminder for a staff meeting stuck to the fridge with a magnet in the shape of a starfish. "They'll need to know."

"We'll take care of it," Adele assures him, resting a hand against his back.

"Okay." Dylan turns back toward the bedroom. "Thank you."

Adele kisses his check. "I'll be out here if you need anything."

Getting into bed alone isn't any easier than it was last night. Dylan slips into his side of the bed and reaches out to where Landon should be, silently hoping for the impossible: that Landon's fingers will meet his. He closes his eyes, pulls up the covers and curls into his pillow, ignoring the ache in his shoulder. He pictures Landon's smile, the way he always sticks his tongue out when he's concentrating, the infuriating way he scrunches his nose when he argues, the way his hair clings to his temples after a shower, the way he kisses Dylan as he dashes out the door, always running late for something.

He holds these images close and imagines clutching them to his chest, more important than any possession. He's scared he'll never have a chance to experience these moments ever again. Scared that he'll forget. Scared that every happy memory will be replaced by *this*—the fear and confusion, the constant feeling of dread in his stomach, the pictures of flowers and the clocks behind bars, the smell of antiseptic and the *whirr-click* of machines trying desperately to keep someone alive.

It's not what Landon would want, for *these* memories to be the last Dylan has of him: his face purpled with bruises, his head wrapped in gauze, his body dressed in a horrible hospital gown. It's not what he would want, but it might be what he gets.

It takes three more days for Dylan to feel as though he can breathe again. Three days for the iron rods across his chest to loosen, for the haze of confusion and disbelief to clear in his mind. Things start to make sense again, and he feels as if he's no longer stumbling blindly into the unknown. He feels like a semblance of an actual human, capable of interacting with others.

Early on Tuesday morning, Dylan walks into the hospital and up to Landon's room on autopilot. He's not expecting the flowers, the cards, the balloon with dangling yellow string, all pushed into a corner on the countertop across from Landon's bed.

The flowers are fake. A few years ago, Dylan had tried to send some real ones to his great uncle when he was in the hospital for gall bladder surgery, and learned that flowers can be harmful to the sick. *Life is strange that way,* Dylan thinks, stroking a plastic petal. How things meant to comfort can end up causing more harm than good. He thumbs open one of the cards; it's from Abbi, one of Landon's coworkers. It's very kind, addressed mostly to his family, an offer to help in any way she can. There are a few others, from cousins, a couple of college friends. One is addressed to Dylan, and he opens it with curiosity, eyeballing the signature. It's from his Aunt Patty.

I'm very sorry to hear what happened to you and your friend. I'll be praying for a quick recovery.

Dylan can't help the small laugh that escapes him, bitter on his tongue. His mom's sister is old-fashioned and has never understood or acknowledged what Dylan and Landon are to each other. She lives two states away, and his only real contact with her is at family gatherings. But after this...

He shakes his head and lets the card fall back onto the counter.

"This didn't happen because you're my friend," he says, turning toward Landon's bed. He sets his bag down, sits in the chair and pulls as close as he can get amongst the machines and equipment. Landon looks the same; the bruises fading into yellow are the only indication that time has passed, that anything is different at all. It's odd to see Landon so still, day after day; only the pillows the nurses keep putting under his back cause him to change position.

He doesn't even look like Landon anymore, Dylan thinks, and guilt twists inside him. Not the Landon he knew.

"Good morning," a voice says from behind him, and Dylan jumps. He cranes his neck and sees Helen enter the room, followed by Logan, Landon's older brother.

"Jesus," Logan exclaims, his voice full of disbelief and eyes wide as he takes in Landon. His gaze flickers to Dylan, to Helen and back to Landon.

Logan swears again and Helen doesn't reprimand him; her own lips are drawn into a tight line. The oldest at just over thirty, Logan has always been the most rebellious of the three siblings; he moved to New York just out of high school to fulfill his dream of starting a band and pursuing the underground music scene. More times than Dylan can count, Landon has griped about Logan's lack of responsibility and his parents' less than warm reaction to it. To no one's surprise, Logan didn't succeed at starting a famous band, but had settled for managing a bar and playing gigs when he could get them. And then there was a kid, a little girl named Jay, born to his longtime girlfriend, Paige. It had been a divisive time for the family, but eventually they had grown tired of fighting and settled on silent disagreement.

"Is he…" Logan starts. He reaches out to Landon but stops, pulls back.

"They're keeping him sedated," Helen explains. "To reduce the stress on his brain. He's not in pain."

Dylan looks at the floor, avoiding their eyes. Helen clings to that fact, that Landon is not in pain, and repeats it to everyone as if it's the one thing that comforts her.

"Christ, this is just…" Logan trails off, his voice thick, as if he's holding back tears. "I'm the one that's supposed to make the family cry, not you."

Dylan bites the inside of his lip and considers leaving. But Logan looks straight at him. "He's doing okay, right? They said he's going to be okay?"

Logan runs a hand over his hair. It's lighter than Landon's and Lana's, almost strawberry blond, and pulled back into a messy ponytail. But his eyes are the same hazel as Landon's, and Dylan can't help but stare back.

Dylan picks at a thread coming loose at a corner of the hospital blanket. "His brain isn't swelling anymore, but it hasn't gone down yet either. They're still waiting."

"Shit," Logan says in a sharp whisper, and Helen glares at him. He apologizes quietly—Dylan can tell he doesn't mean it—and dabs at the corner of his eye with his shirtsleeve.

They sit in silence. Dylan lets Helen have his spot at the head of the bed, and then finds he's staring at Landon's feet, like lumps under the blanket. A few nurses come and go, writing down vital signs and hanging new bags of medication; a respiratory therapist pops in, looks over the ventilator and adjusts a few numbers on the screen. They're going down on the settings, she explains, smiling at them. It's a good thing. It's progress.

To Dylan, it doesn't look like anything but a few numbers on a screen.

"You used to be such a little shrimp," Logan says, after the silence has stretched itself thin. He laughs quietly and takes

Landon's hand. Dylan hopes that, somehow, Landon knows how many people have held his hand in offerings of strength and love. "I used to tease you about it. Remember when I drew that comic about you called Shrimp Man? You would get so mad. You'd get *so* mad and you'd try to fight me, with your scrawny little arms. And when that failed, you'd hide my things instead, or make up embarrassing stories to tell in front of my girlfriends."

Dylan smiles at the image of a tiny Landon trying to exact revenge on his older brother.

"He never told me you called him those names," Helen says.

"That's because he wasn't a snitch," Logan responds, giving Landon's hand a small squeeze. "He was tiny and vengeful, but he was loyal. Especially to family."

Logan glances up at Dylan when he says this. Then he looks back at Landon, following the tube that runs from Landon's lips to the ventilator. The sharp clench of guilt squeezes Dylan's insides once again, and he can't stop the thoughts that this is *his* fault, that Landon wouldn't be here if it wasn't for him, and that this is why Logan's family keeps glancing at him so guardedly.

"He fought back then, and he'll fight now," Logan says. "I know he will."

They're on the news that night. First at five, and again at ten. Dylan finds out at a quarter after five, when his phone explodes with texts and calls from close friends, from people he barely remembers and from numbers he doesn't recognize. He doesn't answer or respond to any of the texts. It's comforting to know that so many people care, are full of kind words and want to offer their help. But it's also overwhelming. Dylan doesn't know what to do with the sheer volume of communications, so he stares at his phone with each incoming text, each unanswered call until Adele gently takes the phone from his fingers.

"You don't need to talk to anyone you don't want to," she says and slips the phone into her bag. "They'll understand."

That night, after he gets home from the hospital, he turns on their small TV and adjusts the rabbit ears until he picks up a grainy image of the local news. His dad is staying with him tonight, despite Dylan's insistence that he doesn't need a babysitter. Adele has been staying most nights, on a makeshift bed made up on the couch, but she has a yoga class to teach in the morning and can't afford to cancel it. Dylan insisted she teach it, not realizing that his father would follow him in instead and plop down on the couch-bed despite Dylan's complaints.

His dad doesn't say much. Growing up, Dylan always thought his dad saved his words for the plays he wrote, knowing that Sam hoped with each one to make it big. But instead, he became more silent after every flop. When Dylan was ten years old, one play had a mildly successful run, even a few positive reviews, and Dylan remembers how proud he felt, bragging to all his friends, that his father was a famous playwright. Unfortunately, famous was a bit of a stretch, and one success wasn't enough to support their small family, so his dad had taken up writing technical manuals for car manufacturers instead.

Dylan has always wondered if there is a connection between his father's quietness and the draining exactitude of writing car manuals.

Sam makes them tea while they wait for the ten o'clock news: chamomile, to calm the mind and body. Dylan accepts gratefully; even though it's too hot out for tea, he's glad to have something to do with his hands. His heart is racing as he waits.

It's a short segment, barely a minute. A newscaster reports the night that completely changed their lives with a neutral expression and a steady voice. Feeling exposed and bare, Dylan shifts uncomfortably on the couch as the anchor uses phrases like "terrible tragedy," "critical condition," "futile search" and "no leads." She uses their names, but no pictures of them, and she ends the story with some statistics on the rise of hate crimes in the area, moving on to a story about the rising cost of peanut butter.

With a knot in his stomach, Dylan blinks at the TV. It seems so stark and clinical, the way the newscaster had put it, everything laid out as if it makes sense and isn't the jumbled mess of a situation that Dylan is caught in. She hadn't talked about the pain he feels every day, walking into that hospital and seeing Landon as still as the day before and the nurse's sympathetic smiles, or the constant ache of missing the person he was going to spend the rest of his life with.

Sam turns off the TV, leaving them in uncomfortable silence.

"The whole world knows," Dylan says, barely above a whisper. "Everyone knows."

"I'll talk to them," Sam says, in the decisive way he has whenever he makes his mind up about something. "I'll ask them to stop running any stories about you."

Dylan nods and runs his finger along the edge of the couch pillow. It's light blue, patterned with a bicycle print, one of the first things he'd picked out with Landon when they moved in.

"It still doesn't feel real, you know?" Dylan stares at those stupid bicycles until they start to blur. "I still feel like I'm going to wake up, or realize I'm watching a bad episode of reality TV."

"It'll get easier," Sam says, looking at Dylan. "I know it doesn't seem like it now, but it will."

"I don't see how it can," Dylan whispers, embarrassed at how his voice cracks. "Not while Landon is in there."

"He won't be there forever."

"What if he doesn't get better?" Dylan challenges, stabbing his thumb into the pillow.

"Then you'll deal with it. But for now, it doesn't hurt to have hope."

Everything seems so stagnant and desperate. Hope seems impossible. He doesn't want to hope, doesn't want to imagine a time when things are better only to have the possibility ripped from his grasp. He's just trying to live from moment to moment and day to day, trying to focus on the truths of the situation and trying not to wish for things that might not happen.

"I'm going to bed," he says, tired to his bones. Exhaustion is a deep ache, pulling at every tendon and sinew. His dad looks sad but he nods and watches Dylan stand up as though he wants to say something else. But he doesn't. He just offers Dylan a small smile.

"I'll be out here," he says, hesitating before adding, "Don't be afraid to wake me up if you need something."

"Thanks, Dad." Dylan knows how hard is father is trying, even if he doesn't really know what to say.

He disappears into the bedroom, shuts the door and pauses to take in a deep breath before crawling beneath the familiar covers. It's only been three days, but he's already getting used to going to bed alone.

CHAPTER 3

A week passes, slowly. Time works differently in the hospital, dragging and jumping, minutes passing in hours, hours passing in seconds. Landon's improvements often happen in the same way, one day yielding nothing, the next marking changes visible even to Dylan. The swelling in his brain starts to decrease, the monitors alarm less frequently, the bruises turn shades of yellow and green. The nurses smile more, greet Dylan each day with positive updates as they fill him in on Landon's night.

Dylan tries to smile back, tries to be excited about each piece of good news, but it's difficult when Landon is still sedated, when the *whirr-click* of the ventilator is a sound so familiar Dylan doesn't hear it anymore. There's talk of a second surgery to put back the piece of his skull that is still missing and close the window that kept Landon's brain from suffocating itself. This is a *good* thing, a sign that things really are getting better, but Dylan can't bring himself to believe.

Lana is there almost as often as he is; her classes are out for the summer and her coworkers at the art store are willing to cover her shifts. Dylan enjoys having the company. Only able to stay away from his family and his job for so long, Logan flies back to New York. Leaving is hard for him, and he promises to come back as soon as anything changes. Landon's father drives back to Madison to make arrangements with his firm and has to spend a week at home before he can come back. Helen spends a lot of time talking with insurance companies, meeting with doctors and specialists and sitting quietly beside Landon's bed.

Dylan's boss gives him two weeks off in addition to his paid leave, and Dylan develops a daily routine—a routine he hates more with every passing minute, every stale cup of coffee, every overhead hospital announcement. He can't think of anything else, doesn't even worry about the project he was supposed to be leading at work; his focus is solely on Landon—Landon, who always claimed that Dylan's mind never left work, even when he was home. They'd fought about it, more than once, and Dylan idly wonders if Landon would be proud of him now.

The hospital staff weans Landon from his sedatives for short intervals in the daytime, and each time Dylan holds his breath. A tiny, flickering flame of hope starts to light in him that something will change, that Landon will open his eyes, or move, or squeeze Dylan's hand, anything to let Dylan know he's still in there. But nothing happens, and the nurses' reassurances—that Landon needs time; that his brain is still in shock and trying to heal—fall on deaf ears.

Lana clings to these words, and whispers quiet encouragements to Landon during these times, holding his hand and telling him how much she loves him. Dylan watches and wonders if he should be doing something similar, if something isn't working right inside of him, and why he can't bring himself to feel something.

Maybe there's only so much a person can take, before they can't anymore.

* * *

"I'm sorry I'm late," *Dylan says, his chest heaving as he shuts the door behind him and kicks off his boots by the entrance. Rain drips down his face, soaking uncomfortably into his shirt, and the bag of flowers crinkles in his hands as he makes his way into the living room. "Did you get my..."*

A smile tugs at his lips. Landon is sprawled out across the couch, a book lopsidedly open on his chest, his lips parted in sleep, the green cone of a party hat strapped to his head, and Dylan can't help the laugh that escapes him as he creeps forward and settles himself above Landon on the couch. Landon's eyes blink open at the shift; a sleepy smile grows on his face.

"You look like a drowned cat," Landon murmurs, brushing a wet strand of hair behind Dylan's ears.

"You look like you just turned five," Dylan shoots back, raising his eyebrows at the cone strapped to Landon's head. Landon sticks out his tongue, and Dylan wonders if he's been spending too much time with the kids at work, but in a moment of forgotten maturity he decides to retaliate and shake his head, raining droplets of freezing water on Landon's face. Landon scrunches his nose and

swats at Dylan, causing him to lose his balance, roll off the couch and land on the floor with an ungraceful thud.

"Are you okay?" Landon asks, leaning over the edge of the couch, sounding concerned, and if Dylan were a better person he might feel bad for what he's about to do, but the temptation is too sweet. He reaches up to grab Landon's arm, pulling him down on top of him.

"You're all wet," Landon whines, but he doesn't pull away and is content to pout.

"Only because I got stuck outside getting you flowers."

Landon's eyes grow wide. "Flowers?"

Dylan doesn't respond. He wonders how, after three years, Landon can still amaze him with his ability to be so happy and adorable and free. He wonders how he ever managed to be lucky enough to come home to this every day. But Landon stares at him expectantly, so Dylan rolls over and stretches to grab the flowers from where he set them, next to the couch.

"Happy Birthday." Dylan presents the flowers. Landon clutches them close to his chest. The yellow of the daffodils makes his eyes glow, and the purple of the lilies brings out the blush on his cheeks. Holding the flowers up so they don't get crushed, he cranes his neck forward to kiss Dylan's lips.

"They're beautiful," Landon says when they pull apart, thumbing the edge of a petal. Dylan doesn't think he'll ever get over how genuinely touched Landon always seems by these simple gestures, by flowers and kisses and texts sent with X's and O's.

Landon springs to his feet, and Dylan rolls over on the floor. Landon makes his way across their tiny apartment to pull the crystal vase, a housewarming gift from Landon's mom, from the top shelf in the kitchen. He fills it with water before carefully arranging the flowers.

"I wish flowers could last forever." Landon's voice sounds light, the way it gets when he really means something, and Dylan pushes himself to his feet, ignoring how damp and uncomfortable his clothes are, to walk over and bump Landon's shoulder with his own.

"Nothing lasts forever."

Landon looks at Dylan and raises an eyebrow. "Someone's a little ball of sunshine today."

"Someone is soaking wet and on the verge of hypothermia," Dylan retorts, and Landon gives him a contemplative look before wrapping his hands around Dylan's shoulders and manhandling him back to the bedroom.

"Well, then I think someone should take a shower and warm up."

Dylan turns around and nuzzles the crook of Landon's neck; a shiver makes its way down his spine.

"Maybe you could join me and I could give you your birthday present early."

"Present?" Landon pulls away, looking at Dylan with a frown. "I thought we agreed we were too broke to do presents this year."

"Sex, Landon," Dylan deadpans. He has to bite his lip to keep from laughing. "Your present is sex."

"Oh." Landon blinks and steps forward, glancing up and down Dylan's body in a way that never fails to make Dylan's knees tremble. "I like that present."

"I thought you would." Dylan presses a gentle kiss to Landon's lips and slips his hands under the hem of Landon's T-shirt. This time, Landon trembles.

Later, his hair still damp, dressed in a baggy T-shirt and sweat-pants, his body loose, Landon is perched on the kitchen counter. He watches Dylan make his birthday cake and contemplates.

"What are you thinking about?" Dylan asks, cracking eggs into a bowl.

"About why you won't cook naked for me." A smile pulls at Landon's lips. Dylan shoots him a glare before reaching for the spatula, bends over a little further than necessary, takes a few seconds longer than he really needs.

"You just saw me naked for at least," he glances at the clock, "an hour and eighteen minutes."

"It's my birthday?" Landon tries, blinking hopefully at Dylan. Dylan just shakes his head and continues to stir the cake mix.

Landon eventually gets distracted and tells him about his day. His job as a child life specialist at the hospital can be taxing, but he always finds something positive to talk about. Today it's Play-Doh sculptures and ukuleles, and a little boy whose hand he held on the way to surgery. He loves his job; there's a light in his eyes for every kid he's helped, every child whose day was made even a little bit better by his presence. Even on the hard days, when he comes home with slumped shoulders and his eyes rimmed in red, he never talks about leaving, never mentions finding an easier job. He just works even harder the next day.

Dylan offers Landon the spatula once he's through mixing, and Landon licks the batter off in one long swipe; some catches on his lower lip and drips down his chin. He ducks his head and his cheeks are red with embarrassment, but Dylan just steps forward and rests a hand on Landon's thigh as he wipes the batter from Landon's chin with his thumb.

Dylan moans exaggeratedly and winks at Landon as he sucks the batter from his thumb. A glint appears in Landon's eyes as he watches, and he sticks his finger in the cake batter before Dylan can stop him and swipes it across his nose.

"Oops," Landon says, leaning forward, and Dylan laughs.

"I'm not going to fall for it."

"Well then." Landon sticks his finger in the cake batter again, this time swiping it across Dylan's cheek. Dylan is still, his breath catching, when Landon perches dangerously close to the edge of the counter to kiss away the spot of cake batter. Something warm blossoms in Dylan, deep inside, and he wonders if it's silly that this boy still makes him feel this way despite their struggles, despite the occasional fights and the fact that they're still trying to make it through, trying to sort out where they're headed. Or maybe that's the reason he still feels this way: because they're figuring it out together.

So he lets himself press back against Landon, lets his eyes close and takes a second to just breathe in Landon, the warm, earthy scent of him mixed with the overly sweet cake batter. He gives himself this moment.

And then he attacks, dipping his fingers into the batter and smearing them over Landon's cheeks in a mockery of war paint. Landon laughs loudly, grabs the carton of flour and dusts a handful into Dylan's hair. Dylan blinks in shock and shakes his head with the flour clouding out and falling onto their clothes.

"Oh, you've done it now," Dylan growls. He steps between Landon's knees, wraps his hands around Landon's lower back and pulls him closer. He feels around behind Landon until he finds a handful of sugar, then leans close enough that Landon tilts his

head to the side, baring his neck; his eyes flutter shut—until Dylan shoves the sugar down the back of his shirt.

Landon's eyes pop open and he squirms, but he gives Dylan a wide smile.

"Excellent, a sugar scrub," he says, leaning against Dylan's chest. Dylan nips at his nose, kisses his lips. "People pay good money for these, you know."

"Sugar scrubs off dead skin," Dylan murmurs, his lips still brushing Landon's cheek.

"Mmm, sexy." Landon nuzzles against him and Dylan lets his eyes drift shut as he tries to step even closer. "Dead skin."

"Shut up."

"Never."

Dylan gives Landon's chest a playful shove and he tilts back; his head smacks against the cupboard with a loud thunk.

"Oh God, Landon, are you okay?" Dylan asks, immediately trying to assess the damage, with guilt building inside him: he probably just concussed Landon on his birthday, and that makes him, officially, the worst fiancé ever.

His eyes close of their own accord when something cold and gooey blankets him, dripping off his hair into his eyelashes and down onto his clothes. Cake batter, he identifies when he licks his lips, the entire bowl of it, dumped over his head. His eyes blink open and a glob falls onto his shoulder while a chunk slides down his neck, slipping under his shirt. Landon is giggling like a madman, and Dylan just stands there, sucks in a deep breath and counts to ten.

"The wedding is off," he says, as firmly as he can, taking a step back and wiping cake batter from his eyes. Landon slides off the

counter, pouting. "Nope, don't even try. You can't win me back this time."

Landon whimpers, smoothes Dylan's shoulders with his hands and presses his mouth against Dylan's throat. He draws back with batter on his nose.

"I'm made of stone." Dylan backs up until he hits the wall. "You can't crack me."

"Delicious stone." Landon hums and licks a strip up Dylan's throat.

"Cold, heartless stone," Dylan counters, but he has to swallow a laugh. Landon looks ridiculous with his sultry eyes and the batter smudging his face.

"Maybe I can help you melt a little," Landon whispers. He presses closer and Dylan can feel his heart speed up, staccato against his ribcage.

"I think you're mixing your metaphors," Dylan breathes back. He is already trying to pull up Landon's T-shirt with fingers slippery-sticky with cake batter.

"It's not a metaphor," Landon says, his voice muffled by his shirt as he pulls it over his head.

"That doesn't make any sense." Dylan laughs, and Landon, hair ruffled and cheeks flushed, finally frees himself of his shirt. Landon is already working on Dylan's buttons, his fingers almost frantic, and Dylan doesn't want to wait. He surges forward, presses against Landon and turns him around, pushing him back against the wall. Landon makes a desperate noise and kisses Dylan deeply, as if it's the last chance he'll ever have, and Dylan is acutely aware of the hummingbird beat of Landon's heart. Dylan lets his hands drift down farther, over the smooth curve of Landon's ass, before anchoring him against the wall. Landon seems to understand what he's trying to do, hoists his legs up and wraps them around Dylan's waist.

Landon immediately leans into him, his arms around Dylan's neck, and Dylan supposes it would be hot, except Landon is gripping too tightly, his body slightly off center, and he is heavy, and Dylan can't keep his balance so they topple, falling onto the floor in a heap.

They're both laughing, and have somehow twisted so that Dylan's body is on top of Landon's and he can feel the heaving of Landon's chest. Dylan kisses the long stretch of Landon's throat; Landon's arms slide up to wrap around Dylan's back, anchoring them together.

They finish there, on the floor, covered in sweat and cake batter, their fingers tangled.

"Did that really just happen?" Landon asks, a shell-shocked look on his face, and Dylan can't help the giggle that escapes him. He's giddy in that way only Landon can make him feel.

"I'm pretty sure it did." He lifts his head and looks at the mess of the kitchen and Landon sprawled beside him. Then he shifts onto his side and places one last lingering kiss on Landon's lips. "It sure looks like it did."

Landon surveys the scene before letting his head fall back against the floor.

"No dibs on cleaning."

And Dylan doesn't argue, because right now, everything is pretty much perfect.

* * *

47

They wean Landon from the ventilator on a Tuesday, extubate on a Wednesday. "It's a trial," the doctors say. "We keep the ventilator in the room, on standby, ready if Landon can't tolerate breathing on his own."

But he does. His chest rises and falls in a more natural rhythm now; his sedation is minimal. The gentle hum is gone and Dylan's thoughts are too loud without it. But it's easier, and he can almost look past everything else, past the bandages and wires, past the central line in Landon's arm, past the catheter and monitors tracking every vital sign, because Landon is breathing on his own, he's breathing. And sometimes, if Dylan watches long enough, he notices Landon's fingers twitch, an occasional movement in his cheek, an irregular breath.

Sometimes, in the brief moments he's alone with Landon, when Lana is at work, when Helen is catching up on sleep at Lana's apartment, when Adele is running errands or teaching a class, he closes his eyes. He closes his eyes and holds Landon's hands, and just lets himself feel. He runs his thumb across Landon's hand and feels the calluses, the old, fully formed ones and the newer ones from the guitar Landon had been teaching himself to play. He follows the life line, the length and depth of it comforting somehow, traces over the rough edges of Landon's cuticles, brushes over the back of his hand where the skin between his fingers is dry and starting to crack in the empty hospital air and works his way up bones of his wrist, somehow so strong and delicate at the same time.

It's calm, without the ventilator. Easier, somehow.

"I hope you come back to me," he whispers, his eyes still closed. "I would really like you to."

Dylan blinks, but doesn't cry. Everything feels too heavy, too weighted, to cry. Landon's face is calm, lacking the pinch of his eyebrows that he gets when he dreams. Dylan hopes he feels as calm as he looks, and that everything is peaceful, wherever he is.

"I can't..." Dylan starts. His eyes follow the lines of Landon's face and sweep the curve of his nose, the parting of his lips. "You have a lot of mail. I haven't... I haven't read them yet. The letters. I'm saving them for you."

Landon breathes.

"I... um, I don't know..."

Dylan swallows past the painful lump in his throat.

"I really miss and you. And..."

He stops. He closes his eyes and grips Landon's hand tighter. "Please be okay."

Landon keeps breathing.

When Helen steps into Landon's room, Dylan is sleeping in the chair beside him. Careful not to wake him, she stays as quiet as she can as she enters. He hasn't been sleeping well; she's seen it in the deep circles under his eyes, the exhausted slump in his shoulders. None of them have been sleeping well, and without her nightly sleeping aid she would be counting her hours of rest on one hand.

She sits in the chair opposite Dylan, smoothes a hand over her jeans. She's been borrowing clothes from Lana; she had packed frantically the morning she left home and ran out of clothes long ago. Lana's clothes are the opposite of her normal attire, and Helen always takes pride in her professional wardrobe, always makes sure to make a good impression on anyone she might meet. Now she finds herself in jeans and loose T-shirts, in cardigans and sweatshirts, with her hair pulled back in quickly done ponytails. But she can't bring herself to care; her worry is focused solely on Landon.

She sits quietly. It's easier to breathe here, being close to her son. Knowing he's still here, in front of her, helps her to remember that she hasn't lost him. Not yet.

"You were always so good," she whispers, careful not to wake Dylan. She lets her hand rest on Landon's arm, cautious of disturbing the tubing pumping in medication, the equipment keeping her son alive.

"I'm sorry we haven't always been there when you needed us." She strokes a gentle rhythm on his arm. "But I'm here for you now. Whenever you decide to wake up, I'll be here."

The words seem meaningless. Landon can't hear her, and one promise now won't take away a lifetime of focusing on her career and not her children, but it's all she can do. She can't help the empty, useless feeling inside her, that she failed as a mother, that if she had done something differently, had offered him more support, more help when he needed it, that maybe he wouldn't be here.

It only takes a glance up at Dylan to know that she's wrong, and that unless it is wrong of Landon to love whom he does, there is nothing she could have done. And despite her hesitance to accept Landon's choices, her inability to ever fully comprehend what he was going through, she's always tried to support him and love him, no matter what.

And he truly loves Dylan. He's always been quiet about it, always reluctant to talk with his parents about the more emotional parts of his life, but she could see it in his blush when she asked him about Dylan, the way he started to ramble before catching himself, biting his lip to keep it all in. She wishes he felt more comfortable around them, that he hadn't felt the need to hold everything in, but she never knew how to tell him and instead settled into a quiet politeness with him.

Seeing them now, Dylan rarely leaving Landon's side, she regrets not knowing more about them. She doesn't know what to say to Dylan, or how to let him know that she doesn't blame him. She can see in the guarded way that he holds himself, the way he can't look into anyone's eyes, he's afraid they'll start yelling at him, telling him that this is all his fault, that he's the reason Landon is lying in this hospital bed. *How does Adele manage to be so warm, so open to her family? She's so easily accepted Landon as a part of her son's life, and she can calm everyone in the room with such ease that even Lana is more comfortable going to her for comfort.*

Helen stares at the freckles dotting Landon's arm, runs her thumb over his skin and hopes that somehow, Landon knows that she's there.

That night, Dylan dreams about the attack, a vivid nightmare in colors too bright, with sounds that echo in his ears and fear so real it's electric in his veins, and he wakes up gasping with his heart pounding against his ribs. Stifled and trapped, he pushes the covers off with a frantic desperation and sits at the edge of his bed and tries to catch his breath. His hands are shaking as he buries his face in them, squeezes his eyes shut and tries to force the images out of his head.

It takes a few minutes for his breathing to get back under control, for the tension in his muscles to ebb and for him to be able to look around the room and comprehend what he's seeing. It's almost six-thirty, and the sun is beginning to rise: golden light seeps through the cracks in his curtains. He slides off the bed onto shaky feet, disoriented, his thoughts distorted by the remnants of his dream.

He showers in a daze, going through the motions without comprehending them. Landon's towel is still neatly hung on the bar next to his, and he avoids looking in the mirror as he brushes his teeth. He makes his way out to the kitchen, feels the wooden floor cool under his bare feet, drinks a glass of water and starts to make coffee the way Landon likes it: strong, with a dash of cream. No sugar.

The faucet is dripping, and he stares at it, the hot mug of coffee clutched in his hands, and watches each drop gather, clinging to the metal ring of the tap until the weight becomes too much and it quivers and falls with a quiet *drip*. He watches each drip and wonders if he's reached the end of what he can take, if he's reached the point where he can't process anything more, that point where reality finally sinks its claws in, sapping him of whatever energy reserve he's been running on.

He turns and the mug slips from his fingers, crashes to the floor. The brown liquid seeps into the small kitchen rug and spreads across the linoleum. Kneeling, he wraps a hand around a shard of the broken mug, still hot from his drink. He holds it up to his face and examines the way the porcelain has cracked in a straight line, jutting sharply to a pointed edge. The white of the glaze looks like bone; Dylan wonders if this is what Landon's skull looks like. Sharp angles, harsh fault lines, jagged edges. Dylan looks back down at the shards on the floor, knowing that the mug can never be put back together. There are too many pieces, an unsolvable puzzle. The mug is no longer a mug, just broken ceramic.

Dylan drops the shard, leans back against the cupboards and closes his eyes against the tears. The silence of the apartment is crushing, as though it's wrapping around his throat and seeping into every pore, completely overwhelming him. His breathing becomes ragged; he's not sure why he's feeling as if he's losing all control. He just wants to get through his morning, to get through this mess of his life as best he can. But he can't help it. Tears leak from behind closed eyes and his good hand grasps at the coffee-stained rug; his fingers thread through the damp fabric.

Someone knocks at the door, but Dylan doesn't notice. He's too wrapped up, stifled, consumed by this *thing* rising inside of him, gripping at his lungs and jumbling his thoughts. He hears the click of the door opening, the sound of footsteps padding across the floor. There's a voice, but Dylan can't understand; everything is distorted, as if he's underwater and the world has narrowed to pinpoints in his vision. Someone sits beside him, arms wrap around him and pull him close, and Dylan imagines it's Landon—Landon, who always knows what to do and how to make Dylan feel better.

But it's not, and he's so frightened by the thought that he'll never feel Landon's arms around him again that he starts shaking harder and his lungs refuse to expand.

"Deep breaths, Dylan." His mother's voice breaks through the fog. "Try to breathe."

Dylan wants to obey, but he can't, his body refuses to cooperate and he feels as if he's going to suffocate on his tears as they mix with panic and he gasps for breath.

"Listen to my voice," Adele says, using the calm but commanding tone she reserves for her tougher yoga classes. "Concentrate on my words, okay? Try and relax your shoulders and let your lungs do the work."

Dylan forces his shoulders to relax and focuses on letting his lungs open, on the air flowing in and out. He tries to find a rhythm in each jagged breath out, each faltering breath in.

"Relax and breathe." Adele's hand strokes down his back in a calming rhythm. He sinks into her, buries his face in her shoulder and slowly his breathing comes back under his control.

"It's okay," Adele says in a softer voice. "You're okay."

"I broke the mug," Dylan manages; the words are muffled by Adele's shoulder.

"It's okay." Adele holds Dylan a little tighter. "It's not your fault."

A fresh wave of tears fills Dylan's eyes and soaks into Adele's shirt, and he can't bring himself to be embarrassed, just cries and hopes that when he's finished the world will be different. That things will make more sense. That maybe he'll understand *why*.

It doesn't take long for his tears to be exhausted; he doesn't have the energy to keep them up, and instead he settles deeper into Adele's embrace. He finds comfort in listening to her breathe, in the feeling of her hand on his back, in the smell of the patchouli and lavender oil in her hair.

"I'm sorry," he murmurs after a long moment has passed and shifts to ease the ache in his arm.

"You did nothing wrong." Adele kisses his forehead. She helps him up without another word, and he leans against her as she guides him to the bedroom, pulls back the covers and nudges him into bed. Landon's side, Dylan notices, and finds an odd comfort in it. His head feels like cotton, his cheeks are too puffy and his ears buzz. He lets his mom smooth the covers over him, lets himself drift, lets himself go.

The sun is shining when he wakes up, and he squints, feeling something brush back the hair on his forehead.

"Hi, sweetheart." Adele smiles from where she sits on the edge of the bed with Dylan's phone clutched in her hand. Dylan licks his lips. His mouth feels so parched it's as if he just traveled across a desert under a blistering sun.

"What time is it?" His voice cracks. He pushes himself up and takes a sip from the water bottle he always keeps by his bed.

"It's just after two." Dylan rubs his eyes and stares at the phone in her hand, confused. "Helen just called."

Dylan's eyes snap up. He takes in the way she's smiling at him and tries not to let his thoughts go where they so desperately want to go. "Landon opened his eyes. Not for very long, but she said he looked around before he fell back asleep."

Dylan sits up straight, his heart in his throat.

"He's awake?"

"It's not like the movies, honey." Adele speaks slowly, as if she's choosing her words carefully. "This is a step forward, but he's not going to wake up like you want him to."

Dylan nods, looks at his hands and feels silly for jumping to such a conclusion.

"But he looked around." He tests the words on his tongue. "He opened his eyes."

Looking back up at his mom, he wonders if maybe hope isn't such a bad thing after all. "He's improving."

"He's trying his hardest," Adele says, and Dylan can't help but echo her smile. Adele cards his hair with her fingers and gently works out a few tangles. "I'd like you to come to one of my classes. I think it could help."

Dylan squeezes his eyes shut. Adele's fingers leave his hair. Her profession has always been a sensitive topic between them. He used to go to her yoga classes, had loved the stretch and burn of his muscles when he was younger. But then he grew older and saw how, with every flop of one of his father's plays, his mother would have to take on more classes, have to find more students, have to work even harder to make sure the bills got paid. Until his father took on the technical writing job. Dylan had hated the knowledge that they were barely scraping by. He couldn't help but resent his mom for not finding a better paying job, or his dad for not working in an office and never having to worry about money. That's when he stopped going to her classes, and while he regrets the things he said as a teenager, there's still tension between them when his mom brings up the topic.

But maybe it's time to let that go. He opens his eyes and sees the way Adele is looking at him, cautious and caring, and Dylan knows she only wants what's best for him. She's just trying to help.

"Okay." His voice is barely above a whisper, and Adele gives him a soft smile, then presses a kiss to his forehead.

"Let's go to the hospital."

Landon doesn't open his eyes again that day, but Dylan isn't upset. Just the knowledge that he did it, that it happened, is more than Dylan has hoped for, and he doesn't want to expect too much. He knows that Landon isn't going to just wake up and tell him he had a lovely nap, but he's ready to go home now. It takes time. Landon needs time.

Instead, Dylan brings his laptop to the hospital and nestles himself in the chair that's quickly becoming so familiar. It's awkward, typing with only one hand—his left arm is still strapped against his chest as his shoulder heals—but he manages. He connects to the hospital's wifi, stares at the Google icon and hesitates before typing in the two words that haven't left his mind all day. For the first time, he wants to know, wants to learn everything he can about what's happening to Landon: about the possibilities, about all the terms the doctors have used that he doesn't understand. He needs to know.

The words "brain injury" bring up over seventeen million results. Dylan blinks at the screen; he doesn't know where to begin. He finds information on strokes, on trauma, on hemorrhages, and it's so overwhelming that he closes his eyes and takes a deep breath. It makes him feel better to start to understand what's happening to Landon. Even if everything is still so unsure, still so vague, he's beginning to have a semblance of an idea. He spends the next hour scribbling down questions to ask the nurses, the doctors, the therapists who pop in and out of the room at various intervals during the day.

Knowing his own tendency to get carried away when he puts his mind to something, he forces himself to stop when the paper is full and his hand cramps. He folds the paper in a neat square and tucks it into his pocket. Information is still bouncing in his head, on the verge of overwhelming him, but he doesn't let it. Instead he sits back in the chair and watches Landon. The bruise on the left side of his face is starting to shrink, the eye is less swollen and the sickly hue of his skin is fading into a healthier color. Dylan can almost imagine that he's just sleeping.

There's a quick knock on the sliding glass door before a nurse walks in; her dark hair is pulled back into a sloppy bun. It's Elena, one of the nurses Dylan has become familiar with. She greets him with a wide smile

"How are you doing today?"

"Better, I think." Dylan answers honestly and, for the first time, he smiles back.

"Smiling is a good look on you," she says, her accent smooth and calming, and Dylan blushes and looks down. Adele asked her where she was from, once, and she told them she'd moved up from Colombia a few years back, had followed her family and joined a good nursing program. Dylan likes how gentle she is with Landon, always making sure to talk to him softly before she does anything; her touch is natural and caring.

She listens to Landon's heart and lungs, shines a light in his eyes and swabs his mouth with antiseptic, narrating her actions all the while to both Dylan and Landon. She picks up one of Landon's hands and pinches the end of a finger and Landon lets out a soft groan and feebly tries to pull away. Dylan sits straight up, his eyes wide.

"Is that… was that…"

Elena sets down Landon's hand and looks up at Dylan with a smile.

"He's responding to painful stimuli. It's a good thing."

Good. The word floats in Dylan's head, and he barely pays attention as she finishes her assessment. Instead, he stares at Landon's hand, watching for any further movement. The fingers twitch, just a tiny motion, and Dylan breath catches. It is such a minor thing, but it's so much *more* than what he's had, it becomes something to cling to and focus on.

"How… um, how is he doing?" Dylan asks, and Elena looks up, a guarded surprise in her eyes. Dylan hasn't been very vocal; he has let his parents or Landon's parents ask the questions and hear the explanations. He wonders if he's been a horrible fiancé, if the nurses have talked about how Landon deserves better. And part of him thinks that Landon probably does, while another part fills with determination to be more involved, to not get so caught up in his own head again—to be here for Landon, in more than just a physical sense.

"He's doing really well," Elena answers. "His vital signs are stable, his labs have been within normal limits and he's been tolerating the adjustments we've made with his medications. It's hard to fully assess brain function right now, until he wakes up a little more. But his scans are improving every day."

Dylan nods, trying to imagine what's happening inside Landon's head, the way his brain is fighting to survive.

"Do you…" He licks his lips, clears his throat. "Do you think there'll be lasting, um… lasting damage?"

Elena's eyes soften. "That I can't answer for you. But I do know, no matter what happens, Landon will have all the love and support he needs."

"He will." Dylan directs his promise toward Landon. He squeezes Landon's hand, and this time, the fingers move.

Two days pass before Landon opens his eyes again. Dylan has a follow-up appointment that morning for his shoulder. The joint is still stiff and sore, and he's instructed to wear his sling for another two weeks, until his next appointment. It's a nuisance, but Dylan is only mildly annoyed; he's gotten pretty good at doing everything one-handed, and he's more concerned with Landon's recovery than his own.

It's early afternoon when he finally gets to the hospital, later than he would like, and his knee is bouncing during the entire drive. He walks quickly. Adele follows close behind him; she's been his source of transportation lately, driving him to and from the hospital. His dad takes over when she has a class to teach. On their way in, Adele greets the hospital staff, many by name. Dylan tries to offer a few smiles, but this still doesn't come easily to him, not when he's so anxious to get to Landon.

Helen is standing outside the room, talking softly to a nurse. She turns when he approaches. She looks as if she hasn't had a good night's sleep in weeks. Dylan's sure they all look like that, worn-down versions of their past selves.

"Is everything okay?" Dylan asks, the words almost catching in his throat as he looks at Helen and the nurse.

"Why don't you go in?" Helen asks with a weak smile pulling at her lips.

Dylan hesitates. He wants to ask more questions, and worry knots his gut, but Adele puts a hand on his back and nudges him into the room. Lana is sitting beside the bed, and when she looks up at him he sees that her eyes are wet. The head of Landon's bed is raised halfway and the blankets pool at his waist. His half-lidded eyes open slightly as Dylan steps into the room.

"Oh." The word escapes him in a breath, and he falters, struggling to process what he's seeing. Lana lets out a wavering laugh and bites her lip. Dylan steps closer and slides into the familiar chair beside the bed. Landon's eyes follow him, his gaze unfocused, as though he's half asleep. His face is just as expressionless as it was when he was sedated.

"Hi," Dylan manages, reaching forward with a shaking hand. Landon's fingers curl when Dylan takes them in his own, and his eyelids close in a slow blink. "Welcome back."

Dylan's heart thuds as Landon's eyes settle on his face. He wants so badly to believe that Landon understands.

"I missed you," Dylan says, his voice thick with emotion. "We all missed you."

Landon's eyes start to slip closed, and Dylan wants to beg him to stay, wants to plead for some sort of reaction, any sign that Landon hears him. But he can't, and as Landon's eyes shut and his fingers go lax in Dylan's, a warm sense of relief fills Dylan, a tiny ray of sun fills his chest.

"He's been in and out all morning," Lana says after a silent moment. Dylan looks up to see her wipe her eyes with the sleeve of her cardigan.

"Good… that's good, right?" Dylan asks, feels Adele's hand on his shoulder, a gentle squeeze.

"He hasn't been responding to anyone, just looking around, but…" Lana gazes at Landon fondly. "They said he might need more time. His brain…"

Dylan nods when Lana trails off, understanding. The trauma to the left side of his brain is so severe that the likelihood of him recovering without any long-lasting effects is minimal. It's hard, to know something is wrong without knowing exactly *what* is wrong. The not knowing throws another wrench in Dylan's need to organize and plan. He wants to be ready for whatever Landon is going to need. Whatever extra support, therapies, doctors—Dylan knows he'll give *everything* he has to help Landon recover. Whatever it takes.

Chapter 4

The physical therapist's name is Matt, and he's tall, with blond
hair and muscles that look as if they could rip through his shirt.
Dylan has to force himself not to stare, even when Matt's smile
flashes teeth unnaturally white, even when his biceps flex and
strain at the sleeves of his scrubs. Matt is friendly and has an
excitement about exercise that makes Dylan believe that he really
does run fifteen miles a day for fun, something both inspiring
and slightly irritating.

Matt is all about involvement, and directs Dylan to help with
therapy in the small ways that he can. At first this made Dylan
uneasy; something about Landon seems so delicate now, so
breakable, and he was afraid of hurting him. But now Dylan
looks forward to Matt's visits and the opportunity to feel as
though he's helping Landon, even if it's just massaging his hands
or helping him curl his fingers into a fist, or holding a leg steady
while Matt does most of work.

Today Matt announces that they're going to sit up. At first Dylan doesn't understand what he means; the head of Landon's bed is already elevated to over forty-five degrees, and the nurses like to prop pillows behind him, until he's in a little nestlike chair-bed. But then Matt lowers the foot of the bed until it's flat, rearranges pillows and clears a spot at the edge of the bed.

"Today the edge of the bed," Matt announces, teeth flashing. "We'll work on building some neck support, and hopefully soon we'll make it into a chair."

Landon stares at Matt the same way he has stared at everyone else over the past two days, only this time his eyebrows scrunch together; his gaze slides from Matt to Dylan, back to Matt.

"You're looking good today, Landon." Matt takes a few of Landon's fingers in his hand. "Can you squeeze my fingers for me?"

Dylan's breath catches in his throat as Landon's fingers twitch with the slightest squeeze to Matt's hand.

"That's great, Landon." Matt looks at Dylan with a wide smile.

"He…" Dylan starts, and stands up cautiously at the edge of the bed. Matt offers Landon's hand and Dylan takes it. He feels Landon's fingers, so delicate in his own. Landon looks up at him, his eyes still tired but full of more clarity than Dylan has seen in a long time, and gives Dylan's fingers a light but purposeful squeeze. Dylan squeezes back.

"I'll talk to the occupational therapist," Matt says. "Let them know about his improvements today."

"Thank you."

Matt smiles and runs a hand through hair that Dylan could only begin to describe as *messy-chic*. "All right, let's get sitting."

Together, Matt and Dylan help Landon turn in bed and dangle his legs over the edge; their arms support his back as they get him upright and take a seat at either side of him. Landon manages to keep his head up for almost a minute before he begins to sag, and Dylan guides him to lie against his shoulder.

A memory floats into Dylan's mind of last winter, when the flu had been particularly brutal. Landon always seemed to catch everything that was going around from the children he worked with, and Dylan used to tease him that he was equally dramatic. He remembers Landon bedridden with the flu, moaning, "This is it, this is the end." Dylan kissed his sweaty forehead, pulled him up into a position similar to the one they're in now, plied him with Gatorade and saltines and cuddled with him until Landon admitted that maybe the world wasn't ending.

"You're doing great." Matt's voice pulls Dylan from his thoughts. He makes sure Dylan is supporting Landon before sliding off the bed to work on leg movement exercises. In the next ten minutes he has Landon flex and stretch his toes and move his ankle in the slightest circle. Then he switches to passive exercises, to help Landon keep a normal range of motion.

They're only little things, but to Dylan they seem like leaps, and by the time they have Landon situated back in bed, Dylan can tell Landon is exhausted. His eyes are fighting to stay open. But at least they're fighting for *something*.

Matt leaves with a smile and a promise to be back tomorrow, and for the first time, Dylan feels genuine optimism about the future.

Lana leans against the fence with a cigarette between her lips. The wind, a cool breeze in the August heat, stirs her hair. She closes her eyes, takes a drag of the cigarette and holds the burn of smoke in her lungs until her chest aches. It's easier to focus on the little things: the birds singing from trees high above, the sound of cars passing by, the quick beating of her heart.

It's easier.

She can hear footsteps behind her, a soft crunch of gravel.

"I didn't know you smoked," Dylan says, leaning against the fence beside her.

"I don't." She flicks the ash from the end, offers it to him. Dylan hesitates, eyes flickering from her to the cigarette before he finally accepts it and places it clumsily between his lips. He takes a drag, too deep, and starts coughing; his lips turn down in distaste.

Lana laughs, a small sound, and she takes the cigarette back.

Dylan laughs too, with a sheepish smile on his lips. "Landon would've killed me if he knew I did that," Dylan says, resting his forearms against the fence.

"Our mom used to smoke." Lana stares down at the pavement. "Landon was the one who made her quit. Well, she told us she quit, but I think we all knew she just started hiding it. It drove him crazy."

Lana drops the cigarette to the ground and crushes it under her toes.

"I thought it might help," she says with a shrug. She looks back up.

"Did it?"

"Not really." Lana looks back up at Dylan. The afternoon sun brings out the warm undertones in his skin, and she can even make out a few freckles along his nose. Nothing like Landon's freckles, but she's never noticed them before. His lips look soft and pink, as if he's recently been biting them, and she remembers Landon going on about those lips when he came home from school and they stayed up late watching trashy TV together. He always blushed when he realized what he was saying.

Now she's lucky if he even opens his eyes when she's in the room.

"Are you leaving?" she asks, and Dylan shakes his head.

"Just needed some air." He drums his fingers along the top of the fence. They're half a block from the hospital; the fence borders a small patch of grass outside an apartment complex. She'd come for a walk with a snagged pack of cigarettes from her mom's purse in hand; she needed something, anything, to clear her head.

"A speech therapist just saw Landon," Dylan says, after a moment. Lana looks up at him, waiting. "He said a few words, but they didn't make any sense."

He kicks a rock and watches it roll into the grass. Lana understands; it's been a few days since Landon began waking up with any frequency, and the repercussions of his injury are becoming more and more apparent.

"What did they say?" Lana asks, but she isn't sure she actually wants to know.

Dylan draws in a deep breath and turns his face to the sun with his eyes closed.

"Some of the same," he says. "It's hard to know lasting damage this early, but…"

Lana looks up at him. "But there will be. Lasting damage." It's not even a question. They all know.

Dylan swallows, his Adam's apple bobbing.

"Yeah. There will be."

His voice is soft. Lana knows how hard it is to stay together, to feel as if you're about to dissolve at any moment when the world no longer makes sense, when everything impossible has suddenly become everything that's real. When someone you love is never coming back.

She wraps an arm around Dylan's waist and leans against him with her head resting against his shoulder. He hugs her back, and together they watch the sun begin to set, both lost in their own thoughts but not alone.

When Dylan goes back to Landon's room, the light is still on and he sees a stack of laminated cards on the bed between Landon and Helen. Helen looks up as Dylan enters.

"We were just going through the cards the speech therapist left for Landon," Helen explains, as Dylan takes a seat on the other side of the bed. Landon's gaze travels from Helen to Dylan; his fingers twitch toward Dylan's hand. Dylan wraps them in his own, kisses Landon's cheek.

"I'm sorry I left, I just…" He trails off, unsure of how to justify his sudden need for space, the knot in his stomach that had threatened to overwhelm him as he watched Landon struggle through the simple tasks the therapist had presented.

"It's okay," Helen assures him, pushing the cards into a neat pile before passing them to Dylan. "You're here now."

Dylan smiles as Landon squeezes his hand.

"I'm going to head to Lana's for a shower and a nap. You need anything?" Helen asks, standing and gathering her bag and coat.

"We'll be all right." Dylan shakes his head. "Thank you."

"Well, you let me know." Helen kisses Landon's forehead. "Goodbye, honey."

She touches Dylan's shoulder lightly before exiting the room, leaving them alone. Dylan thumbs through the cards, aware of Landon's gaze. Landon looks tired, and a frown creases the space between his eyes. He keeps shifting his legs under the covers.

"What's wrong?" Dylan asks, concern growing in him. Landon makes a small noise that sounds as if it might be a word, but it's impossible to make out. Dylan picks through the cards and finds a set of faces in various stages of distress. He lays them out for Landon to look at.

"Can you point to how you're feeling?"

Landon glances at the cards and pushes them away with clumsy hands.

"Okay…" Dylan is at a loss. He bites his lip and pulls out the rest of the cards, laying them across Landon's lap. There are a variety of pictures on them, showing activities, basic personal needs and different body parts that could be causing him pain. Landon looks over the cards; his eyes flutter shut and open again before he pokes at one.

"Pillow?" Dylan glances at the card and at the pillows behind Landon's back. The more awake Landon's become, the more particular he's been about his pillows, always struggling against them, making sure Dylan and the nurses are aware when he's uncomfortable. Dylan helps Landon lean forward, and readjusts the pillows behind him into a shape that looks a little more comfortable. Landon settles back with a smile on his face.

"Better?"

Landon looks back at the cards; his lips purse in concentration. His fingers drift over one, fumble with the edges of it before he manages to grip it between his thumb and index finger. The card has musical notes on it, drifting over a drawing of a radio.

"Music?" Dylan questions. "You want to listen to music?"

Landon blinks, turns his head to look at Dylan and nods. A smile tugs at Dylan's lips; an almost giddy excitement builds inside him at this new level of communication, at being able to understand what Landon wants, and Landon being able to *show* him what he wants.

Dylan pulls his phone out of his bag, finds a playlist of acoustic guitar solos that Landon had been trying to master and turns the volume up just enough for them to hear but not enough to give Landon a headache.

Landon's shoulders relax, and his gaze flickers between the phone and Dylan. He looks content. Almost happy. His hand slides across the bed until it bumps against Dylan's. Landon's thumb brushes against Dylan's ring, sliding over the smooth metal before brushing the skin of his knuckles.

"I have your ring." Dylan keeps his voice quiet, steady. "It's at home, waiting for you to wear it again."

Dylan lifts Landon's hand, kisses the soft skin of his fingers. Landon's eyes meet his, and Dylan pretends he understands. The guitar music drifts over them, and Dylan's heart is warm with the knowledge that Landon was able to communicate with him, even just a little bit.

Landon stays awake for a good part of the day, watching as people move in and out, his eyes always finding Dylan's. He even rolls his shoulders at one point, a small grunt working its way from his throat. A pillow is folded uncomfortably behind him and Dylan keeps helping him adjust to a more comfortable position.

Helen joins them later in the day; her eyes are tired, but her hair's been washed and she looks refreshed. A large coffee is clutched in her hands. Dylan updates her on the day's achievements and Helen takes Landon's hand, tells him how proud she is of him. They sit in silence, and Dylan pages through a magazine Adele brought earlier in the day, something about organic living, but he can't focus on it. His thoughts are too caught up in the day, in what these small improvements could mean. Is this just a small step in a long recovery? Or is this how Landon's life is going to be, now, an existence of hand squeezes, picture cards and broken words?

The thoughts race in his head until he closes his eyes and drifts in and out, fingers still laced with Landon's, until a noise, almost a high-pitched whine, breaks through the tired fog of his mind and he opens his eyes and sees Helen looking at Landon with an expression of concern.

"What…" Dylan starts, and then he sees Landon's lips twitch, his fingers start to tremble.

"Landon, sweetie?" Helen says, and Landon's eyes crack open, his throat works out a choked gasp. Dylan can tell something is wrong: Landon's face is tense, his eyes move back and forth impossibly fast. Dylan pounds the call light.

A nurse enters the room just as Landon begins to shake; guttural moans escape his lips. Dylan freezes. He doesn't know what to do, doesn't even think he can move. The nurse presses an alarm on the wall. More people flood into the room. Questions are directed at him, and he doesn't know how to answer. Helen responds instead, her voice muted and metallic in his ears.

He doesn't understand what's happening; time is slowing down and speeding up all at once, and his eyes are locked on

Landon convulsing on the bed. It's nothing like the movies, where everything is romanticized, made pretty by lights and makeup. On TV, doctors swoop in with a magic cure or heroic fix, and everything is okay again. Mystery solved, lives put back together in forty-five minutes.

But reality is ugly. Reality is Dylan forgetting to breathe and his head swimming as he watches Landon arch off the bed, his face red, aborted grunts escaping his lips, harsh and animalistic. It's nothing like anything Dylan's ever seen before, and he's sure this is the end and he never got to say goodbye.

People push around him, and he feels their hands on his shoulders, trying to guide him from the room. He can hear himself protesting and he feels hot; his stomach is churning but he can't leave, he never got to say goodbye, he needs to say goodbye, he needs to be here.

He's in the hallway, hunched over, a hand on his back, as he heaves into one of those blue hospital puke bags.

"Deep breaths, Dylan, just like that, keep breathing," a voice says in his ear, soft and comforting, and Dylan tries to obey, forces his lungs to do what they're meant to do. He blinks and clutches the blue puke bag as he coughs, drawing in air through his burning throat. Her face wet with tears, Helen rubs soothing circles on his back. A nurse he doesn't recognize is on his other side.

"It's okay," Helen whispers. Dylan's not sure if she's trying to reassure him or herself. "It's okay. It's going to be okay."

The words are repeated like a mantra, one that Dylan's not sure he can believe. He's barely holding on. Every time things start to look up, every time he starts to actually *hope*, something happens to tear it away, leaving him grasping and unbalanced.

Helen pulls him into a hug, and Dylan realizes he's crying, and it's awkward because he's so much taller than her, but it doesn't matter. Helen's arms stay wrapped around his waist, and his head falls to her shoulder, and he cries. He cries out of fear, worry, out of loss, and love and an *ache* that just won't go away.

They wait in the hallway, surrounded by the bustle of the ICU and the smell of antiseptic that Dylan can never seem to get out of his clothes. A patient, pale and gasping, is wheeled past them; a woman clings to his hand, whispers comforts that Dylan can't make out. He wonders with a strange detachment if the patient is dying, and how much time he has left. He wonders if the woman with him is his wife, girlfriend, sister. What she'll do when he's gone.

He wishes he could feel something for them, that he could muster up the energy to feel something for anyone in this place, but he's not sure he can, not with his emotions colliding, exploding, *suffocating* inside of him. He doesn't know if it's empathy or apathy he feels toward the man and woman, but he wishes he knew. All he knows is that every thought, every pang in his chest, every beat of his racing heart goes to Landon.

Landon. As if the world is changing orbit and Landon is the stuttering sun.

Dylan's not sure where the world will go if the sun goes out.

They talk to the doctors. Dylan nods as though he understands when they use words like "tonic-clonic" and "post-traumatic epilepsy," when they talk about neurons and synapses, scarring and abnormal electrical activity. He wants to understand, he *needs* to understand, but right now he feels fuzzy, as if someone has stuffed his brain with cotton balls, and all he can think about is getting back to Landon. He'll research later; he's become good at researching, he'll ask questions and take notes and learn as much as he can.

Later. Right now, he just wants to be with his fiancé.

Landon is sleeping when they're finally allowed back in. He looks the same as before. Maybe his face is a little paler, the rings under his eyes a little darker, maybe a bruise is forming on his arm where it hit the bedrail, but nothing else about him betrays what just happened. Dylan pulls his chair back to the bed. He feels as if he's vibrating, as if he's still moving, even as he sits. So he focuses on the little things: Landon's eyelashes, the nasal cannula snaking under his nose, the gentle parting of his lips, the freckles dotting his skin, the rise and fall of his chest with every breath.

He doesn't know what to say, just listens as Helen cries softly, her hand clutching Landon's, and wonders if the world will ever slow down so he can think again.

Sleeping seems like a good idea.

The room is dark when Dylan wakes up. He's hunched forward, his arms forming a makeshift pillow on Landon's bed. There's an ache in his back, and drool that he quickly wipes off his cheek, but he feels rested, his head clear. A blanket he doesn't remember grabbing slides off his shoulders as he sits up; he arches his spine as he stretches back into the chair… and freezes.

Landon's eyes are open, half-focused and following his movements. His fingers twitch on the blanket but otherwise he remains still, only his quiet gaze betraying that anything is different. Dylan smiles: Landon is still here. Today was scary, but they made it through. *Landon* made it through.

"Hey." Dylan keeps his voice soft. Helen is sleeping in the recliner chair in the corner, and he doesn't want to wake her; she hasn't been getting much sleep lately. He reaches for Landon's hand and tangles their fingers together.

"You've been sleeping for a long time," Dylan says after a moment. Landon blinks, his eyes focused on Dylan's face. *Please stay awake.* "You can sleep as long as you want, I don't mind. I just want you to be okay."

Dylan pauses and then gently kisses Landon's forehead, just above his left eyebrow. Landon moves slightly: the smallest tip of his head, a minuscule bend of his knee, the tiniest scrunch of his nose.

Please stay. "I'll be here, whenever you're ready. Take as much time as you need. I'll wait right here for you, I promise."

Dylan shifts in his seat and bites his lip.

I miss you. "Whenever you're ready."

Landon squeezes his fingers.

Dylan knows he shouldn't be surprised; he's seen the numerous text messages, the calls he's left unanswered. It's been over three weeks since the incident, and he has every intention of getting back to people; every day he stares at his phone, his fingers hovering over the keyboard. But then he stops, unsure of what to say or how to say it, and he knows he shouldn't but he puts his phone away. Tells himself he'll respond tomorrow.

So when Helen enters Landon's room that evening, Dylan is only surprised for a moment to see Tate following close behind. Tate has been Landon's best friend since their first year of college; both were recruited to join the swim team, and they've been friends since their very first day of practice. Even after graduation they stayed close, Landon working as a child life specialist at the children's hospital, Tate as a kindergarten teacher, and Dylan's always been entertained when listening to them complain about the antics of small children.

Tate looks scared now: his eyes are wide and his face is pale. He must have come straight after work, because he is still wearing a slightly wrinkled button-down, his dark hair is nicely brushed and Dylan can see pink and green marker smudges on his hands. Tate takes in the room, his eyes moving from the monitor tracking Landon's vital signs, to the IV pole by his bed, to Dylan, to Landon. Landon's eyes are closed in sleep, but Dylan knows how it must look: the harsh red scars on his head, his thick auburn hair shaved down to his scalp, the faint remnants of bruising still on his cheek.

"Is he…" Tate starts, his voice catching.

"He's sleeping right now," Helen explains, her voice as steady and clinical as a doctor's. "He's been in and out the past few days, so he might wake up for you."

Tate swallows nervously and takes a half step forward.

"How is he…" Tate starts. Dylan lowers his eyes, guilt rising in him that he hasn't been keeping anyone updated. "Doing, I mean."

"He's had some difficulties," Helen says, and Dylan thinks that word can't even begin to cover the fear he felt yesterday during Landon's seizure. "But the doctors say he's improving."

Tate nods, and his lips part as if he wants to ask more questions but is afraid—afraid of the answers, maybe. Anxiety knots in Dylan's gut; he's uneasy about Tate's reaction and he can't sit here anymore. He stands up, mutters an excuse about needing air and leaves. He wanders around the hospital, shaking his hands to try to get rid of the nerves tingling under his skin.

He hadn't expected seeing Tate to have this effect: it is a stark reminder of what their life was like before. Of everything they've lost. He remembers Landon staying up late to study with Tate, remembers going on double dates with Tate and his girlfriend in college, remembers, just a few weeks ago, having a drink out at a local brewery with them. They hadn't talked about anything important, had just spent the night laughing over too much beer. It was fun, lighthearted and something Dylan can't imagine ever doing again. Not anymore.

He buys a pop just to have something to do and loiters outside the building until his head begins to clear and embarrassment creeps in. He knows that if Landon were capable of it, he'd tell him off for leaving so rudely. Dylan smiles, picturing the way Landon's cheeks turned red when they argued, the look he'd get in his eyes when he glared at Dylan. The way Tate would shake his head when they bickered, calling them an old married couple after only a few months of dating.

Tate is alone in the room when Dylan gets back; he watches Dylan enter with unsure eyes.

"I'm sorry," Dylan says, standing near the foot of the bed. Tate stays silent and looks back at Landon. Dylan sits across from him, uncomfortable in the tension that has settled between them. "I should've called you."

Tate blinks, looks up.

"A lot of people have been asking me how he's doing," Tate says, his expression pained. "He's my best friend, and all I knew was what was on the news."

Dylan looks down at the blankets covering Landon and wishes he had a good excuse to give Tate. He doesn't.

"I'm sorry," Dylan repeats. He doesn't know what else to say. Tate lets out a breath and scrubs a hand over his face as if he's trying not to cry.

"I had to find his sister on Facebook to get an update," Tate says. His voice isn't accusatory, and Dylan is grateful, even though he deserves it. "She told me what happened, and I can't even imagine what you went through, but…"

"But you deserved to know."

"He's my best friend. Every day I didn't know what was going on, I felt like I couldn't focus on anything else."

"Landon would be pissed at me," Dylan says, takes Landon's hand in his. "For not calling you."

Tate looks at Dylan for a moment before a sad smile pulls at his lips.

"Yeah, he would."

"I'll do better," Dylan promises, and he really means it. "I'll keep you updated."

Tate looks at Landon's hand clutched in Dylan's.

"Thank you."

They sit in silence, but this time it's more comfortable. A nurse comes in, greets Dylan and introduces herself to Tate before hanging a new bag of medication. Landon begins to stir after she leaves; his face scrunches slightly, his fingers tighten on Dylan's.

Tate's eyes widen, and he glances up at Dylan as if looking for direction.

"Landon," Dylan says, squeezing Landon's fingers in the way that's becoming so familiar. "Someone is here to see you."

Landon's eyes blink open, hazy and confused as they usually are when he first wakes up. It takes him a few moments to start looking around and begin to focus on things around him. He looks over at Dylan first, blinks and shifts his shoulders, wincing. Dylan extracts his hand from Landon's and raises the head of the bed, adjusting the pillows behind him until Landon is sitting more comfortably. It amazes him how quickly he's been learning to read Landon, every expression, every movement, even the way he blinks or twitches his fingers.

"You have a visitor." Dylan motions slowly to the other side of the bed. Landon makes a small noise in his throat, something he's been doing more and more lately, before turning his head so that his eyes find Tate. Tate offers a smile, but it's strained and there's a minute tremble in his hands.

"Hey, Lan," Tate says, voice wavering. He looks up at Dylan as if unsure of what he's doing, and Dylan gives an encouraging nod. Tate lifts his hand, pauses, and rests it on Landon's forearm. Landon's gaze flickers down to the arm before it moves back up to Tate; he looks as though he's trying to understand with an expression of concentration unlike any Dylan has seen before. It makes Dylan's own breath stutter, and he waits to see what will happen.

"It's me, Tate," Tate continues, gently squeezing Landon's arm. "I, uh, I guess I don't know if you remember me or not, but… but I've missed you."

Landon's head tilts, his eyes still searching Tate's. He turns back to look at Dylan, and Dylan smiles at him. Landon looks back at Tate, at the hand on his arm. His lips twitch and his eyebrows draw together. The arm closest to Dylan lifts, just a few inches, but Landon tries to move it across the bed, toward Tate. He can't quite make it over the rise of his body, and Dylan helps, guides his arm over to the other side. Landon curls his fingers into a loose fist, with only his index finger staying out.

They both watch in bewilderment as Landon pokes Tate's hand with a single finger, once, twice. And Dylan can't help it; he starts laughing. It's so ridiculous, and yet so Landon.

Tate, stunned, watches Landon's hand where it has rested near his own and looks up when a sharp laugh escapes Dylan's lips.

It's strange to laugh, after weeks of being so emotionally drained, but it's refreshing. It leaves Dylan feeling lighter than he has in a while.

Landon looks between them. Dylan can't be sure, but he thinks he sees the faintest echo of a smile.

Chapter 5

Landon has it all planned out. Tomorrow. He has tickets *for them to see Dylan's favorite band, has a romantic dinner reserved at their favorite restaurant. He has roses ready to be picked up from the flower shop, rings hidden in the sock drawer, a playlist made for when they get back home. He has a speech written, has spent hours memorizing it, and there's no way he's going to screw up because it's going to be* perfect.

It's going to be perfect because Dylan is perfect, and Landon is so in love, and Dylan needs to know how much this means to him, how much he wants a life together, just the two of them. He's already called Dylan's family—had stuttered his way through his request—because getting the approval of Dylan's parents seemed like the right thing to do. And they gave it to him, Adele laughing and telling Landon he's already part of their family, and it's about time they do something to make it official.

It's all planned out, and he's vowed not to think about it until tomorrow, but he's already nervous, his stomach is fluttering and churning. He can't stop staring at Dylan when Dylan's not looking, imagining him in a suit with a gold band around his finger. He blushes and turns away when Dylan catches him watching and fiddles with his sleeves, pretending to be interested in something in the distance.

"What's gotten into you?" Dylan asks, as they walk to the street fair that had set up a few blocks away for the weekend. Landon shrugs, tries to force down the smile on his face and fails miserably.

"Nothing."

Dylan narrows his eyes. "Why are you smiling so much?"

"Am I not allowed to smile anymore?"

"Nope, I forbid it."

Landon pouts, and Dylan reaches up to poke his bottom lip. Landon snaps at his finger.

"Remind me why I still love you?" Dylan asks, and Landon's stomach flips in a way he'd thought he'd have gotten used to after all these years.

"Because I make you breakfast?"

Dylan squints, his face serious, and nods. "It helps that you've decided clothing is optional while cooking."

"The kitchen gets hot!" Landon protests, crossing his arms. "Maybe if you stopped moving the fan onto the balcony, I wouldn't be forced to cook naked."

"Hmm." Dylan darts forward to kiss to Landon's cheek. "Maybe that's why I keep moving the fan."

They turn the corner, and everything is a flurry of activity and color and music; tables line the street, filled with bright assortments of jewelry and clothes and pottery and everything Landon can *possibly imagine. The air smells sweet, of cotton candy and kettle corn. Children run shrieking around them, and musicians play guitars and maracas at every corner.*

Dylan's face lights up; his eyes dart around to take everything in, and Landon knows this is why Dylan loves Minneapolis, a city where they can feel free to be themselves, where they can walk down a busy street with their fingers intertwined and not worry about anything except which coffee shop they should get their caffeine from, and if they really need to add another throw pillow to their ever-growing collection. It's times like this when Landon realizes that, even though he grew up in Madison, Minneapolis really is his home.

Dylan leads Landon around the market by the hand, stopping to examine homemade jewelry, snag free samples of home-baked goods, or use Landon as a prop to try on scarf and hat combinations, chatting enthusiastically with the few familiar faces they run into. Landon sneaks off to buy cotton candy, half pink and half blue. Dylan steals all of the blue side, laughing when Landon pouts. They share a kiss in the shade of a tree; their lips are sweet and sticky.

"I think you might be my favorite," Dylan says when they make their way slowly back through the market as the shadows start to grow long around them in the setting sun.

"Your favorite?" Landon raises his eyebrows and looks at Dylan; Dylan's skin glows warm in the light.

"Yup." Dylan grasps Landon's hand and swings it between them. "My favorite."

"Good," Landon says thoughtfully. "I think I like being your favorite."

They're at the edge of a park; the music and laughter from the market echo behind them, and Dylan pulls Landon onto the grass, his smile vibrant.

"Your lips are blue."

"Maybe you shouldn't have bought cotton candy then," Dylan replies, still smiling.

"Maybe I like your blue lips." Landon leans in for a kiss. They linger just a moment, aware of the crowd behind them, the people walking by, but unwilling to let the moment end so soon. It's been a busy year, and their schedules have not always matched up; social obligations have filled their free days, and it's been a while since they've had a day like this, open and free, just them. Landon wishes it could last a little longer.

Dylan pulls back, his eyes roaming Landon's face, and he brushes a strand of hair off Landon's forehead.

"Marry me," Dylan whispers, his voice low and serious. Something close to panic churns in Landon's stomach.

"What?" The word falls from Landon's lips and he takes a step back, acutely aware of the ring back home in the sock drawer.

"Marry me?" Dylan tries again, shuffling his feet. "I know this isn't very romantic and it's really sudden, but..." He pauses, and then smiles. "It seems right. I want you to marry me. Pretty please?"

Landon gapes. He knows he looks ridiculous, but he can't help it: He can't believe this. All his carefully made plans and secrets, and now his proposal is spoiled by Dylan asking first?

"No..." Landon starts, before he realizes how that sounds and snaps his mouth shut as Dylan's smile fades.

"No?" Dylan's eyes search Landon's face. "Okay... wow, um. I guess I just thought—"

"No," Landon rushes to repeat. He steps forward and grabs Dylan's hands in his own. "No, that's not what I meant."

Dylan draws his hands away, plants them firmly on his hips and tilts his head. "Please enlighten me as to what else no possibly means?"

"It's just…" Landon starts, still reluctant to spoil his plans. But one look at Dylan's face and he throws his hands up and looks pleadingly at him. "I was going to propose to you. Literally tomorrow. I have a ring and everything."

Now it's Dylan's turn for his mouth to drop open, and he blinks as if he's trying to catch up to this newest turn of events.

"I even got us reservations." Landon's voice is meek. He's feeling like a bit of an idiot. He should have just asked, weeks ago, months ago, instead of spending all this time agonizing about it being perfect. Because, really, when do things ever go the way he expects them to?

"Oh," Dylan says. He licks his lips and steps in closer to Landon. "Oh."

"Yeah." Landon looks down, cheeks burning.

"I see." There's a gentle touch under his chin, lifting his head until he can see Dylan's face. "You've been planning this for a long time, haven't you?"

Landon nods.

"I bet it was a really romantic plan." Dylan lips twitch into a smile. "Very thought out. A definite sweep me off my feet plan."

He kisses Landon, as the warm summer breeze rustles through their hair.

"It was." Landon breathes against Dylan's lips and tangles their fingers together.

"And I just ruined it."

A laugh bubbles out of Landon's chest and Dylan chuckles and draws Landon into his arms. Landon's head falls against Dylan's shoulder.

"You didn't ruin it," Landon murmurs, pressing into Dylan's warmth before drawing back. "Just... expedited it."

"At least we're on the same page?" They both dissolve into giggles. Dylan tugs Landon's hand and they start slowly walking back toward their apartment.

"I promise I'll forget everything," Dylan says, nudging his shoulder against Landon. "I'll act completely surprised."

He kisses Landon's cheek, lingering to whisper in his ear. "And I promise I'll say yes."

"Landon."

A light pressure on his arm and his eyes blink slowly open; the world is blurry as he struggles to focus.

"I knew you weren't sleeping."

The words float through his head, and he registers them but doesn't really understand, can't focus on trying to make out what he's seeing and the noises in the room at the same time. Dylan is sitting next to him with an encouraging smile, and Landon realizes the pressure is Dylan's hand. He tries to smile back, knows the motions, knows what he needs to do, but his muscles have forgotten and only manage a pathetic twitch. It's frustrating, and he lets out a groan, a tiny choked noise escapes his throat. The corner of his mouth feels wet, but he can't figure out why and with the noises in the room around him, with Dylan's hand on his arm and the words leaving his lips, it's just too much. Landon can't process it, so he just closes his eyes and tries to breathe.

Something presses the corner of his mouth and wipes gently. Dylan's voice drifts into his ears like a warm breeze, and even if he's not entirely sure what Dylan is saying, his voice wraps around Landon, holds him and comforts him and he just breathes, slips back into sleep.

There's still a hand wrapped around his when he wakes again, and he gives it an experimental squeeze. His fingers are stiff, slow and clumsy, but he tries and feels the hand squeeze back. A voice speaks and he blinks his eyes open and attempts to process the words.

"Hey there, sleepy."

Not Dylan. He lets his head roll to the side the voice is coming from and sees a girl with long auburn hair braided down the side looking at him with concern. Lana, he thinks, barely able to grasp the name through the fog of his brain. His sister. He stares at her, tries to understand. Dylan was here, he thought he was, but... maybe... everything is hazy and he can't keep anything straight and it's so hard to even *think*...

"Landon?" This is a different voice. He opens his eyes. When did he close them? He doesn't *know*. Dylan is on the other side. "Is it your head? Do you want me to call the nurse?"

No, he doesn't need the nurse; his head is only muddled, confused, trying desperately to sort itself out, but it's been filled with honey and molasses, sticking to the cogs and wheels and making everything so slow. He wants to tell Dylan he's fine, he's okay, but his tongue doesn't move, the words don't come and his lips twitch uselessly.

"Can you answer with your fingers, Landon? Remember, like we've been learning?" Dylan sounds so hopeful. He rests Landon's hand on his own as if he's expecting something, and Landon stares, trying to remember what he's supposed to do. They've been over this, he knows they have, but his thoughts are a puzzle he can't piece together.

So he curls his fingers into a fist because it's the only thing he can think to do, and something that looks like disappointment crosses Dylan's face. But he doesn't get mad, just gives a small nod before uncurling Landon's pointer finger, holding it above the others.

"One finger means yes," Dylan says, holding it there for a moment before uncurling the middle finger, joining it with the first. "Two fingers means no, remember?"

He does, he thinks he does, a shadow of a memory comes through. They've done this before. He tries to concentrate, tries to solidify these movements into a memory that will stick.

"Are you having any pain?" Dylan asks, still holding Landon's hand loosely. Landon lets the words roll in his head, and Dylan and Lana wait patiently while he works to assign meaning to them. He twitches two fingers up.

"You feel okay?"

I don't know, Landon wants to say, but there's no finger movement for that. His world is reduced to yes or no answers to questions he doesn't always understand. He doesn't know why he's here, doesn't know what happened to make everything so *difficult*, to make him feel so tired all the time, to make his whole body feel as if it's being weighed down, to make every movement feel so clumsy and difficult it's as if he's fighting through a river of syrup. He doesn't understand why his head won't stop throbbing, doesn't understand the ache that has settled deep in his bones or why words no longer make sense, why everyone keeps crying when they see him.

But he can't ask, doesn't even know how to ask. The thoughts are only half-formed, and float away as soon as he tries to grasp at them. So he looks at Dylan, at Lana's hopeful face, and twitches a single finger up.

Yes.

Dylan goes back to work. He's lost, the first few days, and his coworkers at the small graphic design company he works for offer him smiles and encouraging words, easing him back with a small project. It helps, a little, but it's still hard, and he stares at his computer, unable to focus, his thoughts stuck somewhere between the hospital and where he actually is. It's not until Tracy, the short, energetic girl who shares the table with him, slides her chair over and starts filling him in that he begins to focus. Her wild blonde hair is barely contained in a bun, and it bobs as she talks. She updates Dylan on all the office drama he has missed; her is conversation interspersed with gentle directions that walk Dylan through the relatively simple project. It helps, and slowly he finds his way back into a forgotten routine from a different life.

The doctor gives him the okay to take off his sling, and his arm is still sore and stiff, but things seem a little easier without it. He keeps in touch, making sure to update Tate, family members and other friends who have sent concerned messages he's left unanswered. It isn't easy, and there are days when it's still too overwhelming, when he just wants to block out the rest of the world, to try to pretend none of this ever happened; but he knows that he can't, and no amount of wishing or denial can turn back time.

They put Landon's skull back together, wean him off his drips and move him to a neuro step-down unit. It's nice to be out of the crazy bustle of the ICU; the new unit is calmer, and just the physical act of moving to a new place makes Dylan feel as though they're getting somewhere. Landon's days are busy with more therapists than Dylan knew existed, but recovery doesn't come as quickly as he had hoped. The extent of Landon's injury is starting to become clearer, more real, and his limitations more defined.

Dylan watches as a speech therapist has Landon practice movements with his lips and tongue, sounding out the small words that he can manage: *yes* and *no* and *cold* and *hurt*, a fractured, childish vocabulary. He listens as they tell Landon that they're going to have to keep the feeding tube in place in his stomach, that Landon still lacks the ability to swallow correctly. He watches as Landon fumbles to grip marbles and place them in a cup, as he gets angry and frustrated and refuses to cooperate.

But he also watches Landon stay awake and alert for longer periods, and start to interact with the people around him. The changes are only little ones, small achievements in a vast sea of limitations, but Dylan has learned that if you don't get excited about the small things, you'll have nothing.

He comes late one day, a week after going back to work. Tracy had insisted on taking him to get a sandwich, with the comment that he's looking too thin and needs to make sure he's taking care of himself. Dylan didn't argue with her; his mother has been saying the same things.

He's late and someone else is already in the room when he gets there, someone with red hair and a laugh that bounces lightly off the walls, her voice full of encouragement: Isla, one of Landon's occupational therapists. She sits on the chair next to the bed, a duffle bag of equipment beside her. They both turn when Dylan enters. Landon almost looks… excited.

"Am I interrupting something?" Dylan asks, trying to keep his voice light despite the guilt he feels about getting here late.

"Only Landon's new talent," Isla says, beckoning Dylan to come forward.

"Oh yes?" He steps forward and kisses Landon's forehead, whispering, "I'm sorry I'm late."

"Do you want to show Dylan what you can do?" Isla asks, passing Landon a red foam ball he hadn't noticed her holding. She stands, motioning for Dylan to sit in the chair she has just vacated, and he does, looking from her to Landon, confused. Landon's fingers press into the foam ball, forming small imprints, and, eyebrows furrowing, he focuses on Dylan. With a grunt so quiet Dylan barely hears it, Landon tosses the ball, which just clears the bed and hits Dylan's knees. The ball hits the ground, but Dylan is quick to pick it up. He stares at Landon with his heart fluttering.

"Toss it back," Isla says, standing behind Dylan as he grips the ball and tosses it gently toward Landon. Landon fumbles a little but manages to grab it. Then he holds it close to his body with a proud expression on his face. It's the most like *Landon* he's looked in a month, and the beginnings of hot tears prick Dylan's eyes.

Landon smiles, the right side of his mouth lifting higher than the left, and tosses the ball back. This time Dylan catches it in a tight grip.

"You…" Dylan starts. He lifts the ball until it touches his chin and a smile breaks out on his face.

"I think we can be done for the day," Isla says. She gathers her stuff. "You did great today, Landon." She touches his arm, smiles and looks back at Dylan. "You can keep that." And with a wink she's gone, closing the door behind her with a click.

Dylan considers, tosses the ball back to Landon. His movements are still slow, sluggish, but this time he barely fumbles to catch it. Dylan's throat feels tight, and he's knows it's silly—Landon's been making lots of improvements, and it's just a cheap foam ball—but something about this short game of catch has eased the ache inside him, has given him a way to interact with Landon through something other than hand squeezes and light touches.

"Scoot over." Dylan helps Landon move slightly to the side and carefully climbs into the small bed beside him. He knows he's not supposed to do this, but right now he doesn't care; he just wants to be as close to Landon as he can.

"I love you a stupid amount, you know that, right?" Dylan says when he's settled, and rests his head on Landon's shoulder. If he closes his eyes he can almost pretend they're back in their tiny apartment, Landon tucked in perfectly beside him, as if it's a Friday night and they're staying in, watching a movie on the couch together. He can tune out the sound of the hospital around them, the announcements being called overhead, and focus on the sensation of Landon beside him, the gentle sounds of his breathing, the warmth of his skin.

He can focus on his fiancé, who threw a cheap foam ball and made Dylan feel prouder than he's felt in a long time. Because it's not just the action, but what the action means: that maybe, someday, Landon might be a little closer to okay. That he will never fail to surprise Dylan, and that Dylan will always be there to give him the support he needs. That he'll always let Landon know how much he loves him.

His thoughts are broken when something hits his chest, and he snaps his eyes open and looks up at Landon. There's a real smile on Landon's face, and the ball has rolled off the bed. Dylan realizes that Landon has just thrown the ball at him, as if he was trying to get Dylan's attention.

Dylan smiles, picks up the ball and flips it back.

The doctors schedule a care conference two weeks after Landon is transferred to the neuro unit. Landon's parents are there, and Dylan's parents, along with a room of therapists, doctors and a few nurses. They want to talk about Landon's future, about realistic expectations and long-term plans. He needs full-time help, they say, at least for now, from someone skilled and able to provide the care Landon needs.

He'll need ongoing therapy, so he has to be someplace where he can access the rehab center many times a week. He'll need someone who can give him his medication and manage his feedings, someone who will know what to do if he has another seizure, another emergency.

They talk about care facilities, places Landon can stay and get the care he needs. They talk about rehab centers far away and list so many options Dylan's head spins and his gut clenches uneasily. The thought of Landon living somewhere else, even somewhere else in the city, isn't one that Dylan wants to entertain. Logically, he can understand their points; they're only trying to decide what's best for Landon; they all care about his recovery.

And it's hard, because Landon can't speak for himself, can't tell them what *he* would want, where he would want to go, and they have to operate under assumptions and the belief that they're doing what is best. They can't ask Landon, who wouldn't be able to understand what they're asking. But Dylan knows Landon. He's lived with Landon for four years, loved him for longer, and something deep inside him knows that Landon wouldn't want to be shipped off, and that forcing him to live somewhere unfamiliar, surrounded by people he doesn't know, away from his family and friends, will only make things worse.

It's not what Landon would want.

But Dylan stays quiet. He doesn't know how to properly convey this in a room full of people with fancy degrees who use expensive-sounding words. Nothing final is decided, but Dylan leaves with a stack of brochures and information sheets clutched in his hands, and a feeling of dread deep inside.

* * *

It takes three days for them to talk about it again. Landon has another seizure while Dylan is at work. He only hears about it after he gets to the hospital in the evening. They're still adjusting his medications, trying to find the right doses, and this leaves Landon exhausted, his eyes struggling to open each day. Dylan clutches his hand even tighter, offers even more encouraging words, and tries not to think about saying goodbye.

It's a Saturday night when they broach the topic. Helen and John had asked Dylan if they could come by the apartment that evening, and he'd spent the last few hours cleaning and making everything look presentable. Dylan's parents arrive with homemade pizza and iced tea made from the mix that his grandparents had sent from India in a small care package. Adele tries to get Dylan to sit, but he can't. It's important for him to have a clean apartment, for Landon's parents to see that he *can* take care of things, that he's not always as hopeless as he might seem. It's silly; they've been to the apartment before; they've seen the laundry waiting to be folded, the dishes in the sink, the coffee pot that desperately needs to be scrubbed. And yet Dylan has never felt so nervous about a visit from his in-laws.

There is a knock on the door, and Dylan jumps, unlatches the chain lock and lets Landon's parents in.

"The elevator is out of order," John remarks.

Dylan nods, feeling his stomach sink. "It's been out for a couple weeks," he says reluctantly. John and Helen share a look. This is already not going the way he wanted.

"I was just about to pour some iced tea, would you like some?" Adele asks, and rests a calming hand on Dylan's shoulder. Both John and Helen agree, and Dylan leads them into sit on the couch, where the pillows are perfectly positioned and the blanket draped over the back is without a single wrinkle. A leg bouncing with his nerves, Dylan sits in a chair tucked in by the bookcase, while Sam flips through a magazine at their small kitchen table. Adele brings out the iced teas and hands the sweating glasses to Landon's parents before pressing one into Dylan's tense grip. She makes Sam put the magazine away, and he does so with an uncomfortable look on his face; important conversations have always made Dylan's dad uneasy, and Dylan knows he would rather be anywhere else than here, right now. Dylan would too, if he could.

"How is Landon doing this evening?" Adele asks, settling into a chair at the table, breaking the silence.

"He was sleeping when we left, but the nurses had him listening to music for a while. He seemed to enjoy it," Helen says, setting her iced tea on the coffee table. Dylan can see the condensation pool against the wood, and his fingers itch to direct her to a coaster but he refrains.

"We've been thinking," John says, putting his own drink down on a coaster. "We want Landon to come back to Madison with us."

And there it is. Dylan feels his stomach bottom out, can feel his mother's concerned eyes on him. He doesn't move yet; he's been preparing for this, but he still doesn't know how to react.

"We've done some research," Helen continues, looks imploringly at Dylan. "There are good doctors back in Madison, and we've already talked to a neuro rehab facility that's willing to take him as a patient."

Dylan sits for a moment before clearing his throat. "Where would he live?"

"With us." Helen's voice is calm, but Dylan can detect a note of tension in it, a wavering uncertainty.

Dylan chews on his lip, a habit that Landon had always chastised him for, and stares at the floor. It's a four-hour drive to Madison on a good day, and the thought of Landon being that far away makes his stomach twist.

"Please excuse me," he says. He sets his iced tea on the floor, stands and makes his way across the living room to the bathroom. He closes the door behind him and leans against it, attempting to catch the breath that's trying to escape him. Panic curls inside of him in tendrils that wrap his lungs, and he pulls away from the door and splashes his face with water. His fingers tighten against the cool porcelain of the sink and he stares at Landon's toothbrush, tucked beside his, at the vanilla mint toothpaste he always insists on buying even though Dylan thinks it tastes disgusting.

He can't imagine a life without this, without Landon's toothbrush and gross toothpaste. Without his shirts tucked in the closet next to Dylan's, without his stupid breakfast bars taking over the pantry and his coffee addiction making the apartment smell like the local café. Without their petty arguments over whose turn it is to take out the trash, and who's working too much, and whether they should watch reruns of *Say Yes to the Dress* or *True Blood*. Without the little notes that Landon sneaks into Dylan's lunch or sticks on the bathroom mirror when he has to leave early for work or the surprise cupcake delivered during Dylan's lunch break. Without the late night karaoke and the lazy morning sex, the *I love yous* and the *I'm sorrys* and the promises not always kept, but always made in earnest.

There's a quiet knock on the door. Dylan dries his face on a hand towel and cracks open the door. Adele is standing outside.

"I'm all right." He knows she doesn't believe him, but she doesn't say anything, just pulls him into a hug.

"It's going to be okay," she assures him. Dylan wishes he could believe her. "Just tell them what you think is best."

He nods, and they make their way back into the living room. Helen and John are waiting, watching as he enters the room once more. They look nervous, and Dylan takes a breath, trying to stand tall in his resolve.

"I think Landon should stay here."

John looks as if he's about to argue, but Dylan gets there first.

"His doctors are all here, and there's an outpatient facility he can go to. All his friends are here, his whole life is here, I…" his voice falters and he stops and swallows past the painful lump in his throat. "I'm here. He wouldn't want to move away from his whole life, please, I know he wouldn't."

"He can't live here." John motions around the apartment. "I know you want him to, but this place is too small, we couldn't possibly fit a wheelchair in here. And the elevator doesn't even work. It's not practical."

"I'll move," Dylan says quickly, takes half a step forward, desperate. "I'll find a new place; I'll find a house with enough room. I'll build a ramp. I'll make sure he fits."

Helen purses her lips, John's eyebrows draw together and they share a glance before turning back to Dylan.

"You work full-time," Helen says. "You can't just quit your job to take care of him."

"I'll hire someone," Dylan responds without a pause. "I'll hire ten people if I have to. I'll make sure he gets the best care. Please." He looks at them, willing them to understand. "Please don't take him away."

"We'll be here," Sam says, and Dylan is surprised. "We can come over and help out, and they can always come to our place."

Helen looks reluctant. Her hands are clenched. John's mouth opens and closes; his brow is furrowed.

"I promise I'll do everything I can to make sure he's okay. Anything he needs. Just… let him stay."

Silence settles over them. Landon's parents are deep in thought, but Dylan's heart is racing; adrenaline pumps through his system. He *needs* to know, needs the reassurance that Landon will stay—and that there will be fewer *withouts* in his future.

"How about we take a day or two," Adele says, directing the conversation with the steady voice she uses in her classes. "Think our options over. There's a lot to consider."

Dylan wants to glare at her; he doesn't want to take a day or two. But he stops himself and looks at the floor, too much on edge to say anything.

"Of course," John says, taking Helen's hand in his own. Dylan closes his eyes. The hand he wants to hold is miles away, tucked in a hospital bed. "We don't want to make any rash decisions."

And so Landon's parents leave with the agreement to take some time and think over every option. To make sure Landon will be getting the best possible care.

Adele sits on the couch beside Dylan after the front door closes and rubs her hand up and down his back in a comforting motion.

"You're very tense."

"Am I making the right decision?" Dylan asks, looking at her.

Adele pushes a curly lock of hair behind her ears. "Do *you* think you're making the right decision?"

"I think I am. I can't stand the thought of Landon being so far away, after all this, and… I *love* him, I would do anything for him."

He grabs Adele's hand. He wants her to understand the true weight of his words.

"I know you would, sweetie," she says, smiling at him. "But Landon's going to need a lot of help, and it's going to be a big commitment."

Dylan nods, steels his jaw. "I can do it. I *want* to do it."

"Then I believe you can," Adele kisses the top of his head. "You should get some sleep, it's getting late."

It's only nine, but Dylan doesn't argue; he's drained after the events of today. He gives his mom a hug, says goodnight to his dad and makes his way back to the bedroom. He stays up for another hour, looking through affordable home listings online, making bullet points of everything he could possibly need. He knows that caring for Landon won't be easy, but right now, it's the only thing he wants to do.

Slowly, Landon becomes more aware of his surroundings. This new room is different, the tan walls have been replaced by blue and his bed is near an even bigger window. A vase of flowers has been set under a picture of something that tugs at Landon's mind, and he spends long hours staring at that picture, the answer just out of his reach. He stares until his eyes burn, until Dylan asks him if he's okay, and all he wants to do is ask what that picture is, what it *means*, but he can't.

The words never come.

People bustle in and out all day, poke him and move him and try to get him to do things he always fails to do. He's busy, and it makes him exhausted in a way he's never felt before, as if a weight is pressing down over his entire body. It's too much, and most of the time he wants to be left alone, only wants to see Dylan and his mom and his sister: familiar faces that don't push him, that make him feel comfortable. People who kiss his cheeks, hold his hand and make him feel safe.

Days become nights, and nights turn into days, and most of the time Landon isn't sure what's what. So he settles for focusing on what he can understand: the blue walls, the vase of flowers. Dylan in the chair next to him, fast asleep and snoring softly. The picture of a boat on the wall, and…

Landon starts, blinking his eyes rapidly. The word is clear in his mind and breaks through the sticky, consuming layers that have been holding everything back. It's a boat; he's figured it out! Success blooms warm inside of him. He's not sure why, but he needs to tell someone; there is a pulling need in his gut, the realization coming with a sense of clarity he can't remember feeling before. Has he ever felt this awake in his life?

His head rolls to the side, where he can see Dylan snoozing in the chair, exhaustion lining his face. He needs to wake Dylan up. There's no rational thought behind this need, it just exists. He *needs*, and Dylan is the only one who could understand.

Landon tries to reach for him with a shaky hand, but he can't lift it more than a few inches off the bed, and Dylan is too far away. Maybe he should try knocking against the bedrail? That seems like something he could do, and it might make enough noise to wake Dylan. Except his hand is too heavy, is getting even heavier the longer he moves it, and he can't muster enough strength to do anything other than weakly grip at the rough plastic of the bedrail. He flexes his fingers around it and feels the ache in his muscles, tries to steel himself.

His lips twitch; his tongue presses against his teeth as he tries to recall the motions he's been forced to practice. The sounds he can make are only a vague semblance of the words he wants to say. A grunt makes its way loose, and an itch tickles at his throat. He coughs to clear it. Dylan stirs, but doesn't wake up.

Landon makes a frustrated noise, balls his fingers into a fist to help him focus.

"Lan." Not really what he wanted, and the sound is barely audible even to his own ears, but it's a start. He coughs again and digs his fingernails into his palm. He runs over the sounds he knows he can get out, trying to concentrate on how each one feels in his mouth.

"Hi." The word makes its way out in a whisper, and he focuses even harder, willing Dylan to hear him.

"Lan," he tries again, this time with a little more force behind the word. "Wake." This sounds more like *ake*, but Dylan's eyes blink open and a frown crosses his face.

"Bo..." This one is a bit harder, and it takes Landon a moment to create the *t* sound, but when he does Dylan sits up straight, his eyes wide.

"Landon?".

"Boat," Landon tries again. He's already tired from this exercise; the word comes out softer than before.

"Bow?" Dylan misinterprets. Landon grunts in frustration, and tries to motion toward the picture on the wall.

"The boat picture?" Dylan asks. He still looks as if he can't believe what's happening. "What about it?"

Landon lifts his shoulders in what he hopes is a shrug; his eyes slide shut for a brief moment before he opens them again.

"Were you trying to get my attention?"

Landon dips his head in a nod.

"Hi," he whispers again, confused when tears shine in Dylan's eyes and are quickly wiped away.

"Hi," Dylan says back, kisses Landon's cheek.

Landon lets himself drift back into sleep, content.

Dylan takes Landon to the hospital courtyard, a small garden area frequented by families and the occasional patient. He thinks Landon likes it out here, the fresh air, the escape from fluorescent lights and constant noise. A patient care tech goes with them;

someone always has to be near in case something happens. She too seems to enjoy the brief escape, and sits on a wicker chair close by, but far enough away to give them some privacy.

Dylan parks Landon's wheelchair beside a bench and takes a seat. It's a hospital-issued wheelchair, sagging from overuse, but they've ordered a nice one for discharge, custom-made for Landon's needs. It's strange, thinking of his energetic fiancé confined to a wheelchair—another thing in a long list of changes that Dylan will need to get used to. A nurse has showed him how to hook the feeding tube to the small button in Landon's stomach, and Matt has him getting Landon from bed to wheelchair in an almost-smooth motion. Isla has them working together to get Landon dressed, so that Landon does as much as he can while Dylan fills in the rest; this mostly means that Landon lifts his arms so Dylan can slide a shirt over his head, shifts from side to side while they work on a pair of sweatpants and curls his toes while Dylan slips his socks on. It's not much, but it's something.

"It's nice out today," Dylan says, squinting up at the sun shining overhead. The end of August has brought signs of an early fall: the heat of summer fading away, the leaves hinting at hues of red and orange. It's been almost a month and a half since the attack, and Landon's doctor projects that it will only be another two weeks until he can go home—two weeks that sound so long, and yet not long enough. Two days have passed since Dylan's discussion with Landon's parents, and they still haven't arrived at a solid answer. Each hour makes Dylan more anxious.

"Nice," Landon echoes in his stilted voice, shifting in the chair beside Dylan. He twists just a little, hand reaching out for the flowerpot situated slightly behind them. His fingers are clumsy, and his hand barely clears the edge of the pot, but he grasps at a small yellow flower, breaks it off at the stem. He turns, his eyes searching out Dylan's as he offers him the flower.

"For you," Landon says, the words quiet but there, a phrase he couldn't have said a few days ago. Dylan takes it, brushes his thumb over the soft petals and then reaches to tuck the flower behind Landon's right ear.

"Thank you," Dylan says, and Landon lifts the right corner of his lips into the uneven smile Dylan is growing to love. The tech doesn't say anything, despite the sign close to them that clearly states *Don't Pick The Flowers*, and Dylan is grateful. Some things are more important than silly rules, and Landon reaching out is one of them.

His hair is starting to grow back a little, and in the sunlight Dylan can see the faint auburn hues that Landon has always denied are there. The thick scars winding along the left side of his head are less visible. The bruising has faded, the chapped lips and dry skin from his stay in the ICU have resolved, and he's starting to actually look like *Landon* again. But there's a droop to his shoulders, an ever-present confusion in his eyes, an unnatural stillness that has settled over him that wasn't there *before* and that makes it impossible for Dylan to pretend that none of this has happened.

But maybe that's not what he wants, he realizes, watching Landon close his eyes and turn his face toward the sun. He doesn't want to pretend anymore, because what happened *happened*. No amount of wishing or wanting can change the past, no amount of screaming and crying at how unfair this is can heal Landon's brain, can right the wrong he's been trying so hard to escape. *This* is his life now, this is *their* life; and pretending it's not is disrespectful to everything that Landon is going through. There is no past-Landon, no future-Landon. There is just Landon, the man he loves with every beat of his heart, with every breath he takes. Landon, the man he promised to marry, to stay beside no matter what.

Landon, who needs his help now, who has to rely on everyone around him to achieve the smallest of things, but is still the same person Dylan fell in love with, all those years ago. There's no use pretending, no point in wasting time with futile wishes, nothing to be achieved by *what ifs*. Dylan realizes now how special every moment is: every second he gets to hold Landon's hand, every word of encouragement he gets to whisper in his ear, every day spent sitting together, just… being. Living. Breathing.

A throat clears, breaking Dylan from his thoughts, and he looks up to see Landon's dad standing off to the side.

"The nurses said we would find you here," he says, and Dylan sees Helen stepping up beside him, squeezing Landon's arm in a silent greeting. She looks at the flower tucked behind his ear and smiles, her face calm and relaxed—as if a decision has been made, and she no longer has to worry.

"Landon likes the fresh air," Dylan says, and Landon blinks, his fingers curling in his lap. Dylan wonders if he has something to say when he does that, if there are words floating around in his head with no way out.

"We've done some thinking," John says, settling on the bench beside Dylan, a few wrinkled papers clutched in his hand. Dylan holds his breath and braces himself for what he's sure he's about to hear.

We're taking Landon home.
You can see him on weekends.
Good luck living by yourself.

105

"There are a few houses in St. Paul I think we should look at," John says, passing the papers to Dylan. Dylan looks at them silently, his brain struggling to process what this means. "Some of them are already handicapped accessible, but there are a few promising options that we could easily fix up."

He points to one; the paper crinkles in Dylan's tight grip.

"I like this one. It's affordable and it wouldn't be too hard to build a ramp up to the front. It's only one level and the kitchen and living room are open. Lots of room for a wheelchair and anything Landon needs."

Dylan blinks and looks up at John and Helen, his eyes wide.

"He can stay?"

Helen smiles, nods.

"You were right." She lets her hand rest gently on Landon's shoulder. "This is Landon's home now, and he wouldn't want to leave. He wouldn't want to be somewhere you're not."

Dylan stares down at the pages in his hand, the pictures of potential future houses—a future home for both for them. Together.

"Thank you," he says, his voice barely above a whisper. A laugh builds and bursts out of him. "Thank you so much."

He stands up, a surge of energy in his veins. "I'll take care of him, I promise I will. He'll get everything he could possibly need, and I'll find someone to help him, and you guys can come stay whenever you want and we can take trips back to Madison, when he's doing better, of course, and…" Dylan cuts himself off, realizes he's rambling, but everything seems so much brighter all of a sudden. Both Helen and John are smiling and Landon is looking up at him curiously, as if he doesn't really understand what's happening but can sense Dylan's excitement.

Dylan takes Landon's hands, touches a kiss to his cheek.

"We'll find a house that I know you'll love," he says, hoping that Landon understands. "No one is going to take you away. We're going to show them that they didn't win. We're still together, and no one can change that."

He hears a sniff, and senses Helen is trying to wipe her eyes discreetly, but he doesn't look away from Landon. He kisses him once more, this time on the forehead. Landon squeezes his hands, his grip firmer than Dylan has felt before, and he thinks that, somehow, Landon knows.

CHAPTER 6

The first time Janessa Little meets Dylan he looks desperate, like a cat that climbed too high and needs someone to show him the way down. He worries his bottom lip constantly; his hair, which falls in a wavy mess over his forehead, looks as though he was going to style it and then gave up; and his clothes are wrinkled. She guesses that folding laundry has been on the end of his to-do list. His eyes are wide and cautious, and size her up as if he's not sure whether to approach or run.

She's read about Landon, about his injury (traumatic), his rehab (extensive), his prognosis (hopeful) and his needs (total). She's memorized everything there is to know about him, because this is a big job and she had to make sure it's something she wants to commit to. But she hasn't researched Dylan, doesn't know anything about him aside from the metallic tone of his voice over the phone, that he's a graphic designer at a small independent company and that he's completely in love with Landon. But now, with Dylan sitting here before her, looking as though he really needs a good hug and maybe quite a few cookies, she realizes she knows nothing important about him.

They're meeting in the small coffee shop in the hospital, sitting on facing overstuffed couches, Janessa on one, Dylan on the other, his mother and Landon's mother on either side of him. It's a little intimidating. She takes a nervous sip of her coffee, certain that this is the most uncomfortable job interview she's ever been to. It doesn't help that Dylan and Helen look just as uneasy as she does. Adele smiles at her encouragingly and she relaxes, just slightly.

"Tell me about yourself," Dylan says and leans forward on the couch. She can hear the springs squeak.

"Sure, okay," she takes a breath and tries to sit up as tall as she can. "I'm twenty-four years old and a certified caregiver, I worked as a CNA for five years and—"

"Janessa," Dylan cuts her off and she stops, heart starting to race; what if she said something wrong, and they already know she's not what they're looking for? She might as well have a big *Nope* on her forehead, because she knows they're never going to look at her and trust her with a job like this. She should have gotten rid of the teal in her hair, and probably the purple while she was at it. Hadn't her grandmother just told her, "You're never going to get a job looking like some sort of neon hooker, Jenny"?

She'd kept the colors in defiance of her rigid family, out of her dislike for the name Jenny, but now, steeling herself for rejection, she wonders if maybe her grandma was right. Dylan smiles at her as if he can sense what she's feeling, as if trying to reassure her.

"We read your resumé, we know your qualifications. Tell us about *you*."

"Oh, um. Okay." Janessa wrings her hands in her lap. Most days she considers herself a confident person, and she doesn't usually let herself be caught off guard; but there's something about the way Dylan looks at her, as if he's hoping for something in her, as if she's some missing piece that will help pull their lives back together. It makes her want this, makes her want to help him—to help this family, however she can.

She really doesn't want to screw this up.

"It's just, this is new for me. For us," Dylan says before she can answer. "I never thought… I never imagined we'd be doing something like this, and I just want to make sure I find the best possible fit for Landon."

Adele takes Dylan's hand and gives it a comforting squeeze.

"Of course." Janessa nods. She wants to take a sip of her coffee to break the tension, to give herself a moment to collect her thoughts, but her hands have started shaking and she doesn't want them to see how nervous she is. "About me. Well, I'm originally from Mankato, but I moved up here a few years ago to study art at the Minnesota College of Art and Design. I considered myself an artist for a long time, actually, but now I just sell a few things on Etsy."

"What happened?" Dylan asks, looking at her intently.

Janessa shrugs. "I realized I like helping people more than I like painting pictures. I know that sounds cliché, but it's true." She gives a shaky laugh and runs her finger along the edge of her cup. "My youngest brother has Down's syndrome. Growing up I spent a lot of my time taking care of him. He means the world to me, but for a long time I wanted to get away, you know? But then I did, and I realized that when I was helping him, that's when I felt the happiest. I still go home and see him, and he's doing really well, but he helped me realize this was what I wanted to do with my life. Help people."

"What's his name?" Adele asks, and Janessa feels herself relaxing just enough to lean back a little in her seat.

"Andrew. He's almost eighteen now."

Dylan nods, his eyes wary, as though he's still trying to figure out if she has ulterior motives.

"So what made you apply for this position? What makes you want to work with Landon?"

Janessa takes a deep breath. This is it. This is the important part. This is what decides if she gets the job.

"At first I was drawn to the position because I have some experience working with patients with, um, brain damage." She doesn't miss the way Dylan flinches and looks down at his drink with sad eyes. "But after I read your story, about what happened, I couldn't stop thinking about it. If something happened to my brother… I don't know what I'd do. Reading about what you and Landon are going through, it made me want to help, in any way I can."

"Thank you, Janessa," Helen says, reaching across the small coffee table between the couches to touch her arm. "You seem very kind."

She's not sure how to take this, the gentle smile on Helen's face, the way Dylan is still staring into his coffee. This family is damaged, hurt and struggling, and maybe it's too much to ask, maybe it's too big a change for them right now; maybe they'll never find the perfect person for Landon. But she wants to try. She won't let herself back down.

"Please." She tries to meet Dylan's gaze. "I haven't even met Landon yet, and he's all I've been able to think about for days. I remember hearing your story on the news and feeling so *angry* about what happened, and it makes me want to put on spandex and go all vigilante on their sorry asses. And aside from being a superhero, I want to help in whatever way I can, because you and Landon deserve someone who cares. And I care."

Dylan's eyes finally meet hers. He has a contemplative look.

"Do you want to?" Dylan asks. "Meet him, I mean?"

There's a tone of cautious hope in his voice, as though he's still not sure what he thinks about her, but is willing to give her a chance.

"Yes, I would love to," she says, and her heart hammers an anxious rhythm. Dylan stands, followed by Adele and Helen.

"This way." He motions for her to follow. They take the elevator up two levels, make their way down a hallway and around a few corners before they stop in front of a simple wooden door, decorated with pictures that look as if they were drawn by young children, and a sign that says *Fall Risk*.

"Landon works at the children's hospital," Dylan explains when he catches Janessa looking. "Some of the kids drew these."

"They're very nice," Janessa says. She touches a picture of a purple dragon with the words *Get Better Soon* scribbled underneath.

It's cozy inside, with wood paneling and soft lighting; the walls are a rich blue. Sunlight streams through partially open blinds and a duffle bag sits in the corner, small stacks of papers and books are on a table, a few trinkets are on a shelf by the bed. It looks homey, comfortable; clearly people spend a lot of time here.

Helen steps close to the bed. "Good morning, sweetie."

Landon blinks as if he's waking up, slowly, hazily. Janessa has seen pictures of him, but they were from before: a smiling, healthy Landon in a park, Landon holding hands with Dylan in front of a Christmas tree. The boy in front of her looks fundamentally the same, but somehow… different. His eyes are shadowed and tired, his smile is uneven, and it's obvious his pale skin hasn't seen the sun in a long time. Red scars wind over his left ear—just visible beneath hair clipped short—the only obvious sign of what Landon's been through.

"We've brought someone to meet you," Helen says, taking a seat in the chair pulled up beside Landon's bed. Landon's eyes trace the room, stopping when his gaze meets Dylan, and Dylan smiles, his whole demeanor lighting up when he looks at Landon. He rests a hand on Janessa's shoulder, guides her forward.

"Landon, this is Janessa. She might be helping us out when you come home," Janessa's mouth feels dry, but she swallows and smiles and nods toward Landon.

"It's so nice to meet you." She takes a step forward and commands herself to stop being nervous. Landon is just a person who had something really horrible happen to him, who may need some extra help now but still deserves to be treated with as much kindness and respect as anyone else. "I've heard so many good things about you."

Landon's eyes move over her face, examining her. His expression doesn't change but his fingers twitch and his hand lifts a few inches off the bed in her direction. So Janessa reaches out, and lets her hand wrap around Landon's. His skin is warm and soft, as if someone has recently put lotion on him, and she gives his hand a small shake and smiles when he squeezes back.

"Hi. How… are you?" The words come out as a stilted whisper, and while Janessa's surprised to hear them, she tries to not let it show.

"I'm very well, thank you." She lets go of his hand, and Dylan straightens out the blankets that have bunched around Landon's feet. She can see how careful and tender he is with Landon, the fondness in his eyes when he looks at Landon, the way Landon looks at Dylan with nothing but trust in his face. And she knows. *This* is love; this is what she wants to help preserve, what she wants to help them to fight for.

She clears her throat and stands tall. "I was reading about you a little, and I saw that you've been teaching yourself to play the guitar." She's aware of Dylan's eyes on her, of Helen and Adele watching her closely. "My best friend and I have a band. We call ourselves the Damned Damsels, and we're really not that good, probably because we're a guitar-harmonica-tambourine band, but we make it work."

Dylan chuckles, and Janessa blushes.

"I bet, if this works out, that you could give me a tip or two. Or, if you have some sort of vendetta against tambourines, we could do anything else you want. We could paint pictures or go to the park all day or sit around in our pajamas; that's generally my favorite thing to do." She looks over at Dylan and winks. "Only when he's not around, though. He doesn't seem like a pajama party kind of guy."

Landon shifts and makes a small throat-clearing noise, his lips working silently. Janessa gives him a moment.

"Yeah," Landon manages. It sounds like a question. His eyes flicker from Janessa to Dylan. Dylan smiles encouragingly.

"Awesome," Janessa says, her mind already beginning to race with everything she could do with Landon. "We could do some finger-painting, maybe? I have a lot of art supplies. Stickers, glitter, feathers, you name it. And you look like someone who appreciates the daring of combining feathers and glitter in their art. Actually, you probably know better and will completely show me up as soon as we crack open a bottle of paint, I can already tell."

She shoots a look at Dylan, who is gazing back at her in amusement, before she leans close to Landon, lowering her voice just slightly.

"I'm sorry, I talk a lot when I'm nervous. Especially around someone as hot as hubby here." She nods toward Dylan, and Landon lets out something that sounds a lot like a laugh. Dylan's eyes snap open wide.

"Well, you are pretty hot," Janessa says to Dylan with a playful shrug, feeling lighter than she has all day. She already knows she could get along with Landon and that she wants to work with him, to keep a smile on both of their faces.

Landon nods in a way that makes Janessa think he's agreeing with her, and Dylan shoots him a look that she can imagine him using *before*—maybe when they would argue over which celebrity is better looking, or when Dylan would catch Landon checking him out in public. Either way, it makes her laugh, and Landon reaches out toward Dylan. Dylan threads their fingers together and lets Landon hold on tight.

Adele stands by Helen and whispers something in her ear. Helen nods.

"We're going to go grab some more coffee and look over some paperwork, give you guys a bit to talk things over?"

"Okay," Dylan agrees. "Thank you."

"It was very nice to meet you, Janessa. I think Landon would be very lucky to work with you." Adele draws Janessa into a quick hug before they leave; the door closes quietly behind them.

Landon is still watching her, but his eyelids are half closed. Janessa thinks he looks tired, clinging to Dylan's hand as though he's trying to stay awake, as though he wants to understand what's happening around him.

Dylan motions to the now-empty chair and lets Janessa sit before taking his own seat.

"So, I don't want to make any final decisions today, but if you are still interested in working with us, could we go over a few things?"

"Of course," Janessa agrees, addressing both Landon and Dylan.

"We've made an offer on a house in St. Paul, and we're building a ramp and making sure it's completely accessible to Landon," Dylan explains. His voice has a new edge, as if he's trying to take control but is still uncomfortable, unsure. "You'd be staying with Landon while I'm at work, taking him to his appointments and to therapy. We've been working out a schedule and it looks like he'll be coming here three to four times a week. There will also be some things we'll need you to help him with at home."

"Totally understand."

Dylan shifts, and a hesitant expression crosses his face.

"He'll, um, he's going to need help with his, uh, personal care, so you'll have to be comfortable doing those things as well."

"Completely comfortable," Janessa assures him. She's not sure how much Landon understands, but he looks down at his lap, his cheeks an embarrassed pink. "Whatever Landon needs, I'll be there. I'm fun to boss around, I promise."

She takes a chance and reaches out to touch Landon's arm, and he looks up, his eyes clouded. But a tiny smile reaches his lips, and Janessa can see how new and frightening this is for both Dylan and Landon as they struggle to keep control in completely unfamiliar territory.

"I'm fine doing anything you need me to do, both of you. Honestly, I want to be there for you guys, and to help take as much stress off your lives as I can. So if you need me to get groceries, or run to appointments, or kill bees, just say the word. I'm totally comfortable with personal and medical care, and anything else you could need me to do."

Dylan nods, his face unreadable. He looks over at Landon, whose eyes have started to slip closed.

"Thank you," Dylan says softly. "This meeting has gone so much better than I expected."

"Really?" Janessa is touched. Landon's eyes have closed and his breathing has evened out; he seems to have given up the fight to stay awake, and Dylan watches him sadly.

"The first person we interviewed didn't realize we were gay and took one look at us and left. That was… fun."

Janessa clenches her jaw. She knows that there are people like that, but it doesn't make her any less angry.

"Dylan, I'm so sorry. You guys deserve better than that."

"It's just been so hard, you know? I've started to forget that there are decent people around who would actually want to help us and not hurt us, and…" Dylan sucks in a deep breath, his voice wavering. "And I couldn't stand it if someone hurt Landon again. I really couldn't."

Janessa blinks back the tears that have started to prick her eyes.

"I want to help. I know I'm practically a stranger, but I really want to help you keep Landon safe. I want to help both of you."

Dylan sniffs, lifts a hand to wipe at his eyes and laughs shakily. "Well, I've never broken down in front of a stranger like this, so you might already have an in."

"Your secret is safe with me," Janessa says, just as Landon lets out a tiny snore. They both chuckle, and Dylan smiles.

"He's been tired lately. Therapy has been taking a lot out of him." Dylan draws his shoulders up and returns to the poise of the Dylan she first met.

"It sounds like he's been working hard."

"He has," Dylan agrees, and there is pride in his voice. "They're thinking just another few weeks before discharge, and I'd love for you to come by once we close on this house. I could show you around and we could go over a few more things?"

"That would be perfect."

"Great," Dylan says, his smile genuine. He stands, and then hesitates. Janessa reaches forward to shake his hand and he laughs.

"Thank you, Janessa. For the first time, I feel like something might be starting to go right."

"I'd love to try and help things stay right," she responds, and decides: *Screw it.* She pulls Dylan in for a hug; her eyes flutter shut and she breathes him in before letting go, wondering how it's possible for these two to already be affecting her so much.

"Tell Landon I really enjoyed meeting him?"

"I will." Dylan looks back at Landon. "I think he liked you."

"I look forward to seeing both of you again," she says, before finally exiting the room.

They close on the house. It's in St. Paul, in a nice area with low traffic and an abundance of trees. Logan flies in from New York to help them move; it doesn't even take an entire day, and their tiny apartment barely holds enough to furnish the house. They had to make some compromises on the house for cost; and while it isn't completely handicapped accessible, they do the best they can. Logan helps to build a ramp up the three front steps; they install handrails in the shower and make sure furniture is arranged in as open a pattern as possible.

It's not a large house, but it has a decent backyard with a wooden deck and an awning with a porch swing. It's not fancy, or like anything Dylan ever pictured them owning, but he already loves it and could easily call it home. He hopes Landon will like it.

Lana starts school again. Dylan knows she's busy, but she comes by as often as she can, helps to unpack and organize the kitchen and criticizes Dylan for the way he arranges his closets.

"Go by season and style first and *then* color, you nitwit," she tells him, shaking her head and muttering something about how she thought gay men were supposed to have an intuition about these things. Dylan pretends to protest, but he lets her go about her rearranging; he knows that she's stressed and that it helps her to have something to do. She comes up with a practical way to organize Landon's clothes, on shelves stacked up from the closet floor so that he can easily reach them.

When Dylan isn't at work or fixing up the house, he's at the hospital, learning everything he can about how to care for Landon. Janessa comes sometimes, too, and the nurses show them how to give medications, how to transfer from bed to chair and what to do in case of an emergency. Dylan immerses himself in research, checking out every book the library has on living with a brain injury. Sandy, the friendly librarian, promises to order more, and Dylan replaces the ones he's already read with a new stack she's prepared for him. He learns everything he can—he wants to be as prepared as he can possibly be when Landon finally comes home.

Landon seems to sense that something is changing. Dylan tries to explain, but Landon still has trouble retaining information, and he doesn't think he'll understand until they're actually there. But Dylan makes sure to tell him every time he visits, because even if Landon doesn't understand, it's not fair to keep things from him.

And, slowly, things start to come together, September begins to melt away; the date of Landon's discharge looms ever closer.

Logan walks down the hallway and stops outside the door. He waits. People are laughing inside, but he can't bring himself to go in just yet. It's wrong, and he's sure it makes him a terrible brother, but he has a hard time seeing Landon like this—his little brother, the one who used to beg for piggyback rides as a kid, the who was always climbing trees and coming home with scraped knees, the one who liked to sneak into Logan's room late at night and ask for stories. Landon always liked the stories about dragons, but only if the dragons were nice.

At the time, Logan had found it annoying and he remembers telling his friends to ignore his dweeby little brother when they came to visit, remembers yelling at his brother to scram more than once. He wishes he hadn't, now. But there's no point in these regrets, no way of turning back time and changing things.

He doesn't like the way Landon sits so still, rarely moving except for the occasional twitch of his hand or tilt of this head. He doesn't like the silence, the way he can tell Landon doesn't always understand what they're saying, or the lost look in his eyes when they talk. He doesn't like the way Landon needs help with the simplest things, the few broken words he can manage, or that his brother is being fed through a damn tube in his stomach because he can barely eat. He doesn't like the fake sympathy from the hospital staff, the promises that things will get better.

Maybe it's because he's been gone and is coming back into this situation with new eyes, but this scenario has the word *wrong* flashing above them all like a neon sign. And he hates it.

"Logan?"

His eyes snap open and he sees Lana's head peeking out the door.

"You coming in? The nurses decided to have a little party for Landon since he's leaving this week."

"Yeah." Logan straightens his faded Led Zeppelin T-shirt. "I'm coming."

Blue and green streamers hang from the ceiling, framing the window, and a few balloons drift in the corner. A giant cookie sits on the counter with the words *We'll Miss You Landon* written on it in blue frosting. Logan remembers his daughter, Jay, begging for a giant cookie for her birthday last year, and he thought it was a sign of changing times that children no longer wanted cake. Jay had asked him why she couldn't come to visit her Uncle Landon, and he'd told her it was because her uncle was still very hurt, and he couldn't have too many visitors right now. She'd pouted, and sniffled, and had pressed a bracelet she'd made into his palm and asked him to give it Uncle Landon.

He clutches the bracelet now, feeling the glittery purple and orange beads in his hand. There are a few nurses in the room, and someone Logan's pretty sure is a therapist. She leans to wrap Landon in a hug and Logan thinks he sees tears shining in her eyes.

"I'm going to miss you," the girl says, resting her hand on Landon's shoulder. "I'm not going to have anyone to read books with anymore."

She pulls away and hugs Dylan just as tightly.

"You guys are going to do great." She brushes a tear from her cheek. "I can tell."

"Thank you," Dylan responds with a smile, but his shoulders are tense, his posture is too straight. "You all have been so wonderful, we couldn't have done it without you."

Logan can feel his mother watching him so he moves to the side and takes a seat in the corner of the room with the bracelet clutched in his hands. People come and go, all offering hugs and kind words, and make Dylan promise to visit again sometime soon. Landon looks different than the last time Logan visited; he's sitting in a chair, his hair is long enough to cover most of the scars on his head and he holds himself a little straighter. His eyes seem clearer. He looks happy, as happy as he can, and he seems to understand that something is happening, that all of these people are here for him. He even whispers a few greetings and goodbyes, but Logan can tell Landon is getting tired; his eyes are starting to slip shut between visitors.

Dylan and a nurse help Landon back into bed. He is awkward and stiff while they move him, and only really able to help once he's settled in and can pull the blankets from his knees to his waist. Logan stares at the floor and tries not to think about how unfair this is.

"Fuck it." He leaves, unable to sit in there anymore, not with the anger he feels, not with everyone standing around pretending all of this is *okay*. It's not fucking okay, and why isn't anyone else getting mad about it?

He walks halfway down the hall before he stops, turns back and stops again. The bracelet digs into his palm. He runs a hand through the hair his mom is always telling him to cut. He wants to scream, wants to punch the wall, wants to break something, but there's nothing for him to do, so he stands there, squeezes his eyes shut and tries to calm his racing thoughts.

"What was that about?"

He can hear Lana stomping down the hall after him, her stupid flip-flops slapping the floor with every step.

"What the hell, Logan?"

"Go away, Lana."

"No."

He opens his eyes at that and sees her standing next to him, her face livid. She points her finger at him, jabs in the chest.

"You cannot do that," she says, every word enunciated. "You can't just come here and pretend you know more than all of us, and then leave like that."

"Jesus, Shortcake," he says, even though he knows how much she hates being called that. "Calm down."

"You." She stops and turns away from a moment. "You haven't been here, Logan. I know it's hard for you to see this, but news flash, douchewad, it's hard for *all* of us!"

Logan stares at her. He doesn't think he's ever seen her this angry.

"I have been here every single day. And every single day it almost *kills* me to see my big brother like this, but you know what? I do it, because I love him. And I support him, because I can't imagine doing anything else. I don't know why I expected that from you."

"Lana, that's not…"

"Don't even start with me, Logan," Lana cuts him off, and Logan realizes she's backed him against the hallway wall. "You *always* leave when things get hard. You left as soon as you could after high school. You left Landon and me at home when things were at their worst and you didn't even hesitate. Things get hard and you only think of yourself."

Logan clenches his jaw. He doesn't know how to refute this.

"How do you think Dylan feels, watching you leave like that, huh? How do you think *Landon* feels? For fuck's sake, Logan. You get to leave in a week, pack up your nice little bags and go back to your nice little family and you know what? We're still going to be here. So you better get your head out of your ass and start acting like a big brother who actually gives a shit."

Lana pokes him one last time in the chest before marching away as fast as her flip-flops can carry her. Logan watches her. She reenters Landon's room after glaring back at Logan one last time.

His head falls back against the wall with a muffled thunk and he stares up at the ceiling and lets out a long breath through his nose. *Dammit.* He looks down at the bracelet in his hand, the tiny heart and star beads mixed in with the glittery ones, and remembers how proud Jay was when she finished it.

"Okay," he whispers to himself before rolling his shoulders and heading back toward Landon's room.

Everyone is silent when he enters: Dylan, sorting through papers on the small table; Lana, her face still hard; and his mother, sitting by Landon's bed. Helen doesn't look at him; her eyes are focused on Landon, on the blankets covering him.

Logan takes a seat in the chair on the other side of Landon, and Lana gives him a warning glare. He ignores her and turns to see Landon watching him.

"Little Jay-Jay made this for you," Logan says, unfolding his hand from around the bracelet. "She wanted to make sure you got it."

He holds the bracelet forward and Landon stares at it, his expression confused, before looking back at Logan.

"It's for you," Logan says, offering it again; but this time he takes Landon's hand, sets the bracelet in his palm and curls his fingers around it. "She said it will help make you better. Seven-year-old logic." He shrugs and Landon's fingers tighten on the bracelet. He brings it closer and opens his hand, his eyes narrowing as he looks at it.

"You don't have to wear it, but..." Logan is so bad at these things, these... emotional speeches. Maybe Lana has a point.

Landon's fingers fidget with the bracelet before he stops with an annoyed sound in his throat, his lips working as if he wants to say something but can't get it out.

"He wants you to put it on him," Lana says, words clipped.

"Oh." Logan feels stupid, but he reaches forward and helps Landon slide the bracelet over his wrist. It's almost too tight, and the elastic stretches under the beads, but it fits. Landon runs his fingers over it and looks at Logan, smiling. And when Landon stretches his hand out toward Logan, he wraps his own hand around Landon's and holds it as tight as he dares without hurting him.

"It's... nice. Pretty," Landon manages, each word a struggle. But it's something.

Logan looks up at Lana, and she dips her head at him, no longer looks as though she wants to murder him. Logan considers that a win.

Things are changing. Landon's not sure how he knows, if it's the way people look at him, the way they hold his hand too tightly or the *goodbyes* being said in his ear; if it's the way that Dylan looks at him, affectionate and nervous, or the way Lana and Logan have started glaring at each other and the tense silence in the room. He wants to ask, wants someone to explain things in a way that will actually *stick*, actually make sense.

It's getting better, waking up is a little easier, awareness filters in a little more clearly. The questions never seem to stop, though; people he doesn't know constantly ask him things he doesn't always know the answer to. But even when he gets frustrated, his family is there with comforting smiles and encouraging words.

Sometimes, when he's not letting himself drift, he goes over the things he does know, and tries to cement them in his mind, to keep the facts from slipping through his fingers once again.

Hi, how are you?

My name is Landon.

I'm at the... hotel.

No.

I'm at the hospital.

I hurt my head.

Even thinking is hard now.

It comes and goes; some days are better than others, with purposeful movements, achievements that result in warm smiles and kisses on cheeks. Some days he feels too heavy to do anything; his head throbs and his eyes are weighted, the words he wants to say are just out of his grasp. He's different… everything is different now, and somehow he knows it's all going to change again.

The room is growing dark, now, and Dylan kisses his cheek and runs a hand over the back of his neck. It feels nice, and Landon lets himself lean into it. He likes the comfort of having Dylan near.

"You're coming home tomorrow," Dylan says, his voice as soft as the dimming sun. Landon blinks, the word *home* brings forward images of a cramped space, a tiny bedroom, dishes piled in a small sink. Home. It sounds nice, and he likes the way Dylan smiles as he says it.

"Get some sleep." Dylan kisses his cheek again. Landon sleeps and dreams of home.

CHAPTER 7

The first night in their new apartment is sweltering. Dylan presses a cool bottle of water to his forehead and groans in relief when Landon angles the fan so it's pointing directly at him.

"Please tell me why we decided to move on the hottest day of the year?"

Landon grabs his own bottle of water and collapses onto the couch beside Dylan.

"When is the air conditioning unit being installed?" Landon pants. With a grimace, he pulls his sticky shirt away from his skin.

"Tomorrow, thank God."

"Good." Landon nods and leans against Dylan.

"No, get away," Dylan protests, pushing at Landon. "You're too hot."

Landon laughs, but flops over without protest.

"You know, we don't officially live here until we've had sex on at least... ninety percent of the surfaces."

"Is that so?" Dylan glances around their apartment. It's not very big, with creaky old floors, a single small bedroom and a living room that blends into a tiny kitchen, with just enough room for a couch and a table, and an even smaller balcony. The ad described the place as quaint, and Dylan decides that's a pretty accurate description.

But, it's Dylan and Landon's first place together, just them, no other roommates to worry about. It's their first place together as adults, college graduates with real jobs, ready to start the next chapter in their lives together. Dylan couldn't ask for much more.

"It's a fact," Landon says, rolling onto his back and propping his feet up on Dylan's knees.

"It's too hot for sex." Dylan wipes a bead of sweat from his temple and makes a face. "And we're not even getting our bed until tomorrow."

"Who said anything about a bed?" Landon smiles mischievously and pushes himself back up. "I count at least... five other potential surfaces."

"Tomorrow," Dylan groans and slides bonelessly down on the couch. "It's too hot to exist."

Landon shifts until he's crawling over Dylan, straddling his hips and sliding his hands under Dylan's shirt.

"Come on, we only have one first night in a new place." Landon leans down and kisses Dylan's lips, his jaw, his throat. "I bet I can make you change your mind."

"Landon, you sex fiend," Dylan says, but the words don't have any weight, not when Landon is sucking so deliciously just above his collarbone. Dylan rests his hands on Landon's back, presses Landon against him despite the heat. This time, he relishes the fire *in his skin, flames licking up everywhere Landon touches, every place he kisses.*

"Okay," Dylan concedes, his chest already heaving. "I'll give you two surfaces."

Landon pulls back, a wide smile on his face.

"Make it three and it's a deal."

"I wasn't aware this was a business transaction." Dylan laughs at Landon's goofy expression, the one he gets when he's trying to be sultry but can't quite hold in his excitement.

"I don't think you understand the importance of tonight," Landon says, tracing a line down Dylan's arm with his thumb. "We only get one first night. This is special."

"Every night with you is special." Dylan lifts his head for a kiss, his lips part and their breath mingles.

"Shut up, you sap," Landon says, and deepens the kiss. "Now sex me up."

"Oh my God." Dylan laughs, shaking his head.

"You love me," Landon says with a smile.

"For some reason, yes."

Landon's lips on his own cut him off.

They make it to four surfaces.

It's the last night of September, and Dylan stays at the new house. He can't sleep, but instead lies awake and stares at the ceiling, listening to the creaks of the house around him. New places always have this effect on him; unfamiliar surroundings fill him with nervous excitement, making it impossible to shut his brain off and try to sleep.

It's different, this time. Tomorrow, Landon comes home. Tomorrow, their whole lives change. He's been preparing and he's ready, Landon's ready, there's nothing the hospital is doing for Landon that Dylan can't do for him at home. But still there's a seed of doubt, rooting itself inside him and making him wonder if he really is ready for this, if he's capable of being the person Landon needs him to be.

With a groan, he rolls over in bed, pulls the pillow over his head and tries to block the thoughts.

He can do this.

He has to do this.

There never was a choice, not really.

The pillows are wrong. He's rearranged them, put them in the closet and pulled them back out again, but no matter what Dylan does, they stay wrong. He groans, plucks them off the couch once more, glares down at them. They're too big, he decides, they take up too much space. *How is Landon ever going to feel at home if the stupid pillows take up the entire couch?*

He turns to throw them back in the closet—maybe he can hunt down smaller pillows—when a hand on his shoulder stops him.

"The pillows are fine," Adele says, and Dylan feels as if he's cracking, as if any added pressure could be the breaking point and he'll shatter all over the nicely mopped floor. "Everything's fine."

She has to be lying. Everything is not fine. Landon's coming home today, and Dylan didn't sleep last night, and there are so many things he wanted to do before this happened, so many things to be done before the pillows decided to mock him and throw off his entire day.

Adele takes the pillows and places them back on the couch. Dylan stands there, arms hanging by his sides. Somehow they look better now that someone else has arranged them. Maybe it wasn't the pillows—maybe it was just him.

"It's going to be okay," Adele says. She guides Dylan to sit on the couch, and he sinks into the pillows behind him.

"I think…" Dylan looks up at his mom. "I'm scared."

"Of what?" Adele takes a seat beside him.

"That I'm not going to be good enough, that I'll let Landon down somehow. That he'd be better off somewhere else."

"Honey. You won't be doing this alone. If it's ever too much, or if you ever need help, there are so many people who would be happy to help you."

"I know that, I just…"

"I know," Adele says. "You'll be okay, I promise."

Dylan leans against his mom. He lets her put an arm around his back and pull him close, and tries to believe her.

It's nearly three in the afternoon when Dylan hears a car in the driveway. He stands, looking anxiously at the door. Adele stands beside him and gives his arm a quick squeeze.

"You're very brave," she says, and lands a kiss on his cheek. He can hear them outside now, and his stomach gives a nervous flip. "Landon's very lucky to have you looking out for him."

Dylan looks at his mom, and she smiles at him just as the front door opens. Lana comes in first, followed by Landon, sitting stiffly in his wheelchair as Helen pushes him. The door closes behind them and Dylan wonders if Logan and John are held up by traffic; they were driving separately, bringing the belongings Landon accumulated during his hospital stay.

Helen pushes Landon into the living room. His eyes are wide; his gaze flickers around the room, takes everything in.

"I haven't painted yet." Dylan wonders why he sounds so apologetic. "You can help me pick the colors, if you want to."

He bites his lip, knowing how stupid he must sound. It's silly to be nervous; he's been with Landon every day for the past two months, it's not like this is new. There's no reason to feel as if he's swimming without a shore in sight.

"It's… warm," Landon says. His voice is so quiet that Dylan has to strain to understand, but he knows Landon is probably as nervous as he is.

"A tour?" Helen suggests, and Dylan is grateful for someone else to take control of the situation. He trails behind while they show Landon the house and hopes Landon can imagine it feeling like home. The living room is much bigger than the one in their last place, and their couch looks almost pathetically small in the open space. The kitchen is just to the left, with a bay window and vast counter space occupied by only a measly coffeemaker and a plastic toaster. A shaded porch wraps around the house from the living room to the bordering bedroom, which is big enough for their bed and all of Landon's equipment. Dylan points out the pictures he hung on the wall: a photo of a vibrant orange autumn forest that Landon took, next to their favorite unofficial engagement photo that Lana shot after they announced the news.

The bathroom is smaller than Dylan would prefer, but he assures Landon that they'll make it work, and they have a second bedroom and a laundry room to make up for it. Landon smiles at Dylan's excitement over the laundry room and nods along to all the possibilities for the extra room, but nervous tension shows in his face and in the way he grips the handles of his wheelchair.

"It's different from our apartment," Dylan says, when they're back in the living room. He remembers how excited they had been to find that apartment, something reasonably affordable in a part of town where they both wanted to live. It hadn't been a perfect place; the sink was always clogging and they didn't have a dishwasher and the elevator only worked half the time. But it fit them. It fit their life.

This is different, they didn't pick it out together, and they'd always planned on getting their first real house after they were married. It's a house of circumstance, a place that fits their needs, a house that will work for their purposes. A place they'll have to learn to love.

Despite that, Dylan knows he made the right choice—that this is the best place for Landon—but he wishes he could feel more confident, that the niggling worry deep in his stomach would go away. He wishes that Landon could tell him to calm down, to stop worrying so much, that everything will be fine. He misses Landon: the Landon who didn't always say the right thing, but always knew how to make him laugh. The Landon who would make jelly bean cupcakes when he was feeling sad, who would be waiting with a large glass of wine and a marathon of *Kitchen Nightmares* after a long day at work. The Landon who could talk to him, hold him, make jokes about his family behind their backs. And Dylan feels awful for thinking this, because Landon is right here in front of him. Landon is doing the best that he can, and none of this is his fault.

But that doesn't stop the loss he feels, the ache deep in his bones or his need for the person who had been beside him through every challenge, through all the hard parts of his life in the past seven years.

Landon was never supposed to be the struggle.

They eat Chinese food that evening and watch *Up,* one of Landon's favorite movies. Landon is on the couch with Dylan beside him, and the rest of the family sprawls on the floor and the few kitchen chairs they've dragged into the room. They need more chairs, maybe a small loveseat. Something to make the living room feel less bare and more like home.

Dylan is too anxious to eat, and pokes through his orange chicken for a minute before setting it on the coffee table. He can't concentrate on the movie, only on the warm weight of Landon beside him and Landon's head, where it rests on Dylan's shoulder, the even rise and fall of his chest. Dylan's hand rests against Landon's leg, and he draws small circles into the soft fabric of Landon's sweatpants until Landon slides his hand over and tangles his fingers with Dylan's. It anchors Dylan, and he feels the weight in his chest lessen just a little; he breathes a little easier.

It's barely eight o'clock when Landon yawns and his eyes struggle to stay open. Lana notices and nudges her parents to help clean up and put away the extra food. She offers to stay and help Dylan get Landon to bed, but Dylan waves her off and tells them they'll be fine. They've already decided that Logan will stay; he's couch-hopping anyway. So they say their goodbyes and promise they'll be back in the morning. Dylan wishes they'd stay away an extra day and give him and Landon some time to adjust, but it's not fair of him to ask, not with Landon's parents leaving soon and Logan staying only a few more days. They deserve time, and he can survive a few more days of this. Maybe it will be good to have the help. He's taken a week off work to help Landon adjust to being home, to help *himself* adjust to having Landon home, to their new house and new life, but it's just *so much*. So much to learn in only a week.

Everyone else leaves, and Logan hangs around in the background, busying himself with cleaning the already clean kitchen, looking for something to do. Dylan doesn't say anything; he knows that Logan is still trying to make up for his absence over the last two months and the way he acted earlier in the week. Dylan doesn't blame him for that. He knows that Logan is someone who needs time, someone who can't just jump in and be supportive or adjust to something as big as *this* without a struggle.

Dylan helps Landon get ready for bed. It's awkward, so different outside of the hospital without nurses hovering close by, without a button to push for help or someone to take over when he doesn't know what to do. There's only him, and he's going to have to be good enough.

It feels odd, Dylan thinks, after Landon has been situated on the left side of the bed as before and Dylan has changed into his pajamas and crawled in next to him, to have someone here beside him. Dylan settles into his side, feeling unsure about what to do now. They never covered this at the hospital. He wants to hold Landon—his fingers itch to reach out and pull him in—but he doesn't want to overstep, doesn't want to make Landon uncomfortable or hurt him.

Landon shifts beside him, a grunt builds in his throat and an awkward limb slides over and smacks Dylan. Dylan startles into a sitting position: Landon is looking at him, his eyes wide and searching. He's trying to roll himself over, Dylan realizes. A smile pulls at his lips as he helps Landon with gentle hands until their bodies are lined up and fit together, close in a way they could never be at the hospital.

"I missed this," Dylan whispers. Landon relaxes against him, his eyes closed and his expression peaceful. "I'm so glad you're home."

And as scary as it is, he means it.

"Me too," Landon whispers, his voice barely audible, his thumb jerking over Dylan's hand. Dylan lightly kisses the back of his neck.

"Goodnight, Landon."

* * *

"Tell me about him," Janessa says on a Wednesday afternoon, as she dumps an entire bag of chocolate chips into the cookie dough. "Tell me about Landon, from before."

Dylan looks up from his computer, where he's been fiddling away at something for work, and leans his elbows against the kitchen table. He closes his laptop carefully, pushes it aside and gives a quick glance back to where Landon has fallen asleep on the couch.

"You don't have to." Janessa carefully stirs the cookie dough. "I'm just curious. I'd like to know more about him."

Dylan chews his lip and draws a circle on the table with his thumb. *How do I describe someone who means the whole world? Someone who has so many facets to his personality it's impossible to tell where to start?*

"Landon…" Dylan starts, and can't help but smile as memories make their way to the surface. "He was sweet, you know? I

137

remember once, when we'd only been dating a few months, he wanted to bring me flowers for my birthday and he didn't have a car, only this run-down bike, and he put the flowers in his backpack so he could surprise me at work, but by the time he got there, God, they were completely crushed. Petals smashed into his textbooks and everything."

Dylan laughs at the memory. "He was devastated, but I remember it being the sweetest thing anyone had done for me in a long time. It didn't matter that the flowers were crushed. Just the fact that he'd gone through the effort to bike twelve miles to surprise me at work was enough."

Janessa smiles at him and spoons fat dollops of cookie dough onto a baking sheet.

"He was the kind of person who would get excited about Netflix releasing a new documentary on whales, or reading long biographies, and he had a weird addiction to jelly beans. He kept a bag with him all the time and was always eating the stupid things. It made me so angry sometimes, because he never had a single cavity."

"Damn his good enamel." Janessa shakes her head at the cookie dough.

Dylan chuckles. "He was a swimmer, too, I don't know if you knew. He had a scholarship for it and everything. He loved to be in the water, and I know he stopped swimming after we graduated, but I think he wishes he hadn't. I remember he once told me that the water blocked everything else out, all the outside noise. When he was swimming, it was just him and the water and nothing else."

Janessa pops the baking tray into the oven and brings a spoonful of cookie dough to Dylan. He savors the sweet taste.

"I wish you could have known him, back then. He always tried to see the good in people, and sometimes it drove me crazy—sometimes I wanted to shake him and tell him to be critical about something for once in his life, but he taught me a lot, I think. About being kind and having patience. What it means to love someone."

Janessa has settled into the seat across from Dylan, and now her chin rests on her palm as she listens. "He sounds pretty dreamy."

Dylan smiles and looks at Landon, nestled on the couch. His mouth has fallen slightly open and his head is snuggled into a nest of pillows; a blanket is pulled up over his shoulder.

"Things weren't perfect, but they were good." Dylan looks back at Janessa. "We were going to get married, travel the world, probably buy a house with a picket fence and adopt a dog, all that jazz."

He shrugs. "Who knows, now. You can't really plan for these things."

"No, you can't." Janessa reaches out to squeeze Dylan's hand. "But you *can* eat cookies with me, and tell me how much you like my hair and then marathon bad TV with your hubby while you guys make those gross heart eyes at each other."

Dylan laughs, a real laugh that crinkles his eyes at the corners and makes him feel refreshed.

"I like your hair," he teases, and Janessa flips it dramatically over her shoulder. "The purple really brings out the color of your eyes."

She sticks her tongue out at him just as the oven timer goes off, and the house fills with the smell of warm cookies when she pulls the pan out of the oven.

"I think I'll keep you," Dylan says with a barely suppressed moan as Janessa sets a plate of steaming cookies in front of him.

"Good. Because you're stuck with me. You both are."

* * *

Things settle into a semblance of normalcy. *Maybe normal isn't the right word,* Dylan muses, as he helps Landon into his jacket. He leads Landon's fingers to the buttons, encouraging him to do them up himself. Landon's fingers fumble. His movements are stiff and awkward; he groans in frustration, tries to pull away. Dylan doesn't let him, but returns Landon's fingers to a button; his hands hold Landon's steady as Landon pushes the button through.

"You've got it," Dylan offers with a smile, and helps Landon with the rest of the buttons. He tries to focus on the small victories.

"Normal" definitely isn't the right word, he decides, unlocking the wheels of Landon's chair and pushing him through the door into the chilly autumn morning. Maybe the phrase is "making do." Adjusting. Figuring things out as they go.

They've taken to walking early in the morning, when the sun is still creeping over the horizon and their breath fogs the air with every exhalation. Landon seems to like being outside: the way the cold bites at his cheeks, the way everything is quiet, so early in the morning, with only the occasional dog walker or jogger passing by. Soon the snow will come, and the bitter cold of a Minnesota winter, and they'll be stuck inside, unable to continue their morning ritual. But for now, Dylan enjoys the way Landon's shoulders relax, the way his face shines in the glow of the rising sun and the way his breathing calms, his expression grows peaceful.

Landon's been home nearly three weeks, and it's been more stressful than Dylan imagined; but it's been good too. They've fallen into something resembling a routine, with the days passing by in a scramble of work and appointments, fixing up the house and trying to figure out how to manage their new lives. It's challenging, but every day Dylan wakes up with Landon beside him—blinking awake with tired eyes, his hair mussed from sleep, an expression of complete trust when he looks at Dylan—and it's worth it.

Dylan closes his eyes and lets the golden blanket of the rising sun cover him, lets it warm his skin. And he lets himself have this moment. He stands still, seeing only the red of his closed eyelids, and tries to pretend that everything is all right, that every day doesn't feel as though he's barely scraping by, as if he's holding on by a thread that might snap at any minute.

Landon coughs, and Dylan opens his eyes, rests a hand on Landon's shoulder, massages gently until the cough stops. Landon's gloved hand comes up to brush Dylan's fingers.

"Should we head back?" Dylan asks, and Landon nods. They turn around and make their way back home.

Janessa usually shows up shortly after seven, always with a twenty-ounce coffee, the only explanation for the amount of energy she has so early in the day.

"Morning, D-money," she sings at Dylan, moving around him to where Landon waits in the living room. Dylan shakes his head when she greets Landon with an excited "Landog, my man," and holds out a fist. Landon curls his own fingers as much as he can and they bump fists, Janessa making an exploding noise as they pull away. Dylan snorts, sure that Janessa has been teaching Landon this with the sole intention of showing it off to *him*.

"He's just jealous he's not as fly as we are," Janessa fake-whispers into Landon's ear, loud enough for Dylan to hear.

"Don't let her corrupt you while I'm gone, honey." Dylan grabs his lunch bag and kisses Landon's forehead.

"Too late," Landon manages, just as Janessa shouts, "No promises!" Dylan shakes his head and heads out the door, already ten minutes late.

Work always seems long, but Dylan tries to appear engaged; he plasters a smile to his face and attempts to be social, to remember who's dating whom and who went on vacation where and what big projects they have coming up. It's exhausting, and most of the time Dylan just wants to pile up his books as makeshift walls around his computer, block out everyone and stare at his screen in silence—but that's not what the old Dylan would do. That's the Dylan his coworkers expect. The Dylan he owes them.

He declines their offers for drinks after work; he doesn't want Janessa to have to stay longer than her full day and doesn't have the energy to socialize anyway. He drives home in silence, taking the time to clear his head, and finds, more and more, that he enjoys the silence and the calm that comes with it. Sometimes he stops at the grocery store, or the drugstore to refill one of Landon's prescriptions, or the library to see if Sandy has any new books for him.

Today he heads straight home, and the smells of baking rolls and a casserole greet him the moment he opens the door. Landon is waiting on the couch; his head rolls toward Dylan and his lips tug into a smile. There's a dusting of glitter on his nose and marker smudges on his fingers, and he looks excited, as though he wants to tell Dylan something.

"What have you been up to today?" Dylan asks, raising an eyebrow as he brushes the glitter off Landon's nose with his thumb. Landon pushes himself up straighter; his gaze flickers to the coffee table. A stack of colored paper is spread across the table, next to a box filled with markers and craft supplies.

"Made you some… something," Landon explains. His voice has gotten clearer with the help of his speech therapist, but he still has trouble finding the right word and often becomes confused in the middle of a sentence.

The top sheet of paper crinkles when Dylan picks it up. Its edges are framed by an assortment of glitter and feathers and glue. In the middle, written in shaky blue marker, in handwriting that could belong to a child, is Dylan's name.

"Did you write this?" Dylan asks, his heart jumping into his throat. Landon nods. Dylan can see practice letters written on the papers spread over the coffee table, the alphabet, written several times over, Janessa's name and Landon's name and the names of family members, but none decorated like Dylan's.

"It's amazing, Landon." Dylan sinks into the couch beside him, and Landon leans against him, his body language relaxed and happy.

"For you," Landon whispers, and Dylan kisses his temple.

"Hey, I didn't realize you were home," Janessa says, emerging from the kitchen. She sits on the armrest beside Dylan and looks at the paper he's still holding. "He did that himself. Well, I held his hand to keep it steady, but the letters were all him."

Dylan lets his fingers brush the paper, feels the roughness of the glitter, the softness of the feathers.

"It's perfect," Dylan says, nudging Landon with his shoulder. Landon nudges back.

Janessa leaves after giving Dylan firm instructions to take the casserole out after twenty more minutes and a warning that if he burns her hard work, Landon will tell her and she'll never cook for him again. She's lying; she'd taken to cooking when she realized that Dylan had been living on Eggos and frozen pizza, and Dylan knows she enjoys it.

Sometimes Dylan's mom calls in the evenings wanting an update on Landon's accomplishments, to schedule something for the weekend or to nag Dylan about coming to a yoga class. Sometimes Landon's mom FaceTimes with the two of them, smiling and waving at Landon from her house in Madison with promises to visit again soon. Sometimes Lana drops by with a movie and microwave popcorn and spends the evening lounging on the couch with Landon, her homework always open and ignored in front of her. And sometimes nothing happens, and they sit on the porch swing in the backyard, or Dylan reads Landon a book, or they marathon reality TV on Netflix until Landon falls asleep with his head resting against Dylan's shoulder, spent from the long day.

Dylan always wakes Landon gently, with a squeeze to his shoulder, a kiss on his forehead or a ruffle of his hair, and helps him brush his teeth and get ready for bed. Only when Landon is firmly under the covers, clutching his pillow and already drifting back to sleep, does Dylan let himself have a little time curled up on the couch with his book and a cup of tea, or in a steaming hot bath, trying his hardest to relax and end the day, no matter how stressful, or how many ups and downs it's had, on a good note.

When he finally crawls into bed with exhaustion seeping into his bones, Landon always finds him. Their fingers curl together; their bodies fit against each other like joined puzzle pieces.

* * *

What Dylan isn't expecting is the anger. Landon's improvements have been vast, his recovery at home exponentially faster than it was in the hospital, but even with those improvements Dylan can see Landon becoming more and more frustrated. Every thing he *can* do reminds him of all the things he can't do, and with every success there's always something *more,* something he wants to do but isn't able to manage.

He's trapped, has a hard time expressing himself and has to rely on others to understand what he needs. Dylan can see how frustrated this makes him, how the Landon inside is trying to break out from the body that won't let him.

There are good days, days when Landon seems proud of his accomplishments, when he lets Dylan hold him and compliment him, days when he smiles and the world seems a little brighter.

But there are bad days too, days when Dylan feels as though he's holding on by a fraying thread, when everything he's worked so hard for seems to disappear in a moment, when nothing is good enough and nothing Dylan says can calm Landon down.

It's a Friday, three weeks since Landon came home, and today is a bad day. Dylan comes home from work early to find Janessa encouraging Landon to work on the tasks his speech therapist gave him, and Landon sitting on the couch with his arms crossed, his jaw tense. Janessa shrugs apologetically and offers to stay longer and help, but Dylan sends her home; she deserves a break after a long week.

"Hey, Landon," Dylan says softly, once Janessa is out the door and he's put his coat away. Landon doesn't look at him, but his eyes are fixed firmly on his knees and his fingers dig into his legs in a way that looks painful. Dylan tries to ease Landon's hands from his legs and hold them in his own, but Landon jerks away and crosses them over his chest instead, still pointedly avoiding Dylan's eyes.

"All right." Dylan acquiesces, pulls his hands back. "What's going on? Are you hurting?"

Landon ignores the question and keeps his eyes fixed in one spot, his gaze hard. It's a stupid question, they both know it; of course he's still hurting, they both are, but Dylan doesn't know any other way to fix this, doesn't know what to do when Landon acts like this. When they fought before, it was always Dylan who would try to avoid it, and Landon the one who made them sit down and talk about it. He always kept a level head, even at his angriest.

"I love you," Dylan tries, moving his head to try to catch Landon's gaze. Landon leans away from him, his body closed off, hands returning to dig fingers into his legs.

"Okay." Dylan stands up. He already feels frayed from a long day at work paired with the constant worry, and dreams about the attack have started creeping into his sleep. The fear that he's not doing enough, that he's not good enough, has left him feeling worn, and he's not sure how long he can keep this up. How long he can keep pretending.

He makes his way into the bedroom. The bed dips under his weight. More and more days have ended this way; Dylan doesn't know what to do, how to help, what Landon needs. So he sits on the bed, pulls Landon's pillow against his chest and buries his face in it and is calmed by the familiar scent of Landon's shampoo.

Until he hears a crash, and his stomach turns over. He rushes back to the living room. The lamp that sits on the end table by the couch is now on the floor, along with the TV remote and a broken glass. Water pools on the hardwood floor. Landon is scowling down at all this with a foreign expression on his face, as if those inanimate objects were the ones that beat his head in and left him like this, shattered pieces of the man he used to be.

Dylan doesn't say anything—no words he could say would help. He crouches down and picks up the fallen objects, carefully piling the broken glass in his palm before depositing it in the trash. Landon flinches at the sound of the glass falling into the garbage can but he doesn't look, just pushes himself back even farther into the couch. Dylan can see the red mark of a scratch on his arm and crescent moons where his fingernails have dug in too deep.

"Landon," Dylan says, the name almost a sigh. He sits on the couch beside Landon and grasps Landon's arm to get a better look. But Landon pulls his arm back and leans away from where Dylan is sitting. His message is clear.

"Please, Landon. Don't be like this. I just want to help."

His words are useless. Landon doesn't respond, just remains stony; his breath becomes ragged as his agitation increases. Dylan can't do this anymore. He's frustrated and tired, hasn't slept decently in weeks, and he just… can't.

Dylan slips into the kitchen, leans against the counter and tries not to cry. He listens as Landon coughs: each harsh breath feels as if it's cutting into him, squeezing his heart. He fumbles his phone out of his pocket and scrolls through his contacts until he finds the number he's looking for.

"Hey, Dylan, what's up?" Lana answers, and Dylan can hear the muffled sound of talking in the background; a laugh breaks through.

"Hi, um…" Dylan feels so *stupid*, but he doesn't know what to say. *How do I tell someone that my whole life is slipping away, like sand sifting through fingers?*

"What's going on?" He hears concern in her voice and the background noises quieten, as if she's stepped outside. "Is everything okay?"

No, Dylan wants to say. Nothing is okay right now.

"I just… I don't know, Lana." He sags to the floor, his back pressed against the cupboards. "I didn't know who else to call."

"What's wrong? Is it Landon?"

Dylan nods, and then remembers she can't see him.

"Yeah, he's just… he's so upset. All the time. And I don't know." His eyes dart toward the kitchen door, the entrance that leads to Landon. "I don't know how to fix it."

"You don't have to fix it." Lana sounds so much like Landon in this moment that Dylan squeezes his eyes shut and scrubs away the tear that escapes down his cheek. "Some things can't be fixed."

He takes a shaky breath.

"I just need to get out." The words surprise him even as he says them. "I need to get away, clear my head. Just for a few hours."

Lana is silent. "Do you want me to come stay with him for the night? I can come over now, give you a break."

Dylan thinks about the laughter he heard in the background; it's a Friday night, and Lana's probably out with friends. He feels bad asking, but he doesn't know what else to do.

"You're busy," Dylan says, but it's only a halfhearted protest, and they both know it.

"It's fine, Dylan," she assures him, and he almost believes her. "I know how hard you've been working to take care of Landon, and how busy you've been at work. You deserve a break."

Dylan exhales. "Thank you, Lana."

"No problem. Be there as soon as I can."

It's nearing six when Lana arrives. She's wearing a pretty blue dress and bright red lipstick; her hair is curled for a night out. She wraps Dylan in a hug, barely three steps into the house, and Dylan lets himself relax in her arms. Nothing is said about her disrupted plans, and Dylan doesn't ask. This is their life now: They're Landon's family, the only family Landon has here, and he comes first. He'll always come first.

"Thank you," Dylan whispers when they pull apart. Lana offers him a smile.

"Anytime." She pulls an elastic band off her wrist and pulls her hair back into a quick ponytail. "Seriously. Anytime you need a break, you call me. I don't want you to wait for this I'm-breaking-down-on-the-phone business, okay?"

Dylan nods; his cheeks warm with an embarrassed blush.

"Good. Glad we discussed this." Lana winks at him as she makes her way into the living room where Landon sits on the couch, his body still tense, his eyes still fixed on the floor.

"Hey, Lanny." Landon glances up in surprise and looks away again.

"I'm going to go run some errands." Dylan shifts on his feet, looking between the siblings. "Lana's going to stay here with you for a bit, while I'm out."

It's an obvious excuse, a blatant ploy to get away. Landon stays tense, and only the slight shift of his shoulders gives any indication that he's heard. Lana's smile falls as she watches them, her hands bunch the fabric of her dress, and Dylan hesitates for a moment before he steps forward, leans over the arm of the couch and lightly kisses Landon's cheek.

Landon doesn't move.

"I'll be back soon," Dylan promises. He already feels reluctant to leave. But if he doesn't, this will just build and build and build until it crushes him. The guilt is already crushing him, knotting in his stomach. He's not strong enough for this, he's not good enough to be who his fiancé needs him to be.

He drives to the Raven, a bar he used to frequent with Landon on weekend nights when they wanted to have some fun, to drink and laugh and forget about their obligations. It's crowded, but Dylan makes his way to the bar, slides onto an empty stool and orders a beer. He hands money to the bartender, one he doesn't recognize. Despite the crowd, he's never felt so alone—as though there's an empty space beside him waiting to be filled.

The beer is too bitter, but he drinks it anyway. He drums his fingers on the bar and taps his feet on the stool. It only takes fifteen more minutes for him to regret coming here, and he's tempted to get up and leave, to abandon his drink, drive back home and promise Landon that no matter how angry he gets, he'll never leave again, not like this. But he doesn't; he needs to prove that he's okay by himself for a while. That he doesn't need Landon the way he so desperately does.

So he sips his drink and tries to take comfort in the blanket of sound surrounding him, the chattering of excited voices, the music drifting from the dance floor, the clatter of shot glasses being passed around. He drinks, feeling the stress begin to ebb from his shoulders, his headache begin to melt away.

"Dylan?" A voice startles him, and he sloshes his beer over the edge of the glass as he turns. Tate steps toward him, his brow furrowing. "What are you doing here?"

Dylan looks back at his glass and tries to figure out how to answer. He isn't sure what he's doing here himself.

"I just wanted to get out for a bit." There. That sounds okay, not too pathetic, but not information-dumping either. Dylan tries to smile, but judging from the concerned look on Tate's face, it's not very convincing.

"Mind if I join?"

Dylan motions to the stool next to him in a *please, sit* gesture. Tate turns to wave a small group of people on.

"You didn't have to leave your friends." Dylan wonders how many people's lives he can disrupt in one night. Tate shrugs.

"It's okay, we were leaving anyway."

Dylan just nods and takes another sip of his beer. Tate orders another round for them both, and they sit in silence for a moment, but it's comfortable. Friendly.

"I miss him," Dylan says, after one drink has become two. He stares into the amber liquid. "I know this makes me, basically, the worst fiancé ever, but I miss him."

Tate doesn't say anything, and Dylan looks up at him, expecting to see him judging, to see a look of disgust on his lips. He just looks sad.

"I miss the way he laughed, and the way he cried at the stupidest movies. I miss all the subtle ways he would try to get me to the pet store so he could convince me to get a dog, or a fish, or whatever it was he wanted that week. It's all those little things that I miss, you know?"

Tate nods, his fingers gripping his drink until his knuckles turn white.

"The Bugs Bunny hat," Tate says, and Dylan laughs.

"Don't even mention the Bugs Bunny hat." He groans, makes a face. "I just… it's eating me up inside, because he's here. He's *here*, and the first days in the hospital I wasn't sure I would ever be able to say that again. And it's my fault…"

His throat closes mid-sentence, his hands clenching into fists, and he can't continue.

"It's not your fault." Tate draws a line down the condensation of his glass. "You know it's not your fault. Landon wouldn't blame you, so you shouldn't blame yourself."

"I know." He's been told this so many times, but it doesn't stop the guilt from sinking its teeth in. "I know. It's just, Landon's been so *angry* lately, and I feel like no matter how hard I try, I can't get it right. No matter what I do."

He can feel Tate's eyes on him but is too ashamed to look up and meet them.

"Do you have to? No one gets everything right, not all the time."

Dylan doesn't answer, just stares at his glass.

"You're going to screw up, it's a given. You'd screw up if none of this had ever happened. Landon will screw up too. But you guys are solid. You'll get through this and move on to the next challenge. You have to stop beating yourself up. There's nothing you can do to change the past. Just deal with what's happening now, you know?"

There's something about Tate's words that makes Dylan push his beer away, and glance up, intrigued.

"At least he's here, right?" Tate offers with a smile. "You guys can figure out the rest."

"He's still here," Dylan echoes, the knot in his stomach releasing, just a little. "I'm going to head back home. Thank you for the talk."

"Landon's my best friend." Tate presses cash onto the bar and stands up with Dylan. "Anything I can do to help, just let me know."

"Thank you." Dylan gives Tate a quick hug. He's not alone in this. He doesn't have to be perfect, because there will be others to help him, like Tate, and Lana, who has the Game of Life spread out across the floor when Dylan gets back home with Landon working to spin the dial.

"Hey." Dylan sinks down on the floor beside Landon. Landon looks at him; his eyes are downcast, apologetic.

"Sorry," he murmurs, and Dylan nudges his shoulder. He lets Landon thread their fingers together, lets him rest a tired head on his shoulder and kisses his hair.

"I'm sorry too," he says, and Lana tilts her head at him, but doesn't pry.

CHAPTER 8

When Dylan pulls into the driveway, his dad is under the car, an old Fiat that he bought ages ago with the intention of fixing it up. He'd never gotten around to it, and it drove Adele crazy that Sam was always buying old cars, convinced that because he wrote car manuals he was capable of restoring them. The repairs always flopped, just like his plays, and sometimes, when Sam was gone, Adele would take the cars into a garage and have them fixed just so Sam wouldn't add them to the long list of everything he'd failed at. He never knew—or maybe he did and just never said anything; but either way, it made Sam happy to be able to fix things, to create something with his hands other than words.

Sometimes Dylan wonders if the cars represent Sam's broken relationship with his own parents, who had never approved of his decision to leave India and become a writer, marry an American girl and have a child who is not only *hapa*, but gay on top of it: the icing on the cake, Dylan figures, in a long line of his father's faults.

"Hey, Dad," Dylan greets him. Sam slides out from under the Fiat; his face is smudged with grease, his hair is a mess, his cheeks are red from the cold.

"Dylan." Sam greets him with a nod, wiping stained hands on his pants.

"A little cold for fixing cars, isn't it?" Dylan asks, his breath fogging the air around him.

Sam shrugs. "Wanted to get it done before the snow comes," he explains, as though this is the most logical thing in the world.

"It looks great," Dylan says, though he knows nothing about cars. His dad tried to teach him to drive a stickshift the summer after he graduated high school, and that ended with sore necks and a tension between them that took months to resolve. Sam nods and drums his fingers against his leg as though he's trying to think of something to say. Sometimes Dylan wishes that the crippling insecurity that came with being a failed writer hadn't torn his dad down to this shell of the person once so warm and friendly Dylan remembers from childhood.

"Just looking for Mom." Dylan motions toward the house.

"She's in her studio." Sam looks back at the car. Dylan smiles at him, leaves him to continue his pseudo-mechanics and makes his way into the house.

Adele's studio is an addition to the back, made of pine, with a wall of windows. It's open and bright, and always smells like nature. The tension leaks out of Dylan's shoulders just from entering the room.

She's instructing a class—prenatal yoga, judging from the number of swollen bellies stretched out on mats of purple and green. Calming music plays from the stereo system Dylan helped install a few years back. Adele doesn't see him at first, and when she does she arches her eyebrows, losing her rhythm only for a moment. Dylan waves at her. His expression is relaxed enough that she doesn't stop class, and he takes a seat on the bench near the back. He waits and lets his eyes close and his lungs fill, breathing when she instructs her students to breathe and letting the comfort of home melt over him.

The class ends shortly after Dylan arrives, and his mom chats with a few of the women who come up to her afterward. Adele's smile is genuine, but her eyes keep flickering to Dylan. Eventually, their yoga mats cleared from the floor, everyone shuffles out the door. Adele mutes the music.

"This is a surprise," she says, and Dylan feels guilty. He doesn't visit as often as he should.

He looks around the room. "Classes going well?"

Adele nods and shrugs on a sweater.

"Next time you want to come to prenatal yoga, at least show up on time," she says, the lightness in her voice assuring Dylan that he's not in for a lecture. He laughs.

"Sorry, I'll remember that."

Adele hugs him. "Come on." She leads him through the house, plucks her scarf from the coat rack and wraps it around her neck. "Walk to the store with me."

Dylan doesn't argue, just buttons up his coat and slips his gloves back onto his hands.

"How's Landon?" she asks, once they're making their way down the street. Long-fallen leaves are slick under their feet.

"He's…" Dylan stops short of the automatic *good* that wants to follow. "I don't know. Sometimes I think he might be happy, but then he gets so angry at me, at Janessa, at himself. And he's been so withdrawn, and… I don't know what to do."

Adele's lips form the thin line they make when she's thinking.

"I know he's frustrated, and I want to help him, but I don't know how when he keeps pushing me away. I'm worried that I'm not doing anything right, or that I'm making things worse."

They turn the corner, and a cold gust of wind makes Dylan shiver.

"I won't say you're doing everything right," Adele says, adjusting her scarf to cover any exposed areas. "Because no one does all the time. But I know you're not making things worse. No one, not even Landon, expects you to do more than *try*, and I know you're trying, honey."

Dylan kicks at a rock, watches it spin out into the road.

"I just want things to feel okay, you know? I want to stop going to sleep at night feeling like I barely held things together today."

"I hate to tell you, but that's just part of life." Adele smiles sadly. "You have to learn to put that behind you, and focus on how you're going to get through the next day."

Dylan pauses.

"I just… I wish I'd never suggested that stupid shortcut."

They stop despite the cold, the traffic driving by and the wind cutting through their clothes.

"Sweetheart." Adele rests her hand on Dylan's arm and then draws him into another hug, this one tighter, warmer.

"I know it's not my fault," Dylan says into her shoulder, his voice shaky. "But I still feel like I ruined his life."

Adele holds him for a moment.

"Don't let this destroy you inside." Her hand brushes his cheek. "You can't live your life carrying that weight."

"I don't know how to get rid of it," Dylan whispers, blinking up at the sky.

"Come to some more classes," Adele says. Dylan has been following up on his earlier promise, dropping by a few of Adele's yoga classes when Lana wants a night with Landon, or Janessa agrees to stay a little late. They feel another gust of cold wind and start walking again. "Bring Landon, and Lana too if she wants. It might not fix everything, but I promise it'll help."

"Okay," Dylan agrees, and Adele looks at him, as if surprised he's not arguing with her about it. "We'll come."

The store comes into view, and Dylan is glad to get out of the cold.

"And Dylan…" Adele picks up a basket from the stack near the door. "Remember it's okay to ask for help sometimes. You have to take care of yourself, too."

"I'll try," Dylan says, and even though he can't make any promises, he means it—if only because he can't keep going on like this. "Now what do you need to get?"

She hands him a list and they make their way through the store, gathering ingredients for something that Dylan can only assume is soup.

"Your father wrote a new play, you know," Adele says as she compares bags of rice. "It got picked up by a small production company."

"Wait… really?" Dylan thinks back to the way his dad hesitated, as if he wanted to say something.

"It would mean a lot to him if you came." Adele places two bags of rice in the already heavy basket.

"Wow, that's… that's great. Of course we'll come," Dylan says, readjusts the basket on his arms.

"It won't be until December, there's still a bit of production work to be done, but I know your father isn't great talking about these things." She shrugs. "I'll keep you updated."

"Thank you." It's been years since his dad has written anything. "Please do."

His mom buys him a tub of tapioca pudding and an assortment of teas to bring back to Landon, despite Dylan's protest that they already have too much tea. Adele informs him that there's never too much tea, and when he leaves an hour later loaded with groceries and a pan of bars, with a goodbye to his dad's legs poking out from under the Fiat, he resolves to follow through with his promises as best he can.

* * *

The snow comes overnight, blanketing the earth in a thick white flurry. Landon sits by the window and watches Janessa shovel the driveway. Her breath fogs the air; she has a blue knit hat on her head. He's supposed to be working on his writing, but his hands ache, and he can't bring himself to sit still. Not today, with the sun reflecting off the snow, making everything seem brighter.

He wants to go help Janessa; he itches to wrap his fingers around the handle of the shovel, to scoop up the heavy snow, to feel the stretch in his muscles. He used to love shoveling when he lived with his parents in Wisconsin. It was calming, somehow, to be out in the cold, to feel the gentle scrape of the shovel on the icy concrete, the wool mittens against his fingers, the snow that catches on his eyelashes.

Janessa sees him watching and waves at him, and he waves back, grips the wheels of his chair and pushes himself back to the table. He picks up the pen he's supposed to use—it's thick, easy to grip— and stares at the paper, biting his lip in determination. His hand slipping only a few times, he writes the word *snow* and even tries to draw a tiny snowflake next to the word. His writing is horrible. The letters are shaky, nearly illegible if he writes too small, but he tries not to let it bother him. It's just another thing he needs to work at.

He can hear the front door open, the sound of Janessa stomp-ing snow off her boots.

"I think your neighbor is hitting on me," Janessa says when she makes her way inside, motions to the paper cup she's holding in her hands.

"Gladys?" Landon asks, thinking of the sweet, gray-haired lady who lives next to them.

"Yeah." Janessa collapses onto a chair beside him. "She keeps making me hot chocolate and telling me that we're welcome over anytime." Janessa narrows her eyes. "Or maybe it's *your* cute little face she likes."

Landon makes a *pssh* noise. Janessa offers him the cup and he takes it, very carefully wraps his fingers around it and lifts it to his lips, taking a cautious sip. It's lukewarm by now, but the chocolate is rich and he closes his eyes and lets himself savor the taste.

"Good, right?" Janessa asks, and Landon nods and sets the cup back on the table. That's enough; he's still wary of liquids, of overwhelming himself and swallowing incorrectly. He hates the way it makes him feel as if he's choking, as if no cough is strong enough.

"We'll have to… um," Landon takes a moment, collects his thoughts. "Go say thank you… sometime."

Janessa raises an eyebrow, and Landon looks at the table. He rarely suggests any activity that involves interaction with others. Since coming home from the hospital, he has felt embarrassed and ashamed of how he looks and how he talks, hates the stares and pity that he gets. And he's not ready to jump back in, not by any means, but he thinks he'd like to dip his toes in a little.

"Sure," Janessa says with an encouraging smile. "We can do that."

Landon nods and scratches a fingernail against the table. Janessa grabs his hand.

"You know Dylan hates that," she warns. Landon withdraws his hand, feeling an uncomfortable twist in his gut at the mention of Dylan's name. Janessa doesn't notice, or doesn't say anything if she does.

"All right, we have," Janessa cranes her neck, "three hours until physical therapy. What should we do?"

They decide on laundry; the hamper is close to overflowing, and Landon pushes himself to the laundry room, Janessa close behind.

"Keep that up and you're going to have some serious guns," she says with a whistle. "Dylan's going to be a lucky man."

Landon scoffs. Her words bring up the thing that's been weighing on him for days.

"What's that noise?" Janessa asks. Landon shrugs and grabs for the laundry, but Janessa pushes it out of the way with her foot. Landon glares at her.

"Come on, my boyfriend gets the exact same look when he doesn't want to talk about something. What's up?"

Landon stares at his knees. He can feel his embarrassment creep across his cheeks.

"Was it what I said? About Dylan?" she asks, and Landon gives a hesitant nod.

"Can you try and tell me what's bothering you?"

Landon purses his lips and takes a moment to think, to grasp the thoughts that flit away. It's like capturing butterflies in a net.

"He wouldn't…" He licks his lips. "He wouldn't want to." He stumbles a bit on all the *W*s, but Janessa doesn't comment, just tilts her head.

"Wouldn't want to what?"

Landon looks at her: Is she really going to make him say it?

"You know," he says. "Do anything. With me."

"Why do you think that?"

Landon pauses, digs his thumb into his knee.

"I can't…" A breath. "I mean. I can't…"

"You can't?" Janessa prompts, giving him a minute to come up with the words. Landon shrugs.

"Anything. I can't do anything."

"You do lots of things," Janessa points out. "Every day, I see you doing so many new things."

Landon digs his thumb in a little harder and Janessa reaches out, taking his hand in hers.

"Are you upset with Dylan?" she asks. Landon shakes his head. He doesn't know how to explain it, this feeling he's been getting when Dylan is close, when he gives Landon a single kiss on his forehead and nothing more, when he holds Landon like he's made of cracked glass, everything he does cautious and reserved.

"With him," Landon manages, looks at Janessa and hopes she understands. "I mean. I can't… be close to him. Like before."

162

Janessa squeezes Landon's hand.

"Oh, Landon. Dylan doesn't care about that stuff. He loves you, and I'm sure he loves being with you in whatever way you can."

Landon looks at their hands and squirms in his chair.

"I care."

Janessa dips her head to catch Landon's eye.

"Have you talked to him?" she asks. "About how you feel?"

Landon shakes his head.

"You boys." She gives a dramatic sigh. "Have you considered that maybe Dylan doesn't want to do anything that will make you uncomfortable? That he doesn't want to do anything you're not comfortable with, and he's waiting for you to take the lead?"

"Me?" Landon frowns.

"Yeah you, ya peanut," Janessa says, her smile warm. Landon draws his hands away, pretending to look offended.

"Look, he's probably just as nervous about this as you are, and you don't want this to build into something it's not. So talk to him, okay?"

Landon nods. "Okay."

"Good," Janessa says, pushes the laundry back toward him. "Now, darks or lights?"

It starts snowing again on their way to therapy. The roads become slick and traffic slows until they're fifteen minutes late. Janessa pushes Landon through the hallways like a madwoman on a mission, making race-car noises at every turn, and Landon hides his face in embarrassment.

Ryan, Landon's outpatient physical therapist, is waiting for them at their usual station.

"Sorry," Janessa says, out of breath. "Landon held us up. You know how he is about powdering his nose."

Landon swats at Janessa's leg, and she lightly punches his shoulder.

"With this weather, everyone is going to be fifteen minutes late," Ryan waves off her apology. "It happens every winter."

Landon doesn't say anything. He still feels self-conscious about the way he sounds, the way his words slur together, the way he stutters and stops, the pauses when he can't remember what he's trying to say. It's so obvious, he thinks, like a giant neon sign that lights up every time he speaks: *Please, Stare At Me.* As if the wheelchair didn't make it bad enough already.

But Ryan doesn't expect chatter, and Landon likes that about him, likes the way he doesn't expect too much of Landon, but doesn't baby him either. He's calm and encouraging even when Landon can't do things and helps push him to do things he didn't think he could.

"Has Janessa been giving you trouble?" Ryan asks, helping Landon transfer from his chair to the padded bench. Landon nods and ignores the playful glare Janessa shoots at him. Ryan starts working on his range of motion, having Landon bend each joint, gets him stretching and moving, warming and loosening up.

"We'll just have to get you strong enough that you can beat her up then, hm?" Ryan says, winking at Janessa. Landon chuckles a little, grips the bench for stability.

"How's the right side been feeling?" Ryan asks, uncurling those fingers. They immediately try to curl again, but Ryan doesn't let them. He bends and stretches each finger, rotating his wrist.

"Still... um, still stiff," Landon answers quietly. Ryan just nods and massages the muscles in his hand. Landon has a brace for his right hand, to help keep the muscles from stiffening too much, but it chafes and he doesn't wear it as much as he should.

Ryan has them play three-way catch with a lightly weighted ball, and Landon knows Janessa only misses the ball to make him feel better. It does.

"All right," Ryan says, clapping his hands on his knees. "I know we usually do the jumpsuit next, but I think you're ready for something different."

Landon looks at Ryan skeptically. What Ryan calls the jumpsuit is actually more like a padded rock-climbing harness, attached to the ceiling and easily moveable. A few weeks ago they hooked Landon in, and he walked the length of the gym, supported by the harness. He shrugged off the victory, as it had been less walking than assisted gliding. But it had been valuable in detecting his weak spots, the way his right knee kept giving out, the way he had trouble lifting his feet high enough to keep his toes from dragging. Dylan was proud when Janessa told him about it, but the fact that he was struggling to do something a two-year-old could do only made Landon feel annoyed.

But he's been trying, doing his exercises at home as instructed, going to therapy twice a week, and working on thinking more positively, no matter how hard that might be.

Ryan stands on his right side and offers him a hand, laying the other across his back in support.

"Janessa, would you be willing to offer assistance?"

Janessa places herself on the other side of Landon, copying Ryan's stance. Landon can feel his heart rate quicken. Unexpected nervousness fills him, making his mind go numb.

"We're going to stand up now, nice and slow, okay?"

Landon's hand tightens its grip on Ryan's as they stand. His weight transfers mostly to the left side. Janessa squeezes his other hand, offering silent support.

"Doing okay, Landon?" Ryan asks, and Landon nods, tries to find his footing. Balancing is tricky; certain movements make the world tip around him, and he feels a nauseating sense of vertigo if he moves too fast.

"All right. Janessa and I are going to take a small step forward and I want you to follow with your right leg, okay? We're here for support if you need it, but I want you to try and do this as much on your own as you can. If you need to stop at any time just pinch my hand or say so, sound good?"

Landon draws a breath and steels himself. He can do this. "Sounds good." Ryan looks at him, eyes wide and encouraging. "You've got this," Janessa whispers in his ear.

They take a half step forward, and Landon braces himself, lifts his right leg and starts to tilt. Janessa supports him so he doesn't fall over, holding his hand tight as his toes brush the floor before he sets his foot down. He's leaning on their arms more than he would like, but Ryan initiates another step forward; Janessa follows his lead. This step, with Landon's weight on his right leg, is a little more difficult; his knee starts to buckle before he tenses, grits his teeth and pushes his left leg forward to meet the right, wavering only slightly as he regains his balance.

"That was great, Landon," Ryan says. He sounds genuinely excited.

"You did it!" Janessa exclaims, patting Landon's hand. "You walked!"

Feeling a little stunned, Landon turns to look at Ryan and then Janessa.

"Can we…" Landon starts. He licks his lips, tries to work up the courage. "Go a little more?"

"Of course," Ryan answers, and they walk a few more feet. Landon's steps are stronger on the left, faltering on the right. But they'll get better, he knows they will, and he finds himself smiling. He *did* it, he walked, when they weren't sure if he ever would.

"I did it," he whispers and feels his cheeks coloring.

"You did," Janessa says, pressing her cheek to his shoulder. Landon can feel himself start to sag; his legs are a little shaky. But Ryan just tightens his grip while Janessa lets go and grabs the wheelchair. As he eases himself back into the chair, sweat beads on his brow, something he would normally be embarrassed about. But right now, exhilarated by his accomplishment, he can't bring himself to care.

Janessa helps him bundle back up in his jacket and scarf and snugs his hat on over his head. They thank Ryan, and he reminds Landon to keep working on his exercises. Next time they'll tackle the parallel bars.

Landon knows he probably looks silly, but he can't stop smiling the whole trip home and doesn't even mind when Janessa stops at the grocery store to stock up on the frozen waffles that Dylan seems to consume by the dozen.

"Dylan's going to freak out," Janessa says when she gets back in the car, groceries loaded into the trunk. "He'll be so proud of you."

The car stalls a little in the cold.

"No," Landon starts, an idea forming in his head.

"No?" Janessa asks, throwing the car into reverse and backing out of the parking spot. "You think Dylan's heart has finally turned to stone or something?"

"Maybe..." Landon says, dragging his tongue over the words. "Maybe surprise him? I could, um... practice and surprise him. Sometime."

Landon nods with a sense of finality. He knows he hasn't been the best fiancé to Dylan; he can see how frustrated Dylan gets, how stressed he looks when Landon gets angry and lashes out, and how much he's struggling to support both Landon and himself. He can't do much for Dylan, can't help out in the ways he wants to and needs more help than he can give; but maybe this could be enough. Maybe this could show Dylan that he's trying, that he's getting there, that someday Dylan won't have to do everything himself anymore—that maybe they'll be a little closer to what things were like before.

"Well, aren't you a little devil," Janessa teases. "But I think it's a great idea. The perfect surprise. Better than rum in your eggnog."

Landon just nods and looks out the window. The smile doesn't leave his face for the rest of the drive.

* * *

It takes two days for Landon to work up the courage. They're in bed, cuddled under a mountain of blankets with a cold winter wind howling outside. Dylan, hair still damp from his shower, is reading a book. Landon leans against him and stares at the words on the page without reading them. He feels tense, nervous, and knows Dylan can sense it by the way he keeps glancing down at

Landon; his lips move as if he wants to say something, but he stops himself before he can.

"Can I ask you an important question?" Dylan asks suddenly, pressing his bookmark between the pages and closing his book. Landon looks up at him with wide eyes, concern building inside of him.

"Will you scratch my back?"

Landon blinks, and Dylan laughs.

"I'm serious," he says. "I've had the worst itch all day and I can't reach it."

He sounds desperate, and Landon can't help but smile.

"Are you... sure?" Landon asks. He hates the way his tongue gets stuck on the words.

"Oh God, yes." Dylan is already working his shirt over his head, goose bumps forming on his skin as it is exposed to the air, and he shifts so his back is toward Landon. Landon puts a tentative hand on his back and feels the solid warmth of Dylan's body, the muscles shifting under his skin. He's lost some weight—they both have, the stress of the year is taking its toll—but Landon thinks he looks just as beautiful as he did on they day they met.

He scratches Dylan's skin, and Dylan leans back against him.

"Oh my God." Dylan moans, and Landon can feel his cheeks heating up. "You are amazing."

Landon won't deny that it makes him feel good to be able to do something for Dylan, to give something back, no matter how little it might be. He also won't deny that the sensation of Dylan's skin under his fingers makes his heart race, almost makes him lose track of what he's doing.

"You have no idea how long I've been waiting for this," Dylan says, and Landon's fingers pause on Dylan's back. Dylan is about to pull away, and Landon doesn't even think, just leans forward and presses his lips against the soft skin along Dylan's shoulder blade. Dylan stills against him and turns around to look when Landon pulls back.

"Janessa said I should, um, show you what I... feel," Landon says. The end of the sentence is choppy, but at least he got it out.

"And how do you feel?" Dylan asks, his eyes wide and full of something that looks an awful lot like hope. Landon can feel his blush grow stronger, knows his cheeks are probably bright red by now.

"Like..." A pause. "Like I wanted to kiss you."

Dylan's face softens, and he tangles his fingers with Landon's. "Can I kiss you?"

Landon nods, and Dylan leans forward to touch his lips against Landon's. It's soft and closed, and not quite centered, but Landon thinks it might be the best kiss he's ever had. When he pulls back, Dylan's lips part, his throat works as if he wants to say something and doesn't know what.

So Landon just settles against him, feels something warm bloom inside him and tucks his feet under Dylan's calves.

"Finish the chapter?" Landon asks. He feels Dylan nod against him. And he knows it may not be perfect, but they're getting there.

CHAPTER 9

Adele's house is warm, decorated in rich reds and blues and purples, and smells like a mix of homemade soap and incense. Lana tightens her grip on the pie she has brought and follows the scent of a Thanksgiving meal into the kitchen. Adele is preparing something at the stove; her hair is pulled back into a thick braid. Dylan and Landon sit at the kitchen table, a pile of potatoes between them waiting to be peeled. Her parents haven't arrived yet, and Lana isn't surprised; no matter how many times they visit, they always seem to underestimate traffic.

"Lana!" Adele greets her, and Dylan's and Landon's heads pop up. Adele hugs Lana and accepts the pie.

"Sorry I'm late," Lana apologizes, tugging at her dress. She hadn't known how formal Thanksgiving with Dylan's parents would be, and had chosen to wear the simple red dress Landon bought for her a few years ago and to tie her hair back with a simple bow. There's a nervous flutter in her stomach and she's not sure if it's left over from midterms or memories of tense family holidays from years past.

"Nonsense." Adele waves away her apology and situates the pie next to a plate piled high with homemade bread. "We still have plenty of time."

Some of the tension leaves Lana's shoulders. Holidays with the Nayars are different, compared to the rigid schedule at the Lewin household. She smiles at Adele and turns to where Landon sits in his chair, pushed up close to the kitchen table. He's holding a half-peeled potato, but it drops into his lap when Lana bends down to give him a hug. He hugs her back. His arms are still a little stiff and awkward around her; his smile lifts higher on the right side than the left. Lana is still taken aback by how different Landon looks; he's still her brother, still has the same hazel eyes that squint when he smiles, the same pattern of freckles across his nose and cheeks and down over his throat, the same messy auburn hair. But he holds himself differently now: his shoulders hunched, his limbs stiff. His face is thinner, and Lana can still make out the angry red scars that peek out at his left temple.

"Hi," Landon says when Lana pulls away. Even his voice is different now. The words are stilted and heavy and interrupted by long pauses, and sometimes Lana has to concentrate to understand what he's saying.

"Hey." She brushes a potato peel from his shirt.

"How are you?" Landon asks, his automatic phrase. Lana remembers that in the hospital, this was one of the first questions Landon could ask; the greeting is so conditioned that he can pull it from a different part of his brain and say it without much thought. At least, that's what the professionals told them.

"I'm great." Lana pulls out a seat next to Landon and plops herself down. "How's my darling little big brother?"

Dylan laughs, and Landon shoots him a look that could only be described as a glare.

"Good," Landon manages. "I'm good."

Lana nods. She figures *good* is about all they can hope for anymore and snatches up a potato. She shares a glance with Dylan, whose eyes are heavy with that tired but hopeful look they so often carry lately, and smiles at him before stealing Landon's peeler and setting to work.

It's another forty-five minutes before their parents show up. Helen, flustered, offers profuse apologies. John stands back and gives Landon a squeeze on the shoulder. Lana's not sure if she's imagining it, but she can sense an awkward tension between her parents: Their eyes never quite meet, and their interactions seem limited.

Helen and Adele finish preparation of the Thanksgiving feast, which is much too elaborate for such a small group of people. Dylan and Lana set the table, and Sam eventually makes an appearance, his fingers stained with ink, glasses perched on the end of his nose.

This might be the oddest gathering of people Lana has ever spent a holiday with, but she stays next to Landon and the knot in her stomach eases with his smiles and gentle questions.

During the meal, Lana observes Dylan. The changes in Landon are obvious, drawing enough focus that it is easy to overlook everything else, and it's only now that Lana can see how much Dylan has changed too. His movements are more cautious, and he always hesitates before he does anything for himself, interrupting his own meal to help Landon. His eyes constantly flicker between Landon and his own food, and for every bite Dylan takes he makes sure Landon gets at least two.

Lana thinks Adele notices too, the way she watches as Dylan pushes away his own plate for the third time so he can help Landon, the way she has to say his name twice before she can capture his attention. She looks proud, but also a little sad, and keeps piling food onto Dylan's plate when he is distracted.

They've both changed; their whole relationship has shifted. They're no longer simply fiancés, they're dependent on each other, and Lana thinks Dylan needs to make sure Landon is okay just as much as Landon relies on Dylan's help. It's a delicate balance, an intricate dance, and they both look as if they're just managing to hold on. Trying to get by as best as they possibly can.

Later, after the sun has dipped below the horizon and everyone has recovered from their food-induced stupor, Adele manages to convince them to participate in a light yoga session. She promises to go easy and lends comfortable outfits to Lana and Helen. Dylan helps Landon change into the sweats he still has in his old bedroom. John sits it out, claiming to have work he needs to go over, and Adele doesn't push. She still hasn't figured out the dynamic in Landon's family; they love each other—that much is obvious—but there's a lingering tension between them and certain topics are pointedly avoided.

The small group gathers in Adele's studio, and she lights a stick of incense and turns on the string of hanging lights that drapes over the windows. They all take places on her extra yoga mats at her instruction. Dylan and Landon share a mat. Excitement builds in her as she helps position Landon on the floor, legs crossed, Dylan behind him, supporting. She's wanted to get Landon on a mat for a while, has some moves that she believes could really help him; and maybe, if this goes well, she can convince him to come back.

She starts them out slow, just some simple stretches they can do from a seated position to open up the chest and the heart. Helen's movements are awkward, the kind Adele sees from students who are afraid to completely let go, to give themselves over. Lana is a little more graceful, has a natural sense of rhythm that helps her move, and while Adele has to make some tweaks and adjustments to her poses, she adapts quickly. Adele makes a mental note to have her come to some classes as well.

She instructs them into a few easy twists, and Landon falters only slightly before Dylan is there, his hands gentle, guiding Landon into the pose. A silent communication exists between them; Dylan never looks away for long, and is always there when Landon needs him. Landon leans back into Dylan's touch, his eyes slip closed, his breath is steady.

This is trust, the kind that only a couple who has gone through something traumatic and terrible and come out on the other side can feel. That's what she sees in them; even if they don't always understand it, it's there.

Landon manages most of the poses; his body becomes looser, his movements more fluid, and at one point he whispers something to Dylan and Dylan shakes his head and laughs, blushing. Adele smiles and instructs them to lie down for their final *savasana,* and Dylan and Landon's hands link across the mat.

After yoga and another slice of pie, Dylan and Landon collapse on the couch, and Lana puts in a movie before curling up on Landon's other side. Barely thirty minutes pass before they're all asleep, tucked together in a giant ball with a blanket shared between the three of them.

Adele chuckles as she hands Helen a cup of decaf, setting the one Dylan requested on the coffee table, just in case. She grabs her own coffee before lowering herself onto a cushion near the armchair occupied by Helen, whose gaze is focused on the three kids—*young adults*—as her thumb trails absently along the top of the mug.

Helen looks different with her hair pulled back into a messy ponytail and still wearing the clothes Adele lent her. She seems more than a little out of her element, but it suits her somehow to be cut away from the rigid exterior she normally presents.

"When did our children start struggling more than we do?" Helen says quietly, her eyes tearing away from the sleeping figures to stare into her coffee. "It doesn't seem fair."

"It's not," Adele answers, her own heart growing heavy at Helen's words. "Nothing about this is fair."

Helen sucks in a deep breath and holds it. .

"I hate that I can't take his pain away anymore, like I could when he was a kid." She lets out a dry laugh. "Kiss it better."

Adele's lips twitch in a smile and her hand reaches to squeeze Helen's knee. Helen looks at her, and Adele can make out the lines around her eyes, the sprinkle of gray hair at her temple.

"We can try." Adele lets her hand fall back to her lap. "But they're stronger than we are. Sometimes they need a shove in the right direction, but they'll make it through."

Helen chuckles, tucks a stray strand of hair behind her ears.

"They'd probably get sick of the kisses anyway," Helen says, and Adele laughs genuinely. Dylan stirs and mutters an unintelligible word before settling back down.

"They seem to have that covered pretty well on their own." Adele takes a sip of her coffee. Helen snorts into her own drink. A comfortable silence settles between them. The movie keeps playing, and Adele pretends to watch it, though her thoughts stray far from the silly romantic comedy Lana chose.

"They'll be okay, won't they?" Helen's words draw Adele's attention back. Adele isn't sure if Helen is asking a question or making a statement, but she nods in agreement.

"Yeah. They will."

Dylan seems reluctant to head back to work on Monday; they enjoyed their two days of solitude with a marathon of old movies and playing Uno and Go Fish when Lana came to visit. Dylan had done some cleaning while Landon worked on the exercises his speech therapist had given him. It was a good weekend, and Landon feels a little more relaxed and thinks Dylan might feel that way too, though he's been hard to read lately.

Monday starts early with a physical therapy appointment, and Landon manages to walk the distance of the parallel bars three times before his right leg can't make it anymore and he almost stumbles to the ground; Ryan supports him just in time. It's frustrating; every step he takes makes him want *more*, makes him want to jump out of the parallel bars and run away from all this. Back to when it wasn't a struggle to do such simple things, when he could do basic human tasks like walking or brushing his teeth without needing help from others, when he could form a simple sentence without losing track in the middle, when he could eat a meal without worrying about texture and thickness and whether he will choke if he swallows incorrectly.

But he can't; there's no going back from this, only forward and through, and all he can do is hope that eventually he'll come out on the other side.

It's nearing three when the doorbell rings. Landon tries to crane his neck from his spot on the couch while Janessa goes to see who it is. Landon can hear voices, talking softly enough that he can't make them out, so he lets his head fall back against the couch and figures Janessa will tell him if it's important.

"Hey," a voice that's definitely not Janessa's says, and Landon turns in surprise. Tate is standing slightly behind Janessa, and he offers Landon a hesitant, nervous little wave.

"Hi," Landon says, shifting self-consciously on the couch. He hasn't interacted much with anyone outside of family and therapists, and while Dylan says that Tate stopped by the hospital a few times, Landon doesn't remember it. He doesn't remember much from the hospital; his memory is riddled with patchy holes and foggy images.

"How, uh, how are you doing?" Tate asks, and it's awkward. Even Janessa looks as though she can sense the unsure tension in the air. Landon looks down at himself, at his right hand folded in his lap, at his legs that can't do what he wants them to, at the small packet of activities he was working on, assignments a third grader could do.

"Good," he answers, because no one really wants to know the truth. Every day he feels as if he's drowning, and some days he wakes up and can't remember where he is. He's afraid his fiancé doesn't love him as he used to, and Landon doesn't blame him, because he doesn't even know if he's really *Landon* anymore, or if he's just a reflection of the person he used to be.

"Good, that's... that's great." Tate shifts on his feet, opens his mouth, closes it.

"Tate wants you to go swimming with him," Janessa says, and Tate looks relieved that she has taken over. Landon blinks, frowns.

"Swimming." He tries out the word and it feels heavy on his tongue. Foreign. He hasn't been swimming in years, nothing beyond a trip to the pool on a hot summer day, not like the competitive swimming he used to do.

"I thought..." Tate starts, looks at Janessa. "I talked to Dylan about it and he thought it could be a good idea. You used to love swimming, and I guess, I thought it could help? Or something, you don't have to, I mean, it was just an idea but..." he realizes he's rambling and cuts himself off. "You used to say you never felt more alive than you did in the water, so. I don't know."

Tate shrugs, his cheeks bright red. Janessa looks between them, her lips starting to curl up.

"I think that's a great idea, Tate," she says. "What do you think, Landon?"

Landon's first instinct is to say no. Swimming would involve going out in public, to a place filled with people who might stare at him, trying to figure out what's wrong with him, or people who tell him how brave he is while offering sympathetic smiles, as though his life will suddenly be easier now that a stranger pities him. The idea knots his gut, but he also knows he can't stay inside forever.

He thinks of Dylan, how he wants to get better for him, how he won't get better if he doesn't challenge himself.

"Okay." He nods, looks up at Tate and hopes Tate knows how much trust he is putting in him right now. "Sure."

Tate looks surprised, as though he wasn't actually expecting Landon to agree. His face lights up in excitement. "Really?"

Landon nods, trying not to show how nervous he is. Tate has a few guest passes to the YMCA a short drive away, and they agree to meet there in an hour, giving them enough time to get ready and swing by Janessa's place so she can grab her swimsuit.

They find Landon's suit shoved in the back of his underwear drawer. It's wrinkled and a little big, but Janessa ties the strings extra tight so it will stay up, and helps Landon slip on a pair of sweats over it. Janessa packs a small bag with some pudding packs, Landon's to-go emergency medication in case of the rogue migraine or seizure, a towel and a change of clothes. The drive doesn't take long, even with the stop at Janessa's apartment, and they get there almost twenty minutes early.

The gym is busy but not crowded and mostly filled with small kids and the occasional adult walking by with a sweaty towel draped over his neck. Landon stands out, sitting in the lobby in his wheelchair, feeling as if he doesn't belong in a place filled with healthy, active people. He shrinks down into his chair. *If I try hard enough, will I disappear?* He almost jumps when Janessa lays a hand on his shoulder and rubs a soothing circle with her thumb.

He touches his head automatically, brushing the scars that peek out at his temple and disappear under his hair. He feels a twinge—whether real or imagined, Landon doesn't know—sets his hand back in his lap, and wishes he had brought a hat.

Tate shows up with a bounce in his step. For a moment, he looks just the way he did in college, back when they would amp themselves up for a meet or before a particularly grueling practice. But then he sees Landon and something in his expression falters; maybe he was remembering the same things, and the harsh reality sank in when he realized things aren't the way they used to be.

He checks them in, and Landon has to write his name in shaky letters on a guest registry. The pen slips in his grip before he gives up halfway through, ready to throw the clipboard on the counter. Janessa grips his hand and helps him finish the letters. It's embarrassing, needing this help when people are watching, and Landon already wants to cry, can feel the pitying eyes of the staff members from across the counter.

Tate leads them to the elevator; Janessa pushes Landon's chair. Landon's jaw clenches. This is why he hates going out in public; this is why he wants to stay at home all day, wants to see Dylan and Janessa and no one else, wants the world to forget he exists. If it forgets, there will be no one to stare.

They use the family locker room, which is mostly empty, for which Landon is thankful. Tate keeps glancing at him. Landon can see the nervous tension in his shoulders and feels bad; he knows Tate is just trying his best to reconnect. He probably debated this for weeks before he mentioned it to Dylan, and is just trying to help Landon do something he loves.

Landon forces himself to relax, even offers Tate a small smile as Janessa piles things into their lockers. Tate smiles back, a little more at ease, and leads them to the pool. It's not the lap pool, as Landon expected, but a smaller pool without lanes. The room is humid, and the smell of chlorine is a familiar burn in Landon's nose.

There's only one other family there, two women with a little boy who looks about four years old. The boy glances over, but his attention doesn't stay; instead, he turns back to splash the women. Janessa snorts, pushing Landon's chair over the damp tile. The lifeguard watches them, but Tate flips him a thumbs up and he nods, sends a thumbs up back.

"I taught swimming lessons here this summer," Tate explains, turning back to Landon. "They let me know when the pool is usually the least busy."

Landon's eyes flicker around the room, land on the stair entrance into the pool and move to the chair lift. Tate must see where his eyes are, because he does that nervous shifting thing again and clasps his hands together.

"It's accessible, if you—"

"No," Landon cuts him off, feels his stomach flip like a dying animal. "I don't..." He looks up at Janessa, begging her to understand. "Please."

"We can get in on the side," she says with a nod. Landon's heart feels about ready to burst out of his chest, and a weird buzzing under his skin makes his fingers tingle.

"It'll be okay," Janessa says softly. She takes Landon's hand and squeezes. He squeezes back and tries to let go of some of his anxiety.

"You, get in the pool," Janessa instructs Tate, and he obeys, slipping into the shallow end closest to them, while Janessa pushes Landon's chair to the edge. *The water barely comes up to Tate's waist, and it's really not that far to go. It'll be okay. I can make it.*

Janessa helps him out of the chair, and he clutches her arms, afraid to fall on the slippery tiles. They move slowly, Janessa helping Landon to sit at the edge of the pool and dip his feet in the water. It's warm, and Landon pushes himself forward until his knees are bent, his calves submerged. Tate's almost as tall as he is like this, and stands just to the side as Janessa parks Landon's wheelchair in the corner of the room. Landon grips the edge of the pool for support and waits until Janessa jumps into the pool.

"All right." She grasps Landon's hand. "Let's do this."

Landon lifts his other hand, and Tate hesitates for only a moment before taking it, his grip firm. With their support, Landon slips into the pool and leans against the wall.

"It's warm," he says with a smile, and Tate laughs a little.

"Yeah, feels nice, right?"

Landon nods, lets his knees bend and sinks lower into the water. Tate jolts forward before stopping, realizing it was intentional. Landon's not worried, just closes his eyes and lets himself enjoy the warm water lapping around him, melting the tension from his body.

"Want to go deeper?" Janessa asks, after Landon has soaked. She looks nice, he thinks, in her pale purple swimsuit. The ribbing on the edges accentuates the curves of her figure. Tate must think so too, and Landon wants to laugh when he sees Tate looking at her, blushing and looking away when she comes up behind Landon and wraps her arms around him, her breasts pressed firmly against his back. If things were different, Landon might tease Tate about it later, because Tate is one of those guys who pines, spends days working up the courage to ask a girl for a date and then chickens out, moaning about it later over video games with Landon.

But their friendship isn't like that anymore, so Landon doesn't do anything except let Janessa guide him into deeper water. It's

183

up to her shoulders before she stops, and Landon gives a few experimental kicks, feeling the water glide around his legs. It's easier to move, here in the water; his joints feel less stiff without the pull of gravity.

"What's the matter, can't swim?" Janessa asks Tate in a teasing voice, and his cheeks turn an even darker red before he sinks under the surface and swims over to them.

"How's it feel?" he asks, shaking water out of his hair.

"It's nice." Landon waves his arm out through the water. "Familiar."

Tate smiles. "Makes me miss those old swim team days."

Landon hums and wiggles his way out of Janessa's arms. Though she still keeps a hand wrapped around his bicep, this gives him more freedom and he lets himself sink under for a moment, lets the water hold him and feels a quiet peace spread through his body. He stays until his lungs burn, until he can feel Janessa start to tug him upward, and he pushes off the bottom of the pool with legs that are a little bit stronger.

He's gasping when he comes back up but it feels good; the ache in his lungs reminds him that he's still alive, he's still here. Water drips down his face and into his eyes, and he blinks. Janessa and Tate are looking at him with concern, but he just smiles and lets himself sink back down until the water comes up to his chin.

"You always had the, um, the good ideas," Landon says, leaning against Janessa for a little extra support.

"Damn right I did," Tate says with a laugh, and Landon splashes him. Tate splashes him back, but the water hits Janessa full in the face.

"Oh no, you did not." She wipes at her eyes. Landon grins and reaches to grab onto the side of the pool so Janessa can retaliate, splashing a wave at Tate before shouting "Race you!" and taking off across the pool. Tate looks surprised for a moment, but after a quick glance at Landon he takes off after her. He wins, of course, even with Janessa's head start, and she pouts when they reach Landon once more.

"No fair," she says. "You have like, muscles and all that to your advantage." She waves at Tate's body, and Landon almost feels bad for him; even the tips of his ears have turned red. He'd tell Janessa to knock it off, but he hasn't felt so good in a long time, so free.

They swim for almost an hour, and Landon even treads water for a short while, but it leaves him feeling exhausted, his muscles ache, and he knows they'll be sore tomorrow. Getting out of the pool proves to be a little harder than sliding in, especially now that he's exhausted most of his energy, and he concedes in using the pool lift, just this once.

"Thanks," he tells Tate, once they're dried off and changed into fresh clothes. "It was, um… it was fun."

Tate smiles. "Anytime, man. I can even get you a discount membership if you want. Just, you know. Let me know."

"We will," Janessa says. Tate's eyes light up, and Landon has to force down a smile. He thinks he should start inviting Tate over more, if only to watch how flustered he gets in front of Janessa. She thanks Tate again, and Landon would say something more but his mind is fuzzy from all the activity and he doesn't trust himself to speak.

The cold winter air freezes Landon's still-damp hair, but he barely notices, helps only half-heartedly as Janessa gets him situated in the car, rests his head on the window and promptly falls asleep.

* * *

Christmas Eve starts with a sun that makes the snow glisten and sparkle, as if it was dusted with glitter overnight. The house seems brighter, warmer somehow, and is filled with the scent of sugar cookies as Dylan makes batch after batch. Landon sits on the floor in the living room, digging through their box of Christmas stuff and spreading it out on the floor around him.

They have only a few hours until Logan and his family fly in from New York, Landon's parents arrive and their house is filled with people, and there's still a lot of work to be done. The Christmas tree needs decorating, the cookies need baking, the house needs cleaning and presents need wrapping. But for now, Dylan enjoys the quiet, the calm before the storm.

He slides a tray into the oven, sets the timer and makes his way into the living room. Landon is untangling tinsel that has wrapped around a garland of mistletoe. His fingers work with more dexterity than Dylan has seen in a while—until the mistletoe slips out of Landon's fingers and he curses, his hands clenching shut.

Dylan sits down beside him and picks up the mistletoe.

"I think it might be a lost cause," he says, and bumps his shoulder into Landon's, hoping Landon understands that *it's okay*, there's no need to be angry.

"Sorry," Landon murmurs, bumping his shoulder lightly back. *I'm trying.*

"Should we decorate the tree?" Dylan looks over at their very sparse, very fake tree. Landon digs through the box and pulls out the ornaments. They don't have many; in the past, content to simply visit family for the holiday, they'd never really made an effort to decorate for Christmas.

Landon pulls out a small ornament in the shape of a dog with reindeer antlers.

"Junior year," he says, running his thumb over it.

"You volunteered at a kennel that year." Dylan says, remembering Landon coming home covered in scrapes and scratches, his clothes full of dog fur. "I thought it was fitting."

"It was," Landon says with a smile. "I kept it by, um… by my bed all year."

He scoots over to the tree and carefully hangs it on a branch.

"Perfect," Dylan says, and they admire it for a moment before sorting through more ornaments. Together they decorate the tree, Dylan helping Landon stand steady when they get to the top, his hands on Landon's waist while Landon places a snowflake ornament as high as he can. Landon leans back against him, his body solid and warm, and Dylan kisses the back of his neck.

Landon turns around until his chest is pressed against Dylan's with his chin hooking over Dylan's shoulder. Dylan wraps his arms around Landon and holds him close, letting them just stand like this.

"I have a surprise," Landon says, pulling away just slightly. "For you."

"A surprise?" Dylan raises a curious eyebrow. "Should I be scared?"

Landon smiles and shakes his head. His hair is getting shaggy, locks falling over his forehead, his ears barely peeking out from under it. It ruffles with his movement.

"Take my hands." Landon's voice is low, and Dylan obeys. Landon's hands slide into his. His fingers are cold, and Dylan holds on as tight as he can.

He waits as Landon draws his shoulders up, standing tall and confident. "Move," He says, a firm instruction. Dylan takes a step back and Landon follows, lifts his right foot and takes a step forward. Dylan has to brace his arms to help keep Landon up, but they keep moving, Dylan walking backwards and Landon following. Walking.

"You—" Dylan starts, but Landon's toe drags on the ground and he stumbles. Dylan steps forward and wraps his arms around Landon, holding him up.

"You're walking." Dylan can barely believe the words as he says them. He remembers the doctors in the hospital saying Landon might never walk again, remembers them saying so many things that Landon has proved wrong just in the few months since he's been out of the hospital.

"I've been pr... um, practicing," Landon says with a shy smile. "I know I'm, uh, I'm not that good yet, but I'm working at... at it."

"It's amazing, Lan." Dylan feels a bit breathless, feels something like butterflies in his stomach, and he wishes there was a way that Landon could know how proud he is, of everything he does. "*You're* amazing."

Landon blushes. "Not that amazing."

Dylan arches an eyebrow.

"Not as, um... as amazing as Gordon Ramsay," Landon manages, his words slurring just slightly.

"Definitely more amazing than Gordon Ramsay." Dylan runs a hand down Landon's arm. "You're much nicer, too."

Landon laughs and lets his head fall against Dylan's shoulder.

"I'm glad you, you think so," he says, his voice muffled by Dylan's sweater. "I know... I know I haven't been, lately."

Dylan can feel him curling against him, can feel the apologetic set to his shoulder.

"It doesn't matter." Dylan lifts Landon's head up with a finger under his chin. "I still love you."

Landon blinks, his eyes searching Dylan's face, before his lips press Dylan's. Dylan takes a sharp breath and sinks into the kiss. Landon clutches his arms, and Dylan's hands drift down Landon's back, feeling the dip and curve of his spine under his fingers.

Landon parts his lips and sucks in air but doesn't pull away. His breath is warm on Dylan's skin. Dylan slides his tongue across Landon's lip and deepens the kiss. His fingers play with the hem of Landon's shirt before they slip underneath and stroke the smooth skin. Landon makes a surprised noise, and Dylan thinks he can almost feel the hammering of Landon's heart against his chest.

His lips linger on Landon's before he reluctantly pulls away, lungs emptying in a rush.

"That was a good surprise," he says, and Landon lets out a shaky laugh, his head falling back onto Dylan's shoulder. Dylan can feel Landon's jaw working, as though he wants to say something, but Dylan knows how difficult it is for him when he's overwhelmed; the words jumble in Landon's head, everything mixes together and it's hard for him to figure out what's what.

"Can't say..." Landon starts, shifting against Dylan. "Planned." He shakes his head, knowing his words don't make sense, and Dylan rubs his back. Landon's knees start to bend, his body begins to sag against Dylan's, and Dylan directs them toward the couch. Landon drops into the cushions.

His face is a little flushed, his lips are red and his eyes are shining. Dylan settles into the couch beside him, and Landon leans against him. Their hands find each other, and only the faint sound of Christmas music coming from the laptop near the decorations fills the silence. This is comfortable, and Dylan knows neither of them is ready for much more, not right now. This is enough. This is good, just being together, finding this intimacy without grand gestures, everything meaningful in its own little way.

They're not ready, but that's okay.

"Now, come on. Christmas isn't going to decorate itself."

They manage to get everything done in time for a knock on the door. Helen and John picked up Logan and his family from the airport, and suddenly the house is full of people. Helen and John immediately make their way to the kitchen with dishes of food they've pulled out of the car and Logan and Paige wait in the entrance with little Jay clinging to her mom's legs. Paige is tall and stunning, with dark skin and thick black hair pulled back into an elaborate twist. Jay is a miniature version of her mother, with wide brown eyes and a bow nestled in her own tight curls.

"Hey, Jay-Jay," Dylan greets her. He bends down and Jay lets him scoop her up in a hug, giggling when he turns her around.

"Oh my goodness, you're getting so big, I can't believe it! How old are you now, twenty?"

Jay covers her mouth as she laughs.

"I'm five, silly," she says, in that *are you stupid?* tone that only a five-year-old can manage.

"Well, nearly twenty then." Dylan winks at Logan. "Did you have a good flight?"

Jay nods, and Dylan puts her down so her mom can wiggle her out of her winter coat.

"They gave me cookies!" she exclaims. Dylan laughs.

"I suppose you wouldn't be interested in making any cookies with me then, hm?"

Her eyes grow even wider. "Please can we make cookies?" she pleads, and Dylan laughs again, leaning down to kiss the top of her head.

"Of course we can. Tomorrow, all right?" He's pretty sure Logan and Paige would not be thrilled if he loaded her up on too much more sugar. She nods in agreement. Dylan shows Logan and Paige where to hang their coats and leads them all into the house. It's Paige's first time here, and she looks around appreciatively. Jay squeals with delight at the Christmas decorations, the presents already under the tree.

"Hey, London Bridge," Paige exclaims, when they step into the living room, leaning to wrap Landon in a hug. Landon smiles and returns the hug tightly. "It's so great to see you. You look really good."

Landon blushes and responds with a quiet "Thank you." He's nervous surrounded by this many people, with the attention directed at him, even if it is only family.

"Jay, don't you want to say hi to Uncle Landon?" Logan asks, nudging Jay from where she's tucked herself behind Logan's legs with only her head peeking out.

Landon waves at her. "Hi, Jay-Jay," he says, and Dylan stands back for a moment and tries not to interrupt the interaction. She's only five, and he doesn't know how much she understood of Landon's injury when Logan explained it to her. Landon looks different now; even if the injury isn't obvious. It's apparent in the way he sits, the stiffness in his right arm, the unevenness of his smile, the way his voice sounds just a little bit different.

Jay buries her face in the back of her dad's legs, and Landon's smile falls, only for a moment; then it's back, but it looks forced. Dylan moves behind the couch, rests a hand on Landon's shoulder and offers him comfort.

"Are you hungry, Jay?" Dylan asks, mostly to break the awkward silence.

"We've had a long day," Paige answers when Jay doesn't move, and her eyes are apologetic.

"Of course. Well, dinner will be ready in about half an hour, and then we can eat, okay?" Everyone agrees that dinner sounds lovely, and Logan excuses himself and takes Jay to the bathroom while Paige moves to the kitchen to help prepare food.

"She's just nervous," Dylan says, when they have a moment alone and he is sitting on the armrest beside Landon. Landon looks up at him and brushes a strand of hair out of his eyes.

"I know," he says. He sounds resigned, but not sad. "It's okay."

Dylan kisses Landon, just a quick one this time.

"Let me know if you need anything, okay?"

Landon nods. "I will."

Lana arrives and plops herself on the couch beside Landon. Dylan's parents show up shortly after that, and there's no more time for private conversations. Dylan goes to the kitchen to help prepare dinner, and someone starts playing Christmas music.

He's setting the table when he notices Jay on the couch next to Landon with an impressive sticker collection spread out over their laps and stickers pressed to Landon's shirt and a few to his cheeks.

"What are you guys up to?" Dylan asks. Lana also has an assortment of stickers stuck to her outfit, and they're all smiling. Jay looks up at Dylan, motions at the stickers.

"I'm showing Uncle Bridge my stickers," she says, her voice proud. She started calling Landon that a few years ago, when Landon proved too hard for her to pronounce and she'd picked up on the London Bridge nickname that Paige likes to tease him with. Landon didn't mind, and it stuck.

"I can see that," Dylan says with a smile. Jay looks at her stickers and narrows her eyes. She looks back at Dylan.

"Do you want one?"

"I would love a sticker." Dylan settles onto the couch beside them. Jay considers her stickers with a serious expression, then peels the back off of a green dinosaur with purple spots and sticks it to Dylan's shirt.

"Now you match," Jay says, accomplishment in her voice. Dylan sees a similar dinosaur sticker stuck to Landon's shirt and laughs.

"We do. Thank you, Jay-Jay."

Jay nods, satisfied. She digs through more of her stickers, rambling about how many more she has at home and how her mom *always* buys them for her on Fridays when they go to the grocery store, and how the mean boy down the street always tries to steal them from her. Dylan asks questions in the right places and keeps Jay chattering while he leans against Landon, peels the stickers from his cheeks and kisses the red marks left behind.

And he thinks: *This is a pretty perfect way to spend Christmas Eve.*

They camp out on the floor that night with Jay snuggled in a fort of blankets and pillows, and watch Christmas movies until she passes out in Paige's arms in the middle of *Elf*. Dylan finds himself nodding off beside them, warm and cozy in the blankets, his eyes slipping shut, breath coming heavy. Lana sleeps on the other side of Dylan, wrapped in a borrowed sleeping bag. Dylan can hear Landon and Logan still moving around, Logan doing some sort of cleaning by the sound of it until Landon whispers at him to stop.

"Dylan will be mad," he whispers, and Dylan's breath catches for a moment, but he keeps quiet and pretends to be asleep.

"What?" Logan whispers back, but Dylan can't hear him moving.

"He's… uh, particular," Landon whispers and Dylan wants to protest, but he keeps still. "He… he likes things a, um… a certain way."

Logan doesn't say anything, but Dylan can hear him sit back on the couch.

"He's just… stressed. I think," Landon whispers. "He's been working really… um." There is a pause, the sound of rustling fabric, as Landon collects his thoughts. "Hard. Working hard."

"So have you," Logan murmurs back. Then silence, and Dylan knows Landon is probably shrugging off Logan's words.

"I wish…" Landon starts, stops. "I wish he didn't have to deal with this. With me."

"Dylan would do anything for you, you know that."

"I know, I just… worry about him."

Dylan squeezes his eyes shut even tighter and forces himself not to move, no matter how much he wants to tell Landon that he doesn't have to worry, Logan is right and all Dylan wants is for Landon to focus on himself, on getting better.

"I know you do," Logan says. "Dylan worries about you too."

They're silent for a while, only the occasional rustle of fabric showing that they're still awake. Then Logan helps Landon lie down beside Dylan on the edge of the blanket fort. Landon scoots until he is pressed close to Dylan. Logan nestles into the couch, and only then does Dylan let himself move, shifting under the arm Landon has draped over him. He feels Landon's breath against the back of his neck. It's nice to be held, and he lets his fingers intertwine with Landon's and falls asleep to the glow of the Christmas tree.

Jay wakes them all on Christmas morning with a squeal, her eyes bugging at even more presents under the tree. Paige makes her calm down enough to eat breakfast before she opens any presents, and she manages half a bowl of cereal before they decide not to torture her anymore. She plays Santa, picking up presents and delivering them to each person before choosing one for herself.

She scores a huge book of stickers from her parents—for a moment, Dylan's worried she might pass out from excitement—a few stuffed animals from her grandparents and a little tea set that Dylan helped Landon pick out for her online. She busies herself playing with her new toys, too enthralled to pay attention to the grown-ups' presents.

Logan and Paige exchange their own gifts while Dylan opens a box from Landon and Janessa marked *To: Waffle Addict.* He laughs when he rips the paper off to reveal a waffle maker. Landon watches him with a cautious smile that turns real when he sees Dylan's reaction.

"This was Janessa's idea, wasn't it?" he asks, and Landon nods. Dylan gives him a quick kiss. "Thank you."

Landon can't quite get the wrapping paper off, so Dylan helps him open a set of journals from Janessa, to help him with his writing. His present from Dylan is smaller, thinner, and Dylan feels a little nervous when Landon opens it and holds the glossy book with care.

"It's a guitar book," Dylan says, when Landon looks up at him. "I know you were learning to play before... and I thought you could take lessons, maybe, or Janessa or Logan could help you learn and maybe it would... I don't know. I can return it if you don't want it."

Landon runs a finger over the cover and flips through the pages. The songs are easy, but familiar, songs that Dylan knows Landon would love to play.

"It's perfect." Landon leans against Dylan. "Thank you."

Landon also gets a set of pens that stabilize as you write with them, a few inspirational books from his parents, a soft green scarf from Lana and a restored record player with some vintage records from Logan. But throughout the day, Dylan spies Landon clutching the guitar book, paging through it and bookmarking songs, and he makes a mental note to dig Landon's guitar out of the closet of their small second bedroom.

Adele and Sam come by in the late morning, and the rest of Christmas is spent building snowmen in the back yard, eating cookies and napping on the couch under a pile of warm blankets.

"Merry Christmas," Dylan murmurs that night, as he crawls into bed beside Landon, exhausted.

"Merry Christmas," Landon whispers back, nuzzling against Dylan.

Chapter 10

"You know what would complete my life right now?" Landon asks from where he's sitting on the couch.

Dylan pokes his head out from the bedroom. "Do enlighten me."

"A gyro from the stand down the street."

Dylan makes his way into the living room and wraps his arms around Landon from behind the couch.

"But it's so far," he whines. Landon turns his head and looks seriously at Dylan.

"We're talking about life completion here."

"Well, in that case, how could I possibly say no?" Dylan laughs. He steps away from the couch to find his keys. Landon slips his shoes on and taps his foot as Dylan wraps a scarf around his neck.

"You know it's like eighty degrees outside," Landon says, looking pointedly at Dylan's scarf.

"It's fashion." Dylan flips the scarf dramatically over his shoulder, and Landon chuckles. "And there might be a breeze."

"Since when did you care about fashion?"

Landon takes Dylan's hand after they lock the apartment door behind them, and they walk past the out-of-order elevator to the stairs.

"Since Tracy started forcing us to read her fashion blog. I don't think she's a fan of how casual our business casual has gotten."

"Well, you look very dashing. Sophisticated." Landon bumps Dylan's shoulder, and Dylan bumps back. They step out of the apartment into the warm summer evening, and Landon tugs Dylan in the direction of the park a few blocks away. The air is humid but not unbearable, the sky hints at a golden and pink sunset, cars pass by with places to be and shops stay open for the last visitors in search of trinkets. Evenings like this remind Dylan of why he loves Minnesota: walking hand in hand with his fiancé, enjoying the gentle calm that comes just before the dark.

"It's nice out," Landon remarks, and Dylan hums his agreement. They turn a corner and walk single file to allow a woman pushing a stroller to pass.

"Tate wants to have a barbecue this weekend," Landon continues.

"Another one?" Dylan raises his eyebrows. Landon nods.

"He wants us to be in charge of booze and asparagus."

Dylan laughs. "I don't think Tate understands how to barbecue."

"Don't tell him; it'll crush him." Landon smiles, his eyes crinkling at the corners. "Besides, I think he's lonely."

Dylan nods; Tate recently broke up with his girlfriend, and has been inviting them over nearly every weekend for some summer activity.

"At least it's not another croquet party. I don't think anyone would survive another one of those."

Landon snorts, his thumb fiddling with the ring on Dylan's finger, and Dylan bites back a smile. Even though he pretends to *be annoyed, he loves the way Landon has taken to playing with their engagement rings, as if he still can't believe they actually exist. That he and Dylan are actually getting married.*

"Why are you smiling?" Landon asks, looking at Dylan.

"No reason." Dylan squeezes Landon's hand, and then they're at the park and the smell of spiced gyros drifts over them in the gentle breeze. There's another couple in front of them, and Landon's hand leaves Dylan's so he can pull his wallet from his pocket. He sifts through it and pulls out a few bills.

Pink streaks the sky by the time they lower themselves onto the park bench, steaming gyros in hand. Landon moans at his first bite, and Dylan laughs.

"Is your life complete now?"

Landon nods. "I think it might be." He takes another large bite; a piece of lettuce dangles from his lips. Dylan just shakes his head and focuses on eating his own gyro. The onion is sharp on his tongue, and the tang of the tzatziki makes his mouth water; Dylan wouldn't quite call this a life-completing gyro, but it is pretty perfect for a serene summer evening.

Aside from the occasional remark and brief game of footsie, they eat their gyros in silence. Landon continues to make obscene noises, and while it's ridiculous, Dylan feels his pants becoming uncomfortably tight. And Landon knows it, if the smile on his face is anything to go by.

Soon the gyros are devoured, long shadows drift over the park and the sun begins to disappear behind the buildings around them.

"We should probably head back," Dylan says. He turns to look at Landon and is stopped short by a pair of lips on his own and a kiss that tastes earthy and warm, like spring and summer, like rain and sunshine mixed into one. The park bench

is awkward, their knees knock together and Dylan pulls away reluctantly.

"We should definitely head back."

Landon springs to his feet and pulls Dylan off the bench. They speed-walk across the park and down the sidewalk in the descending dusk, passing a bar; the smell of beer and the sound of country music seep out onto the street. A few people lingering in the entrance give them a strange look. Landon untangles his fingers from Dylan's and shoves his hands into his pockets until they're past the bar, and Dylan grabs Landon's arm and pulls him into an alleyway, hearing the crunch of old gravel under his sneakers.

"It's creepy back here," Landon protests, trying to tug them back onto the sidewalk.

"Come on, it's a shortcut." Dylan slides his hand down Landon's arm until their fingers wind together. "And no one can see us back here."

Landon glances back at the street before turning to Dylan, a reluctant look on his face. The alley is dark, and the buildings obscure the last of the sun; the light is so dim that even Landon's freckles are hard to make out. Dylan inches closer to Landon and dips his head to capture Landon's lips in his own. Landon's hands find Dylan's scarf, tugging at it playfully, and Dylan presses back against him until Landon's back hits the rough brick wall.

A surprised noise escapes him at the contact, and his hands are on Dylan's chest, fingers curling into the fabric of his shirt. Dylan teases the kiss a little deeper, his tongue tasting the seam of Landon's lips. They should get home, a voice in the back of Dylan's head reminds him; they shouldn't be kissing here in the alley, but a thrill works its way down Dylan's spine with the feeling of Landon's body against him and he can't stop. Not quite yet.

He can sense Landon just about to pull away when the crunch of gravel sounds from behind them along with the metallic scrape of something heavy against cement.

"What do you fags thinks you're doing?"

And then a forceful grip on his arm and pain blossoming in his shoulder as he is jerked away from Landon.

They don't happen every night, the nightmares. Sometimes he wakes up too early and doesn't know why sleep won't come, even though his eyes are gritty with tiredness. Sometimes he wakes up, heart pounding, and can't catch his breath until he feels Landon beside him, feels the steady thrum of his pulse under his skin. Then he can slip out of bed and splash his face with cold water. Sometimes he still sees *them*, the men from the alley, their silhouettes imprinted behind his eyelids, can feel the panic racing through his veins, feel his stomach turning, feel sweat beading his forehead.

It doesn't happen every night, but the fear is enough to keep him up until exhaustion sinks into his bones, until his eyes start to shut of their own accord and the world starts to blend together like watercolor paints with too much water. Because it is fear, real and tangible: the fear of that night, seeing Landon on the ground, a halo of blood around his head. The fear of waking up and, for one heart-stopping moment, not knowing if Landon is alive or dead. The fear of his brain running wild with *could haves*, *what ifs* and *maybes*.

It's not every night, but it's a black cloud over his life, a constant storm inside him. He finds himself avoiding alleys, dark roads with no lights, shadows that hide the unknown. He starts leaving work earlier just so he can make it home before it gets dark, before his heart starts to slam against his chest and his hands start to shake, before he has to squeeze his eyes shut and tell himself *It's okay, it's okay, it's okay.*

The winter is long and cold, and it's wearing him thin. That's what he tells himself every time panic crawls its way up his windpipe, its claws sinking in and refusing to let go. He's stressed at work, he's tired, and he must be low on vitamin D. It'll get better.

It has to get better.

It will.

He cancels more plans and makes excuses every time his coworkers invite him out for a drink, every time Tate or Janessa or Lana suggest he come out with them for an evening, even just to the movies. He can't leave Landon alone, he says, even though Landon is becoming increasingly more capable and is spending half days alone a few days a week, now that Janessa has picked up a second job teaching art classes to kids with disabilities. Home is a safety net, a bubble where nothing can touch him, can touch either of them.

So when Adele calls to say she got them tickets for his dad's play on a Friday evening, Dylan spends a long time in the bathroom staring at the mirror and convincing himself that it's nothing: There's no reason to worry, nothing to get worked up about, it's going to be fine. He spends too long doing his hair, picking out an outfit and helping Landon pick out an outfit, so they're almost running late when they finally leave and the sun has already long set.

The snow crunches under Dylan's feet as he walks from their parking spot three blocks away from the small theater. He clutches the handles of Landon's chair so tightly his knuckles turn white. The buildings cut away into a small alley, and Dylan feels claws digging in, snatching his breath.

"It's okay," he whispers to himself, and Landon turns his head, craning his neck to look up at Dylan. Dylan smiles as best as he can, swallows against the fear and pushes forward. They've gotten Landon a walker and a pair of forearm crutches now that he's been doing so well in therapy, but even though he hates the wheelchair, he still needs it for these longer distances and for the snow and ice that threaten to make him slip and stumble on his already unsteady feet.

It's early January, and the new year has brought a fresh layer of snow and a freezing wind that bites them through even the thickest coats. It wouldn't take long, Dylan thinks, glancing back at the dark alley behind them, to freeze to death lying on the cold, dark sidewalk. For someone to knock them down and leave them, for frost to bite at their fingers and noses, for the ice to gnaw into their bones before anyone could find them.

The claws tighten.

Warmth wraps them up when they make their way into the small theater. Posters line the rich purple walls: the image of a little girl clutching a stuffed rabbit under the title. *Mixed Moonlight*, the play is called, and *written by Samir Nayar* appears underneath. There are quite a few people in the lobby, Dylan is proud to see. He remembers his mom mentioning an article in the newspaper about the play, and he really hopes it doesn't flop. He doesn't think his dad could handle another failure.

Dylan can see Landon's shoulders draw in as he tries to make himself smalle; his fingers dig into the sleeves of his jacket. It's unavoidable; people are going to stare, will look longer than necessary at the man who seems too young to be in a wheelchair with his limbs held stiff and thick scars peeking out from under his hair. People stare at what they don't understand, at things that are different. It's only human nature, but Dylan wishes they would stop. He wants Landon to feel comfortable, doesn't want him to worry about what others think about him, about the little kids who point and ask their parents, "What happened to that man?"

He finds Adele in the lobby, and she wraps them each in a hug.

"You both look so nice," she says, and kisses their cheeks. Dylan brushes her off, but he can see a small smile on Landon's face, see his shoulders relax just slightly.

"As do you," Dylan replies; Landon nods in agreement. His mother rarely dresses up, and she looks very elegant in her pale green dress with her curly hair tamed and pulled up from her shoulders with a few bobby pins. Adele smiles.

"Your father will join us in a bit." She motions them to follow her into the theater. "He's talking to some Very Important People."

"Dad? Talking to people?" Dylan says with exaggerated surprise, and Adele nods.

"He even combed his hair." Dylan whistles. Adele leads them down the row of chairs to a section in the front. It's the handicapped section, with a space between the seats for Dylan to park Landon's wheelchair. Landon's jaw tightens just slightly, his smile a little more forced, but he doesn't say anything and lets Dylan get him situated. They're good seats, really, with a nice view, and Dylan hopes that Landon won't let it bother him too much.

He starts to unwind the scarf from Landon's neck but Landon pushes his hands away, mumbles a quiet "I can do it," and grips the scarf himself. Dylan pulls away, bites his lip and sits in the chair next to Landon. The scarf gets a little tangled, but Landon manages, folds it on his lap and buries his hands in it.

Adele glances at them, and Dylan shrugs. He's completely lost in these situations. He never knows what Landon is going to want, when he's going to need help, or when he's going to snap if Dylan tries to help. Landon's moods change faster than Dylan can possibly keep up, and he's learning how to balance the good and the bad, the quiet, reluctant Landon with the happy, optimistic Landon and the angry, frustrated Landon.

It only takes a few minutes for Landon to calm, and he nudges Dylan's hand with his own. His fingers are icy, and Dylan starts to massage warmth back into Landon's hand. He feels the knots in the muscles under his fingers and makes a note to buy Landon warmer gloves.

His dad joins them when the lights start to dim, and he looks more excited than Dylan has ever seen his father look.

"Congrats, Dad," Dylan whispers to him, giving him a thumbs up when Sam begins to pull at his suit jacket anxiously. His dad smiles and looks too nervous to say anything, but the lights fade out completely before anything else can be said.

The play starts with blue lights, and a little girl sitting in the middle of the stage. She's alone, and everybody's sad, she says. She's lost and doesn't know how she got here, to this odd, magical world. It's enthralling, and Dylan is completely absorbed as the little girl travels through fantastic worlds in her dreams, guided only by her stuffed bunny. The dreams become more vibrant, more surreal and frightening, and Landon squeezes his hand at times, his breath picking up beside Dylan.

Intermission comes just after someone else steps on the stage, an older man with sad eyes and an old, ragged suit, who talks about loss and facing the unknown. Dylan is confused at first, unsure how this fits into the world his father has created, until the other half of the stage lights come up on the little girl lying in a hospital bed with a bandage around her head and a monitor beeping the single, lonely rhythm of her heart.

Then lights come up through the theater, and it takes Dylan a while to move, to wiggle his fingers in Landon's and separate himself from the events onstage. Landon has a thoughtful look. He clutches the program in his other hand, the paper wrinkling under his fingers. Sam stands suddenly and wipes nervous hands on his pants.

"I'll get us some drinks," he says, disappearing into the crowd. Dylan sinks back into the chair. Adele is looking at them.

"It's good." Landon's voice is soft. Dylan nods, feels a lump form in his throat.

The fear of losing someone we love creates demons in us all. The words ring through his head, spoken in the heartbroken timbre of the man's voice before the curtain fell.

"I'm going to use the restroom," Dylan manages, trying to smile at Landon before standing and heading after his father. There's a line outside the women's bathroom, but he dips into the men's side without a wait. He stands at the counter and waves his hand in front of the faucet until it turns on; a measly stream of water splatters into the sink. It's lukewarm, but he lets it run over his fingers, gathers some in a cupped palm and splashes his face. Someone comes in, and Dylan quickly rips off a length of paper towel and pats his face dry.

He feels a little better. The odd twisting in his stomach has settled, and he straightens his sweater, trying to hold himself tall as he leaves the bathroom. He makes it halfway across the lobby before he sees his dad with a drink in each hand.

"Dylan." Sam spots him and hands him a drink. Dylan takes a sip, the taste of dry white wine bitter on his tongue, and thanks him. Sam shifts on his feet, and Dylan can see gray peppering his hair, can make out lines on his face he doesn't think he's noticed before.

"It's good," Dylan says, unsure if he means the wine or the play.

"Is Landon..." Sam starts. He frowns at his own cup of wine.

"He loves it," Dylan responds. It's obvious how bad his dad's nerves are.

"Good. I... good."

And that's it. Conversation finding an end, they make their way back to their seats. Sam hands his wine to Adele, and even though Landon shouldn't be drinking alcohol with the medications he's on, Dylan figures a tiny sip couldn't hurt. Landon makes a face, sputters and hands the cup back to Dylan.

"Not good," Landon says, sticking out his tongue. Dylan looks down at the wine and remembers how Landon used to drink almost anything given to him without complaint. He chuckles, can't help it, and Landon swats at his arm.

"I'm sorry." Dylan looks over at him. "It's not funny."

"Not at all," Landon says, a serious look on his face. The doctor had said his tastes might change, that he might not like things he used to and that things he never liked may become enjoyable. It's an odd guessing game, figuring out what Landon likes and doesn't like now and mentally recategorizing all the things Dylan had committed to memory over their years together.

"A life without wine is…" Landon starts, looking tragically down at the cup in Dylan's hands.

"Well, if it makes you feel better, this wine is shit." Dylan ignores the sharp nudge he gets from Adele at his language. "So it might not be wine in general."

Landon nods, considers. "That is better." He smiles, looks back at the stage. "Yes."

Dylan smiles at Landon's change in mood and takes a swig of the wine just in time for the lights to flicker and dim.

The second half of the play begins with the girl in the hospital bed with the stuffed rabbit under her folded arms. Her family sits at her bedside, and a doctor reveals that she'd been climbing a tree to rescue the stuffed animal her brother had thrown into the branches when she'd fallen and hit her head on the way down. Some of the words echo in Dylan's own memory, the girl's face replaced with Landon's, the stage replaced with the claustrophobic walls of the hospital. He can hear the sounds of people sniffling in the audience, of noses being blown, but he finds his own eyes dry, finds himself oddly calm, now.

He knows how this goes; he's seen it, he's been there and lived it. He knows how it feels, the mind-numbing realization that the person you love most can be ripped away from you in a second. He knows how it feels to wake up every day alone in bed, to have your body go through the motions of a normal life while your mind is somewhere far away. He's been through it, has made it through, is still trying to make it through.

The scene shifts to the little girl again, sitting in the middle of her fantasy world with only her rabbit companion beside her. She can hear her family calling to her, can hear their pleas for her to come back. She cries, but the rabbit doesn't comfort her, and her surroundings grow darker and darker, fading away into nothingness.

She's alone and still she doesn't move.

Dylan can hear Landon sniff beside him, and he grabs his hand once again, holds on tight.

They watch as the family tries to come to a place of acceptance. They don't notice that the world from the little girl's fantasies trails behind them, that the rabbit is in nearly every scene, invisible to everyone but the audience. It's a shadow looming over them, holding them back, and they can't let go, no matter how hard they try.

How do I let go of someone who has become a part of me? How do I let someone go when I know I'll drown without him, the threads of our souls so woven together I'll unravel when they do? How do I let go of someone when I know I don't want to live in a world without him?

Dylan feels Landon's grip tighten in his own, and Dylan touches a kiss to his knuckles.

The lights begin to fade, and for a moment Dylan thinks it's the end. But then the blue light shines and the girl stands up. Her nightgown looks as if it's glowing, and the stuffed rabbit dangles from her hand. She looks over the audience, looks back at the world created by her dreams and gives it a curtsy before walking across the stage and into the arms of her parents.

I'm sorry I made you wait.

Applause roars through the audience as soon as the curtains fall, and even though he feels worn, hollowed out, Dylan smiles at the sight of his dad ducking in his seat, trying to hide his excitement.

The actors come out in twos, each receiving an increasingly loud round of applause, but it's only when the little girl comes out that the audience stands. Landon nudges Dylan until he helps him up, an arm around his shoulder while Landon claps, his eyes red.

Sam joins the actors once they've left the stage and the applause has died down. They follow him into the lobby and watch from a distance as people walk through, congratulating the actors and Dylan's father. Sam holds his head high, looking more confident than Dylan has seen in a long time, and Dylan is glad. He's glad these words are out there and that maybe others can begin to understand, even if only the faintest bit.

"Your father was so worried," Adele says, not looking away from the passing crowd. "How you would react."

"It was difficult." Dylan's eyes travel to Landon, to the scars that creep out across his temple, to his face lined with a weariness that shouldn't be there. "But it was… real."

Landon's eyes are downcast and he stares at his hands, but he doesn't look sad—just thoughtful; his brow is scrunched as though he's trying to remember something just out of his grasp. The crowd is starting to thin as people wrap up in scarves and jackets and brace themselves for the cold. Dylan is digging Landon's hat out of his pocket when someone calls his name and he looks up to see a tall, black woman headed toward them. It's Abbi, Dylan recognizes, one of Landon's former coworkers. The last time Dylan saw her, her hair was in tiny little braids, but now it's loose in its natural curl, making her look taller than she already is.

"Dylan?" She stops a few feet away, her gaze on Landon with a look of surprise on her face. "Landon, hi."

Landon shrinks, his shoulders drawing in, lips pressing together in that way they always do when he is feeling self-conscious.

"It's really good to see you," she says, looking unsure about what she's supposed to say or do. Landon shifts in his chair, and Dylan rests a reassuring hand on his shoulder. Dylan introduces Abbi and Adele, who shake hands and exchange warm greetings.

"Did you enjoy the show?" Dylan asks when Abbi's gaze flickers back to Landon.

"It was great. I read about it in the paper and I recognized your father's name, so I had to come."

"I'm glad you did," Dylan says. "It means a lot to him."

Abbi smiles, her eyes flickering back to Landon.

"We really miss you," she says, the words quick and sudden, as if she didn't think about them before speaking. "Work isn't the same without you."

Landon looks up at her with an expression of surprise.

"We're having a very late staff Christmas party next week—you could come, if you want. Everyone would be very excited to see you."

Landon is quiet for a moment, considering. "I'll try," he says, and bites his tongue before adding, "I'd like to... to see everyone."

Dylan's not sure if Landon is lying for her benefit, or if he genuinely does want to see his old coworkers and friends, but he doesn't say anything, just lets Landon carry on this conversation on his own.

"That would be great." Abbi glances over her shoulder. "And if you guys ever need anything, just let me know. I'd love to help out."

"Thank you." Landon's response is quiet, and Dylan squeezes his shoulder, hoping he knows how proud Dylan is of him for this, for being brave enough to interact with her.

"I'll see you around?" Abbi asks, and Landon nods. His shoulders relax.

"It was nice to see you, Abbi," Dylan says, and Landon gives her a small wave as she turns to leave. She waves back before joining a small group of people across the room.

They wait for a while longer, with the occasional person talking to Adele, but no one else recognizes Dylan or Landon, which is okay. Landon's had enough excitement for the day. Eventually, Dylan's father has talked to everyone he's supposed to, the actors filter back to the dressing rooms, the lobby empties and they can finally leave.

Dylan lets Landon bundle himself up before they exit into the frigid night, and puts on his coat and tightens his own scarf around his neck. And even though Dylan tries not to be scared, he still flinches when they pass the alley.

* * *

The coffee maker is mocking him, Landon decides, glaring back at it. All he wants is to make a nice breakfast for Dylan, just this once, because Dylan deserves a break after everything he's gone through this winter, after everything Landon has put him through. He just wants to show Dylan that he can still help, he can still do things, he's still worth it; and he needs to prove to *himself* that he can do this.

Except, he can't. And the coffee maker sits on the counter, its innocent plastic face staring back at him. It had been hard enough to fill the carafe; he still doesn't have the stability to carry it without falling, so he'd balanced it on his walker and very carefully filled it in the sink before wheeling it back to the coffee maker. Water had sloshed over the top when he tried to fill it, and dribbled off the counter onto the floor.

Then the eggs he'd started on the stove started to smell a little burned, and he scooted down the counter as quickly as he could, trying to scramble them and burning his hand on the pan before he could turn down the heat.

And now the coffee maker is mocking him as he tries to remember what comes next. He'd put the water in and gotten the cups out; the pre-ground coffee beans were in a neat container next to the sugar.

Coffee beans. Yes, that's it. He wrestles the lid off the bin and wraps his fingers around the scoop inside. *You've done this before,* he tells himself, hand trembling as he lifts a generous scoop out of the bin. *Get a grip.*

Coffee grounds scatter across the counter, but he manages to dump the majority into the coffee maker and repeats the process once more before he's satisfied. He closes the lid and presses the power button, and the smell of burnt eggs fills the kitchen once more. With a curse under his breath, Landon makes his way back to the eggs and gives them a stir; the blackened edges stick to the bottom of the pan.

He hears the shower turn off, hears Dylan whistling in the bathroom, and Landon is a little disheartened by how pathetic his breakfast looks. The coffee maker groans and Landon turns back toward it, eyes widening at the sight of the pale brown water in the carafe, the grounds floating around and overflowing. At nearly the same time the smoke detector starts to scream, and Landon's head whips back just in time to see the eggs, a blackened mess filling the air with an acrid smell.

Frustration builds, stings his eyes, and he curses, grabs the nearest thing to him—a porcelain coffee mug—and watches as it shatters on the ground. He slides down to the floor, the shrill ringing of the fire alarm making it impossible to think. It feels as if someone is jabbing a small knife into his brain.

He can hear Dylan's footsteps followed by his confused voice, asking Landon what happened, but Landon doesn't answer; he couldn't find the words now even if he wanted to. He just digs his palms into his eyes, feeling frustration and anger coursing through him, white hot. The old Landon would never have done this; the old Landon was collected, always kept his head in situations like this. The old Landon was stronger and *better*.

The scream of the fire alarm stops, but he can still feel it echo in his ears along with the hiss of a hot pan under a stream of water. The smell of burning eggs is replaced with the scent of soggy ash. And once again, Landon has made more work for Dylan, has left Dylan to clean up *his* mess, has ruined everything he's tried to do.

He can feel a gentle hand on his shoulder, but he shrugs it off, embarrassed and ashamed and so overwhelmingly angry. He wants to punch something, wants to scream and kick and take this boiling rage inside of him out on something, but he also wants to find somewhere deep and dark and just crawl inside, close the door and let everyone forget about him. He wants to stop dragging everyone down, to stop hurting and ruining everything he loves. Everyone he loves.

"Lan." Dylan's voice is quiet, almost hesitant. Landon doesn't move, just digs his palms in until his eyes ache and sucks a sharp breath in through clenched teeth. Dylan sits down beside him, his body almost close enough to touch Landon's, but not intruding. Not pushing.

"It's okay—" Dylan starts, but Landon tenses.

"Don't." The word is sharp, biting, but Landon can't help it. He doesn't want to hear false comforts, doesn't want Dylan to tell him how great he is or how his failures aren't so bad, doesn't want reminders of how far he's come.

They sit in silence for a moment, only the sound of Landon's breathing filling the space. Eventually Dylan moves, and Landon can hear him collecting pieces of the broken mug, sweeping the shards into a dustpan.

"I feel so stupid," Landon says, his voice choppy. He senses Dylan go still, and then his gentle touch, pulling Landon's hands away from his face.

"You're not stupid," Dylan says firmly. "Please don't think like that."

"Then why can't..." Landon loses the words in the avalanche of his thoughts and pulls his hands out of Dylan's and crosses them over his chest. "I can't even think at all."

Tears of frustration prick at his eyes, and he feels pathetic; he can't even talk without crying. This time he doesn't protest when Dylan wraps him in his arms; when he pulls him close, the fight drains out of him.

"Fuck." The word slips out of him, its harshness muffled by Dylan's shirt. Landon presses closer, shakes his head against Dylan's chest.

"I just wanted..." he starts, feels Dylan running a hand down his back. "I wanted to do something nice. For you."

"I'm very touched."

Landon pushes him away and sits back against the counter.

"I couldn't do it." Landon's words are starting to run together, but he can't stop it; he gets so worked up that his brain can't focus on everything he wants it to. It takes everything he has just to rein in his emotions. "I can't even make coffee."

Dylan looks up at the counter, at the coffee maker.

"You were really close." He kisses Landon's cheek. The touch is calming, helps Landon breathe a little easier.

"I forgot the filter." Now that the anger is starting to ebb, shame creeps into its place. Shame over the way he acted, over his inability to do simple things, over always needing Dylan to save him. "And I broke the cup."

"I don't care about the cup." Dylan settles against Landon's side. Landon leans against him, feeling drained. "You could break a million cups, and I'd still love you."

"I just…" Landon protests. He wants Dylan to understand. "I hate… this." He presses a hand to his head, to the side that was broken and shattered, and feels the scars, the dip in his skull.

"I know you do." Dylan winds his fingers through Landon's and a shiver works its way down Landon's spine. "I wish I could take it all away for you. Every day I think about what happened, and every day I know it should have been me. I wish *so much* that it had been me."

Landon makes a noise of protest, but Dylan just pulls him closer and continues.

"You didn't deserve any of this, but you've been so brave, and you've been trying so hard, even if you don't see it. I know it doesn't seem like it, when the little things build up, but you're allowed to make mistakes. And it doesn't mean you're stupid."

Dylan tightens his grip on Landon's hand. "It just means you're human."

This time he turns Landon's head, softly kisses his lips.

"And I love you."

I'm not worth it, Landon wants to say, and he bites his lips. They tingle with the memory of Dylan's kiss.

"I love you too," he says instead, and lets his head fall back against the cupboards. "I'm sorry you... have to put up with, with me."

"Shush." Dylan turns so that his whole body faces Landon's. "There's no one I'd rather put up with."

Landon lets the words embrace him, sink into his skin, pulse through his veins. Dylan helps him back up, and Landon leans against the counter while Dylan dumps out the ruined coffee.

"Now, let's make some breakfast and watch cat videos on YouTube all morning," Dylan says with a smile, and Landon laughs, marveling at how Dylan always knows how to make him feel better. He might not completely understand, but he's trying and, to Landon, that's what counts.

They make French toast and coffee with steamed milk, curl up on the couch together and watch five different videos of cats falling off of things. The stress of the morning starts to ebb when Landon feels the warmth of Dylan's body, their fingers twined together, Landon's toes tucked under Dylan's legs.

He's comfortable here with Dylan, doesn't have to worry about how he looks or sounds, or if he needs a little extra help or some encouraging words. Dylan makes him feel safe, and even though sometimes he still can't believe it, Landon knows that Dylan still loves him, no matter what he can or can't do.

His toes curl at the thought, and Dylan glances over at Landon, eyes searching his face.

"What are you thinking about?" Dylan asks, shifting their hands so he can run his thumb over Landon's knuckles.

"You." A smile pulls at Landon's lips, and he can feel his cheeks growing warm in a light blush.

"Good things I hope," Dylan says in a teasing tone. He leans forward to kiss Landon's cheek, and Landon turns his head to capture Dylan's lips.

"The best things."

His heart picks up speed, and he tugs at Dylan's hand until Dylan gets the hint and presses back against Landon until they both slide down on the couch. Landon nuzzles Dylan, kissing the line of his jaw down to his lips. Dylan returns the kiss, anchoring himself on either side of Landon's shoulders with his arms, and a lock of hair brushes Landon's forehead.

"This okay?" Dylan asks, pulling back after a moment, his lips red, face flushed.

A twinge of annoyance makes itself known: Landon wishes everyone would stop asking him that, would trust him to tell them when it's too much and he needs to stop. But he doesn't say anything, just blinks up at Dylan and nods, unsure his brain can find the words he wants to say anyway.

Instead, he reaches up and slides his fingers over Dylan's waist, over the smooth skin of his back where his shirt has hiked up. Dylan makes a soft noise, his breath warm on Landon's cheek, and Landon's fingers dig into the soft flesh as something hot and electric starts to build inside him.

He arches his neck just until Dylan's lips catch on his, until the kiss deepens and Dylan follows him back down. He's missed this, this closeness with Dylan. They've been close over the past months in so many ways, but not like this. Not with their guard down, with nothing to hold them back.

Dylan's tongue teases the seam of his lips, and Landon allows entrance, relishes the feel of Dylan's body, heavy on his. Before, he wouldn't have thought he was ready; he would have worried about how he looks and what he can't do anymore, if Dylan will be left unsatisfied and comparing him to the Landon from before. But now, there's an ache deep inside, a *need* that's impossible to ignore, to be close to Dylan and find the connection that's been severed for so long.

He's unraveling as fast as he can put himself together, trying to gather all the scattered parts of himself even as they slip through his fingers. But Dylan keeps him contained, and with every lingering touch, every kiss, Landon becomes more whole. He's loved and he's wanted, and in this moment it doesn't matter if his brain doesn't work the way it should.

In this moment, he is truly happy.

Dylan drags his lips over Landon's and down his jaw and throat to the sensitive hollow just above his collarbone. Landon moans, trying to press Dylan against him even harder. And then Dylan pulls away, cheeks red, pupils dilated, hair in disarray.

"We should…" he starts, pauses and looks as if he's trying to catch his breath. "I think…"

Landon tilts his head and waits for Dylan to say something, anything else. He doesn't, just pushes himself into a sitting position and runs a hand through his hair. Landon closes his eyes; a twinge of disappointment grows in his gut, but he pushes it away. This was good—this was enough.

It's enough. It has to be.

CHAPTER 11

Just when the inhabitants of Minnesota begin to give up hope, the snow melts. Winter washes away into spring, the biting wind is exchanged for a warm breeze, and singing birds replace the sounds of early morning snowblowers. The sun is brighter and stays longer, making everything seem a little more cheerful.

But with spring come the migraines. They slam into Landon like a pillowcase full of bricks, making his head throb, his eyes water and his stomach turn. Dylan hangs the thickest curtains he can find over their bedroom window and blocks out as much of the spring sun as he can. Landon spends most of his days curled up in bed, a pillow over his head, buried immobile under the blankets, every breath careful and calculated. They cancel most of his therapy appointments, adjust his medications, try massages and aromatherapy, and once even acupuncture. Nothing seems to help, and the migraines get worse, leaving Dylan feeling helpless and Landon wishing it would just *stop.*

Before the migraines, they'd had a conference with Landon's doctor and a few therapists, who had deemed him capable of spending most of his days at home by himself. So Janessa's time was reduced to only two days a week, allowing Landon to become more independent, to start doing more things for himself. There had even been talk of him starting to work part-time in the fall, and Landon had been both nervous and excited, had talked of nothing else for days.

And then the migraines, like a bolt of lightning striking Landon down when things were just starting to seem better, when he was smiling more, when things were getting easier between them. Now Landon cocoons himself in the dark, and Dylan's nightmares haven't stopped, and everything feels as though it's crumbling at the edges, breaking away every time he tries to hold on.

He takes long meandering walks through the park and sits under the trees on grass that has just started to turn green. He starts drawing again with his sketchbook propped up on his lap at the park, or on the couch, fingers smudged with charcoal and ink. He draws portraits and pictures that don't make much sense. It helps relieve some of the tension, like air leaking from an oversized balloon. And it keeps him from feeling so lost, so helpless when Landon shies away from his touch—even the quietest words cause him pain—or when he emerges from the bedroom only long enough to eat a single piece of toast before he starts wincing, his face scrunching and eyes watering, and Dylan helps him back into the bedroom to bury himself once more under his nest of blankets.

Sometimes, when it's particularly bad, Dylan sleeps on the couch, scared of hurting Landon with any movement, with the sound of his alarm or the soft noises that come with sleep. He keeps the house quiet and does the best he can, but as days turn into weeks, he knows he can't do this alone anymore.

Today there is a knock on the door, and Dylan opens to Landon's mother with a duffle bag slung over her shoulder. He must look rough, because she immediately draws him into a hug. He lets himself sink against her like a rag doll with cotton for bones.

"You look exhausted." Her eyes search his face.

Dylan's not sure if he wants to laugh or cry; exhaustion barely even begins to cover it. "Landon's had a rough week," he says, though she knows; that's why she came out. To help, to be the support that Landon needs and Dylan doesn't seem to be able to give him.

"How is he now?"

Dylan leads her inside, takes her jacket and sets her duffle bag on the couch. He glances at the closed door of their bedroom and wrings his hands. "He's had a migraine since last night. I was going to take him in tomorrow morning if it gets any worse, but I don't know what else they can do."

Helen looks around, her lips a thin line.

"Can I see him?"

Dylan hesitates. He's reluctant to bother Landon, but maybe the presence of his mom and knowing he has support will help.

"I don't think he's sleeping. You could see if he feels up to drinking something."

Helen smoothes her hands over hair pulled back in a tight bun.

"Thank you for calling," she says. "I know how hard you've been working to help Landon, and you can call us anytime. We can't… help him as much as we want to, being so far away, but I can always take time off if you need extra help."

"Of course." Dylan feels a little guilty that it's taken him so long to let them know what's going on. "I will."

She smiles, squeezes his arm and makes her way to the bedroom, cracks the door open and slips inside. Dylan hears a gentle voice, Landon's surprised, "Mom?" and then Helen, whispering something he can't make out. Dylan drops onto the couch and sinks back against the cushions; he can relax for the first time in weeks.

Sleep comes quickly.

* * *

The first thing Landon notices when he blinks awake is that his head no longer feels like it is splitting in half. There's only a gentle ache, a bruise that doesn't quite want to fade, and a memory of something far worse. The second thing he notices is the body beside him, leaning against the headboard, a book perched on its lap: his mom, he realizes, after he blinks the fog from his eyes. She was here last night, had pulled him in like she used to when he was a child and sick with the flu or had a scraped knee. She'd kissed his head and told him to sleep, that she would be here in the morning. He did, and she is.

"Good morning," Helen says, smiling down when she notices him looking up at her. She brushes a hand through his hair and it feels so good that he closes his eyes and lets himself *feel*—feel warm and safe, like an actual human again, if only for a minute.

"Morning," he says, pushing himself up when she withdraws her hand.

"How are you feeling?"

Landon licks his lips; his mouth is as dry as sandpaper. "Thirsty."

Helen chuckles. "Hold on."

She kisses his forehead before sliding off the bed. He watches her leave the door open just a crack. Voices filter in but he doesn't listen, just leans back against his pillow and fills his lungs, letting himself feel whole again.

"Hi," a quiet voice says, and Landon doesn't realize he's closed his eyes until they're sliding open again. Dylan is beside the bed, holding a glass of water. Helen is close behind. She places a comforting hand on his back as Landon accepts the water. It's cool, and he almost moans at how good it tastes. Dylan pulls the cup away from his lips.

"Don't drink too fast," he says, and Landon sighs and stares down at where the water dripped onto the bed in his hurry to drink. Dylan was right, his stomach rebels just a little at the water, but he lets his head fall back and waits for it to pass.

"Thank you." He takes another sip, this time more slowly.

"How's your head?" Dylan asks. Landon tries to smile even though his face feels stiff, as if it's been too long since he's practiced the movements.

"Better." He can see Dylan sag with relief. "A lot better."

"Good." Dylan kisses his forehead. "Good."

Landon makes it out to the living room later that morning and sits on the couch under a pile of blankets, and while it's not much, he feels a little more human. Dylan runs to the grocery store after Helen passes him some money and comments on the distinct lack of food in the fridge, and if he weren't worried about bringing back his headache, Landon would laugh at the sheepish look on Dylan's face.

Helen straightens things up while Dylan is gone, organizing in the manner that only moms can, and Landon watches her for a while, trying to figure out what seems off about her. Something nudges at his thoughts.

"Mom?" he says after a moment. She's dusting off the bookshelves and stops to look over at Landon. "Where's your ring?"

Helen's hand moves to cover the finger her wedding band used to encircle, and she is still for a moment, looking resigned. Then she walks over and sits gingerly on the couch beside him.

"I was going to tell you," she says, brushing a lock of hair out of Landon's eyes.

"Tell me what?" Landon asks, even though he knows. Deep inside, he knows.

"Your father and I are getting a divorce." The words are said as a fact, no heavy emotions attached. Landon's not surprised, not really. His parents' marriage hasn't worked for a long time, not since Landon was in high school and everything started to fall apart.

"I'm living with Aunt Rose for now," Helen continues, rubbing her hands. Aunt Rose is Helen's aunt, an elderly lady who lives twenty minutes from Madison and whose house always smelled like potpourri and gin. Landon remembers going to visit, the way she would pinch his cheeks and tell him he needed to fatten up and get a sensible pair of boots. *Lewin men*, she would say with a curl of her lip, *more string bean than men, really.*

Landon shakes his head, wills his thoughts to stop wandering and forces himself to keep focused on what Helen is saying.

"Are you okay?" he asks, reaching to rest his hand on Helen's. She looks at him with a wavering smile.

"I am." He can hear the honesty in her voice. "It's... hard, but I'm happier now."

She pauses, a sad look crossing her face. "I just wish we had figured this out earlier. I regret what you guys had to go through, living with us."

Landon thinks back to the fights, to hiding with Lana in her room while their parents shouted at each other, the sound of the front door slamming, his mom cleaning up broken glass while pretending everything was all right.

"It's okay," Landon says, even though it isn't. "I'm just glad you're... you're happy now."

Helen looks at him, her gaze softening, and runs her hand across the back of his neck.

"Don't ever doubt how much we love you," she says before withdrawing her touch. "How much we've always loved you."

Landon looks at his lap, at the blankets over his legs. He had doubted, years ago when the words "I think I'm gay" had left his lips at dinner one night, when his dad's smiles had become more strained, when his mom had become more withdrawn, had given him rehearsed speeches about how experimenting was okay, he was only sixteen and still had a lot of growing to do, and couldn't be expected to know everything about himself yet. He remembers feeling alone, as though Lana was the only who supported him, but he knows now that it wasn't true. His parents were reacting to a situation they knew nothing about while the rest of their lives fell apart around them.

"I love you too, Mom." Landon leans against her.

"I've been looking for jobs out here," Helen says after a moment. "So I can be closer to my babies."

"*Mom*." Helen laughs, and Landon sticks out his tongue. "I'd like that. We'd both like that," he adds seriously. He knows how hard it's been for his mom to be so far away over the past few months.

"I'm glad." She kisses the top of his head. "I'm so proud of you, my brave little boy."

Landon scrunches up his nose; he hates when she gets sentimental like this. But he doesn't protest. His head throbs, and he can feel the headache starting to come back; he closes his eyes and wills it to stay away a little longer. Helen must notice. She runs her fingers gently through his hair.

"Let's get you back to the bed," she says, helping Landon up, holding him steady when he starts to stumble. His legs feel as if they're moving through water, and he sags against her as they make their way into the bedroom. The pain in his head grows, folds in on itself, gnaws at his brain and shreds the most important parts of him.

Helen helps him into bed, rubs his back as he gets sick into the garbage pail beside the bed, shakes out two pills for him, tucks him under the covers and draws the curtains until the room is once again dark. The migraine wraps around his brain, its fingers dig in, and he's being pulled away, but he doesn't want to go. Frustrated tears sting as he thinks of Dylan coming back from the store, so hopeful that Landon will still be up and that everything might be better now.

"You're so strong." His mom's voice, barely a whisper, cuts through the haze just for a moment, until the migraine clutches him tighter, like a monster hunched possessively around his brain. "I'll be here."

He sinks under.

A phone rings, vibrates in his pocket. Dylan frowns, confused for a moment, his own phone silent in his hand as he checks his texts before heading out of the grocery store parking lot. He scrambles, pats down his pockets and pulls out Landon's phone; Landon must have worn Dylan's sweatshirt and forgotten it in the pocket. The screen lights up with a number he doesn't recognize, and Dylan swipes a finger over the screen to answer.

"Hello?"

"Hi, is this Landon?" A woman's voice sounds in his ears.

Dylan leans back in the driver's seat. "No, this is Dylan, Landon's fiancé."

"Hi, Dylan, I don't believe we've met yet," she says, and Dylan frowns, thoroughly confused. "My name is Ruby, I'm with the support group Landon's been going to. Might I speak with Landon?"

"He's not available right now." Dylan drums his fingers on the steering wheel. "Can I help you?"

"I was just calling because Landon missed the last two meetings, and I wanted to check in to make sure he's doing all right, and see if he's coming this week."

Dylan looks out the window at the parking lot, processing what she's saying.

"I'm sorry... meeting?"

"The support group meeting?" Dylan finds himself becoming more confused. "Landon has missed a couple and we were worried about him."

"He, uh, he's been having migraines," Dylan says automatically, not sure why he's explaining this to someone he doesn't know.

"I'm so sorry to hear that." Ruby sounds genuine. "Is he doing any better?"

"He's getting there." Dylan is entirely thrown off by this conversation and doesn't know what else to say.

"I'm glad," Ruby says. "Will you tell him the next meeting is Wednesday at eleven if he's feeling up to it? And tell him we're thinking of him."

"Sure." Dylan runs a hand over his face.

"And Dylan, we'd love to see you there sometime too. He talks about you a lot."

"Oh, yeah. Okay."

"All right, tell Landon I called, okay?"

"I will, thank you," Dylan says with forced politeness. He ends the call and sits in the car while the heater finally starts to sputter warm air through the vents, staring at the phone. Landon's been going to a support group, that much is obvious, but… for how long? And why didn't he tell Dylan? None of it makes sense. Dylan doesn't understand why Landon would hide something like this from him.

He warms his hands in front of the heat vents before putting the car in reverse and heading out of the parking lot. The house is quiet, the door to the bedroom is shut, everything is still in that way that houses only seem to be when someone is sick. Dylan sighs and kicks off his shoes, a mixture of disappointment and worry in his gut. He pulls Landon's phone out of his pocket and puts it on silent mode before cracking open the door to the bedroom, where he sees the familiar pile of blankets over Landon and Helen sleeping on the bed beside him. Dylan, careful not to make a sound, sets the phone on the bedside table; his hand hovers over Landon's shoulder before he turns and leaves.

The couch is good enough.

It's nearing three in the morning when Helen wakes. The room is dark, only a sliver of light peeks through from the crack under the door. Landon is still asleep beside her, his breaths long and heavy, and Helen touches a kiss to his forehead before she slips out of bed and silently leaves the room.

The house is chilly, and Helen wraps her arms around herself as she steps into the living room. A single lamp beside the couch illuminates the room in a soft, yellow light; the edges of the room blur into shadows. Dylan is asleep on the couch, his long legs are scrunched in order to fit. He's wrapped in a worn-looking hoodie that that Helen recognizes as one of Landon's, and a thin blanket is crumpled on the floor beside him. Helen picks up the blanket, brushes out the dust and drapes it over Dylan, making sure to cover his feet and tuck the corners in around his shoulders. He stirs, blinking open a bleary eye.

Helen rests a comforting hand on his arm. "Shh, it's okay."

"Landon?" Dylan's voice is still rough with sleep, and she can tell he's struggling to keep his eyes open.

"He's fine, just sleeping."

Dylan nods, his eyes slipping shut again. "Okay."

Helen brushes a hand through Dylan's hair. Its gentle waves are soft against her fingers. Dylan lets out a humming sound, and she can tell he's already dipping back into sleep, his lips parting, the lines around his eyes relaxing. He looks exhausted, and Helen doesn't think he's had a decent night's sleep in weeks.

Between his work and helping Landon, she doubts he's taken any time for himself.

Part of her wishes he'd ask for help, that he'd let them know when he's struggling, when he can't do this all on his own. But she understands, too: He's been trying so hard to prove to them, to himself and to Landon that he can do this; that they made the right choice, that all they need is just the two of them. He's been trying so hard, and he's wearing himself out.

It'll be easier, she hopes, when she can be closer and asking for help won't seem like such an inconvenience. When she can finally give her son and his fiancé the support they've deserved all along.

She fills a glass of water from the tap and looks out the window at the pale moon, shimmering through the clouds as if she's seeing it through water. She lets the silence of the house clear her thoughts and sets the empty glass in the sink before making her way back into the darkness of the bedroom.

Dylan doesn't bring up the call, not at first. Landon stays in bed for another week and Dylan calls his doctor begging for another prescription, for anything to help. They start him on a new medication, and slowly, just as the flowers are beginning to push up from the damp spring soil and birds start to sing on the branches outside their window, the migraines fade.

Helen stays for two weeks, helps Dylan around the house, shops for food and cleaning supplies and makes Landon oatmeal and tea. Landon ventures out of bed, spends more time on the couch and starts going to appointments a few times a week. The relief is evident on his face every day that his brain doesn't rebel against him, every day spent outside the dark of their bedroom.

After Helen leaves, Lana comes over more, spending time with Landon while Dylan is at work, and sometimes Dylan comes home to both Lana and Janessa sprawled in the living room and Landon watching their antics with amusement. Dylan supposes it's only natural that they became friends; with Janessa's loud personality and Lana's loud opinions, they seem like the perfect match. Until their strategies for amusing Landon start to include glitter and rearranging furniture, and Dylan has to banish them all to the backyard.

Two weeks pass after the call and still Dylan keeps it in, chews at his lip and tries to figure out how to bring it up. Landon hasn't mentioned anything, hasn't hinted at missing any meetings, and each Wednesday passes without a sign that he wants to be somewhere else. Two more calls have gone unanswered, Dylan discovers, when he peeks at Landon's phone one day as Landon is taking a midday nap. He feels guilty, looking at Landon's phone, but the desire to know what Landon is hiding gnaws at him. He puts off talking about it.

On Saturday, there's a spring festival at the park down the street. Landon gets up first; Dylan is still tired after a nightmare that kept him awake most of the night, panic gripping his chest, making him cling to Landon to remind himself he was still there.

When Dylan rolls out of bed, Landon has coffee made and is sipping it with a proud smile on his face. Dylan accepts his own; it's a little weak, but otherwise not bad.

"Do you want to go to the park today? See the festival?" Dylan asks. He watches Landon stare contemplatively at his coffee before nodding.

"That would be… fun." Landon looks nervous, but determined. Dylan smiles and sits down next to Landon. He thinks of the phone call and knows he shouldn't let it eat at him anymore.

"So, um…" He starts, bites his lip and tries to figure out what to say. Landon tilts his head. "You got a call, a few weeks ago. From Ruby."

He can see the moment it dawns on Landon, whose expression is controlled as he looks back down at his coffee.

"Have you been going to meetings?" Dylan tries to keep the hurt out of his voice.

Landon clears his throat. "Yeah."

"How?" Dylan knows it's not the right question, but it's the first thing that comes out.

"Janessa drives me. Or Lana." Landon digs his thumb into the table. "Tate did once."

Dylan frowns.

"So everyone knows except me?" Landon doesn't answer, just digs his thumb in harder. Dylan grabs his hand before Landon can make a dent in the table and guides it down to his lap. "Why didn't you tell me?"

Landon opens his mouth, closes it and opens it again. "I just…" he clears his throat. "I need to talk to someone to who understands."

"I understand."

"You don't." Landon shakes his head. "You don't know what it's like to… to have to depend on someone for *everything*, to not…" the words catch and he works his throat, trying to bring them back. "To not know your own body, your own thoughts."

"You could have told me," Dylan says, wishing his voice didn't sound so strained.

"You don't…" Landon looks up. "I wanted… I *needed* to do this on my own."

"Without me? Why?"

A moment passes before Landon answers. "You've… you've done so much for me and I… I was tired of feeling so helpless. I just… I needed to do something on my own."

Dylan thinks he might understand, but it doesn't dampen his hurt at being left out of something so important to his fiancé. It feels like a crack between them, a hairline fracture in the trust and honesty they've always had.

"You could have told me," Dylan says, the words soft as he stares at the table. "I would have supported you."

Beside him, Landon makes a frustrated noise. "Forget it." He pushes his chair out, reaches for his crutches and pulls himself to his feet, only wavering for a second before finding his balance.

"Landon…" Dylan stands, unsure why Landon is suddenly so angry. "Please don't get mad."

Landon can't always help it; his brain doesn't work that way anymore. Emotions come too quickly and too strongly for him to control, but he doesn't want the conversation to end this way.

"You don't get it," Landon says, hands tightening on the handles of his crutches.

"Then explain it to me," Dylan pleads, trying to push down his own frustration.

Landon makes a frustrated noise in the back of his throat.

"I don't know *how*."

Dylan wants to reach out, to wrap Landon close, to tell him that it's okay and they'll figure it out. But he's starting to understand, just a little, that comfort is not what Landon needs. He's spent so long relying on Dylan to make things okay, to make them better again, that he needs to do things on his own now. As much as he can.

"I just… I wanted something for myself."

It still stings, to know Landon purposefully kept something from him, but Dylan pushes the feeling down, for now, and focuses on resolving this in a way that won't turn into a fight.

"Was it helping?" Dylan asks. He shoves his hands into his pockets. "The support group?"

Landon pauses only a second before nodding, a quiet *yeah*.

"Okay." Dylan sucks in a breath and tells himself that's what matters—it was helping Landon, that's what's important. He's about to turn and leave, to head back to the bedroom and pretend to fold laundry or something, when Landon stops him.

"I'm sorry."

Dylan looks back at him, Landon's are eyes shadowed as he stares at the floor, and he leans heavily against the table.

"It's okay," Dylan says, wishing he could really mean it. "I didn't realize I was holding you back."

Landon shifts, his eyes flickering up to meet Dylan's. He doesn't say anything and Dylan leaves with a weight in his stomach, the monster clawing at his throat.

It builds all day, the weird, gnawing feeling that Dylan can't quite place, the one that usually accompanies his nightmares, dark alleyways and crowded streets. It builds as he folds laundry, as Landon keeps starting to say something only to shake his head, attempts aborted. It builds as they get ready to go to the park, and Dylan tells himself to get a grip.

The park is full of people, the air is filled with music, the walkway is dotted with booths displaying homemade crafts. They find a small clearing to the side edged with flowers, and a man sitting on a rock, strumming a guitar. They settle onto an iron park bench. The sun is warm despite the last lingering bite of winter on the wind. Dylan listens to the music and feels a different sort of ache, one that reminds him of years ago—of a street fair and cotton candy, of a kiss and a proposal, of the overwhelming happiness that had wrapped around them, sewing itself into their hearts and pulling their lives together. For better or for worse.

Landon must feel it too, the way he leans against Dylan, rests his hand against Dylan's thigh and draws a choppy heart on Dylan's leg with his thumb. Dylan lets his hand drift down and skim Landon's wrist, his soft skin.

"Dance with me," Dylan whispers, joining their fingers. He stands, reaches to grab Landon's other hand and tugs him to his feet.

"No one else is." Landon looks around, his cheeks flushing.

"So?" Dylan slides his arms around Landon's waist and holds him steady. Landon grips Dylan's arms and moves closer, until the few inches between them are charged and heavy, begging to be closed.

The guitarist changes his tune to something a little more upbeat, and Dylan leads, pulls them farther from the bench and lets them sway with the fabric of Landon's jacket bunching under his fingers.

"I should've… told you," Landon says after a moment, gripping Dylan's arms a little tighter. "I'm sorry."

Dylan doesn't respond, but grabs Landon's hand, twirls and dips Landon, his hand heavy on Landon's back, his eyes flickering over the stretch of Landon's throat. Landon laughs as he straightens back up, and wobbles only a bit before finding his balance.

"I love you." Dylan doesn't think it's been said enough, recently. "But I think we need to work on communication."

Landon nods, leans against Dylan. "I love you, too." The words are freighted with something that almost sounds like relief. "And we will. *I* will."

Dylan smiles and ghosts a kiss on Landon's cheek before they sit back down, but the knot in his stomach grows.

They eat cotton candy, and Dylan buys a necklace he thinks his mom will like. Landon becomes fascinated by a booth selling wind chimes, and by another with homemade soy candles. He talks to a few vendors, ventures farther from Dylan than he has before, and Dylan doesn't remember the last time he looked so confident, so sure of himself. Dylan feels proud of how far Landon has come, of the way his anger and frustration are being replaced by something brighter, something happier, but it also leaves him feeling a little thrown off, unsure.

"There are going to be fireworks," Landon says, excited as a twelve-year-old on the Fourth of July. "We should stay."

Dylan hesitates. The idea of fireworks, of staying as it gets dark with so many people around him, makes the anxious thrumming under his skin grow. But Landon looks so excited, and he actually wants to stay out here, in public. Dylan doesn't want to deny him that. Not after so many months of solitude, of Landon feeling ashamed of how he looks, of how he talks, of the scars on his head. So he swallows the feeling and smiles at Landon as convincingly as he can.

"Fireworks sound great."

They run into Janessa and Lana, oddly enough. Both girls have face paint, Janessa a sparkling rainbow from eye to ear, Lana what looks like a purple cat, its tail winding up to her eyebrow. Landon admires them after they hug, and Dylan laughs and tells Landon he can get his face painted if he wants. Landon brushes it off, but Dylan can see the wistful look in his eyes.

They drag Landon to the face-painting booth. A girl with paint-stained fingers greets them, and Landon takes a careful seat in the rickety chair she has set up. Dylan holds on to his crutches.

"What do you want?" the girl asks, brushing her hair back and leaving a streak of purple behind. Landon chews his lip and considers the display of pictures.

"Surprise me," he says, his words clear, and Dylan is impressed with how sure of himself he sounds; this is a side of Landon he hasn't seen in a long time. Dylan stands back, munches on the kettle corn Janessa bought and watches as Landon sits very still, his eyes closed. He looks serene, with the setting sun golden on his face, catching the auburn glow of his hair. And the knot unravels, just slightly, but enough for warmth to spread under his skin and through his veins, pulsing with the beat of his heart.

"How's it look?" Landon asks turning his head to show off the dark outline of a wolf howling at a full moon.

"Wow," Dylan says, stepping forward. "That's really good."

Landon beams as he looks at his reflection in the mirror the artist holds out, touches the edge of his cheek.

"You're next," Landon says, grinning, and Dylan tries to protest, but the girls wrestle him into the seat and threaten to take away all the kettle corn if he doesn't get his face painted. Dylan agrees with an exaggerated sigh and crosses his arms over his chest while she paints. But Landon smiles at him, stands close and Dylan can honestly say he doesn't remember the last time he had this much fun, the last time things felt so normal.

The brush tickles as the artist works, and Dylan shoots Landon a glare, which Landon returns before sticking out his tongue; and if Dylan weren't so scared of moving and completely messing up his facial masterpiece, he would tell Landon off for acting so childish.

She hands him a mirror and Dylan bursts out laughing when he sees the giraffe, its long neck winding up over his eye.

"It suits you," Janessa says, contemplating the work. "Weirdly tall, provides shade for everyone else, likes to eat wood."

Landon's eyes grow wide, and Dylan manages a choked noise before hissing, "There are *children* here, Janessa." Janessa winks at him, shrugs and daintily eats a piece of popcorn while Dylan shakes his head and pays the artist, giving her a generous tip.

"Don't we look like quite the group," Lana remarks, linking arms between Dylan and Landon. The sun is beginning to dip behind the horizon, and they make their way over to the clearing where the fireworks will be. It's only a small show, if Dylan remembers from past years, like a kiddie version of the Fourth, but it's on one of the first days of spring nice enough to stay outside, so the park is full. He sees families with barely contained small children and teenage couples stretched out on blankets, the more sophisticated perched on lawn chairs.

The sun sinks, and Dylan feels his throat tighten, the lump in his stomach grow. The dim light of evening makes it difficult to keep track of what's around him, and there are so many people he doesn't know, tall men in jackets, and it's impossible to keep his thoughts focused on any one thing. His heart pounds in his chest.

Lana picks a spot off to the side and settles down in the grass, Janessa following. Landon hesitates, his eyes on Dylan, a worried look on his face.

"You okay?" Landon asks, his voice soft, and Dylan nods, but it's a jerky movement, his eyes still flickering around.

"I'm fine," he tries to assure Landon, looking back at him. And then he smells it, the rich, spicy smell of roasting gyros, coming from a stand just to the side of the clearing. There's a short line, and people walk by with gyros in hand, laughing and smiling. The smell wraps around Dylan, so thick in the air that he doesn't know how he didn't smell it before. It invades his nose and his lungs, squeezes at his heart, and he can't breathe, can't inhale, because then he'll smell it, that stupid scent of lamb and onion and sour cream.

And he can see it, can feel it, the hot July summer, the way Landon smiled with his mouth full and sauce on his nose that Dylan had kissed away. He remembers how it had tasted earthy, of meat and cucumbers and lettuce, a taste that was soon mixed with the smell of blood, the damp rot of the alleyway, the men who had reeked so strongly of alcohol it burned Dylan's nose.

There's a hand on him, grabbing his arm, and Dylan can't breathe, can't think—just lashes out as a crack echoes through the air. A crack just like the one the pipe made when it hit Landon's head, a crack like the one Landon's body made when it collapsed to the ground, a crack like the one Dylan's arm made when it was wrenched behind him. There are more hands on him, the smell of gyros surrounding him, and another crack, another and another, and how many times are they going to hit him, they're going to hurt him, kill him, oh God, Landon—

"Dylan!"

Another hand on his arm and he wrenches away, with a thud and an *oof* sounding beside him. It sounds like Landon and Dylan blinks, fingers tangling in the soft grass below him. Grass. He's on the ground; a rock digs into the back of his thigh. He blinks again, looks around and his lungs finally expand and heave; the haze evaporates from his eyes. There are people around him, Janessa and Lana and others with kind faces, concerned and caring. He sees Landon beside him, propping himself up on the ground with Lana's hand on his shoulder; he looks disgruntled and concerned, but alive and okay.

Janessa is in front of him, hovering over Dylan as if she wants to touch him but doesn't want to cause any more distress. A woman Dylan doesn't know stands beside her with a little girl by her side who bites her fingers nervously.

"Hey, you with us?" Janessa asks, voice gentle, and Dylan nods, digging his fingers into the dirt beneath him.

"What...?" Dylan's voice catches in his throat.

Janessa glances at Landon, who reaches over and lays a cautious, gentle hand on Dylan's arm. Dylan leans into the touch and takes Landon's, letting it anchor him. Landon tilts his head, confusion in his eyes, lips a worried line.

"I think you blacked out," Janessa says. "You started hyperventilating and wouldn't respond to us, and then you went down and took Landon with you."

"Landon..." Dylan echoes, his brain still struggling to catch up. He remembers fighting someone off, and a sick feeling bubbles in his stomach. He turns, pulls Landon's hand from his arm to his chest and holds on tight. "Did I hurt you? I'm so sorry, I hurt you, I didn't…"

Landon touches Dylan's lips with his finger, his face showing nothing but concern.

"I'm fine," he says, though Dylan's not sure if he believes him. "I'm… worried about you."

"You sure you're okay?" Dylan presses, searching Landon's face for a sign of anything that could mean he isn't.

"Promise." Landon squeezes Dylan's hand. Something cold is pressed into Dylan's other hand and he forces himself to look away from Landon and sees a sweating bottle of blue Gatorade.

"Drink it," the woman Dylan doesn't recognize instructs him. Dylan does as she says, and only when he brings the bottle to his lips does he realize he's shaking. The cold shock of Gatorade does help to calm him. His head stops spinning, and the ground is steadier under his feet.

"Thank you," he pants, and tries to hand the drink back to her.

"Keep it," she says, with an encouraging smile. "It'll help you feel better."

Janessa thanks her again and she tells him to take it easy before leaving with the little girl trailing close behind her.

"What happened?" Janessa asks, squatting beside Dylan. He feels embarrassed. His cheeks grow warm and he presses his forehead to his knees, taking a second to breathe.

"Low blood sugar?" Dylan tries, but he can tell none of them believe him. And then there is another crack, a loud *boom,* and Dylan flinches, his breath catching in his throat until he realizes it's just the fireworks. *Just fireworks.* Janessa raises an eyebrow at him, and Lana looks at him doubtfully.

"I'm fine," Dylan insists. He lets go of Landon's hand and starts to push himself to his feet. Janessa keeps a steadying hand on his back so he doesn't fall over again. Lana pulls Landon to his feet and helps get his crutches situated, and Dylan's hands curl and uncurl into useless fists.

"Let's go home," Landon says, once he's standing; his face paint has smeared into something that looks like a bruise, and Dylan has to look away. He still feels overwhelmed by the crack of fireworks and the smell of gyros, and it's so *dark*. Dylan just wants to crawl into bed and forget this ever happened.

"I'll be okay." Dylan forces himself to smile at the girls. "You don't need to come back with us."

Lana narrows her eyes, and Janessa looks as if she wants to argue, but stops herself.

"We'll call you if we, uh..." Landon makes the face he does when he's looking for a word, when his sentence has slipped away, just out of reach. "If we need anything."

"Okay," Lana says, even though she doesn't sound as if she agrees. "But I'll stop by tomorrow and make sure you're both okay."

"Thanks, Lana," Landon says, and hugs Lana and Janessa. Dylan is already turning to leave the park; his legs feel shaky and he's not sure how long he can stand here before the panic builds again. He hears Landon say a few parting words before he starts to walk back in the direction of their car, and tries not to feel so embarrassed and *stupid* because he can't do one simple thing his fiancé wanted to do. For the first time in a long time, Landon actually looked happy, was having a good time with people he loves, out in public, and now Dylan has ruined it.

His eyes burn and he stops, takes a breath and realizes he's alone. Turning around, he sees Landon nearly half a block back, doing his best to catch up, every step forceful and deliberate.

"I'm sorry," Dylan says when Landon catches up. The words sound choked, weak. He crosses his arms over his chest and can't bring himself to meet Landon's eyes—the shame is too much. "I'm so sorry."

Landon pauses for only a moment before wrapping his arms around Dylan's waist and pulling him in. A traitorous noise that sounds close to a sob escapes Dylan's lips and he knows he should feel ridiculous, crying on the sidewalk barely a block from their car, but he doesn't care. He only cares about the arms around him, the warm body pressed against him, holding him close. Another firework cracks through the night, and Dylan flinches, fingers digging into Landon's arms just to make sure he's real, he's okay, he's *okay*.

"You're okay," Dylan manages. He looks up, searching Landon's face even though he knows he's being silly, he's overreacting, but he can't help it. The claws around his esophagus tighten, everything is too real, too close.

"I'm okay," Landon says, the words strong and sincere, and Dylan sniffs, his cheeks burning. "I promise."

"I ruined your night." Dylan lets his arms fall to his sides. Landon leans onto his crutches and shakes his head.

"I'm just... just worried. About you."

Dylan lets out a wobbly laugh. Landon's worried about *him*, and it seems so ridiculous after everything he's felt tonight. He lets his head fall to Landon's shoulder and breathes deeply, grounding, orienting, controlling himself. He's okay. Landon's okay. *I'm okay.*

"Let's go home," Landon whispers, nudging Dylan. Dylan lets Landon set the pace the rest of the way to the car.

One step inside the house and Landon sees Dylan deflate, his shoulders falling, head dipping forward like he's been holding something heavy for too long. Dylan kicks off his shoes, hangs their jackets in the closet and makes his way into the living room. He stands there lost.

"Come on." Landon wants to take Dylan's hand but can't, not with these stupid crutches. Instead, he nods toward the couch and hopes Dylan will follow. He does.

"Sit," Landon commands, and Dylan obeys, falling back onto the couch; his eyes are shadowed by tired circles. He still has the giraffe on his cheek, and despite the circumstances, Landon thinks it makes him look adorable. "Hang on." Landon motions for Dylan to stay and makes his way into the kitchen, pours him a glass of orange juice. He knows that what happened wasn't caused by low blood sugar; it was obvious that something else was going on, but Landon figures it doesn't hurt to be careful, or to give Dylan a quiet moment to calm himself, away from the noises and smells and people of the park.

It doesn't take long for him to realize that he can't both carry the drink and use his crutches, and he wants to kick something, wants to lash out in frustration at his inability to do something so remarkably simple. But he doesn't; he's learning to recognize these urges, to control the bouts of anger and channel them into something more productive. So he steels his jaw, leans the crutches carefully against the counter, grasps the glass in his left hand and slowly walks back to the living room. He has to stop once, when the world dips under his feet and a wave of vertigo washes through him, but he doesn't fall; his steps stay steady, and he makes it back to the couch.

Dylan accepts the orange juice, and Landon can see his hands shake as he takes a sip. A sense of unease growing in his gut, Landon takes a seat next to him.

"What are you thinking about?" Landon asks. He wants to reach out for Dylan's hand, but knows Dylan might need some space; he never was the best at opening up.

Dylan licks his lips and runs his thumb along the rim of the glass.

Landon can't help it any longer. He reaches out to lay his hand on Dylan's leg. "You can talk to me."

"I don't..." Dylan looks down at Landon's hand. "I thought talking would be easier once we got out of the park, but..." A dry laugh escapes him. "I think I was wrong."

"It can be easy, if you want it to be," Landon says, searching Dylan's face. "You... you've always made it, um, easier for me even when... when it's the hardest thing I have to do." Dylan sets the glass down on the coffee table and looks at Landon.

"I want to be able to do the same thing for you," Landon adds, and he knows his words are choppy, that his sentence runs together in spots and it's not the best he's ever spoken, but it's good enough. He feels silly that it's been so hard for him to convey this to Dylan; he knows Dylan's been hiding something, struggling with something all on his own. And he can never fully repay Dylan for everything he's done, for how entirely he has been there for Landon, for the many outbursts and breakdowns Dylan has gotten Landon through, for every step and every word that Landon has struggled with while Dylan remained patient and supportive.

"It was the gyros," Dylan says after a moment, looking back down at his knees.

Landon blinks. "The what?"

"We were eating gyros the night it happened." Dylan's voice is thin. He scrubs a hand over his face, smearing the painted giraffe, and it looks sad now, its mouth turned down in a smudged frown. Landon stays silent and lets Dylan draw in a breath, swallow whatever emotions are preventing him from continuing. "And it's just... the smell of the park and the fireworks, they sounded like when..."

He cuts off, his eyes blinking rapidly.

"Sometimes it comes back so intense, and it's like my brain won't stop thinking, won't stop racing with all these memories, and I can't stop worrying because I don't want anything to happen to you and it's just... it's *so much.*" The words come in a rush, and Landon grabs his hand from where it's fallen to rest in his lap and holds on tight.

"I think," Dylan starts, staring at their intertwined fingers, "I think I'm realizing that I haven't been dealing with everything as well as I thought I was..." He shakes his head, his eyelashes damp with unshed tears.

"It's okay." Landon runs his thumb over Dylan's knuckles. "Take your time."

Only the sound of the occasional car driving by outside fills the silence.

"When you were in the hospital, I couldn't *breathe* without you here. I couldn't remember how to be myself anymore, and the thought of losing you... and no matter what I do, all I can think of is *that* night, like my entire existence revolves around it, and I hate it. We're getting our lives back and I want to move on, but it won't let me go and I don't understand why."

His voice cracks on the last word, a tear slipping from his eye, and he quickly wipes it away.

"Sometimes I feel like I can't be happy anymore."

Landon studies the man next to him: his fiancé, the love of his life, the infallible anchor that has held him in place for so long, the man who made it okay for him to not be okay, who lifted him up and helped him get to the point where he is now. Even he isn't immune to the demons that haunt at night, to the insecurities that hack at the soul and the kind of fears that consume and make even the smallest things the most taxing, the act of breathing an Everest, impossible to climb.

This isn't something new. This is something Dylan's been dealing with, something he's been pushing away, feelings he's been bottling up until the pressure is too much to bear.

Landon thinks it's been a long time since Dylan has really felt happy.

"You will be." Landon's thumb grazes Dylan's engagement ring, snug on his finger. "We'll work on it together."

Dylan sniffs. He turns his hand around so his palm meets Landon's.

"And..." Landon squeezes Dylan's hand. "I think you should see a therapist."

Dylan doesn't look too surprised, and Landon wonders if he's been thinking the same thing.

"If I do, would you come with me?" Dylan looks at Landon, eyes wide and uncharacteristically vulnerable.

"Of course." Landon hears echoes of their earlier argument, about the support group he hid from Dylan, and a tendril of guilt nestles in his belly. "I'm sorry… that I didn't tell you."

He looks down at their hands, his pale skin against the darker hue of Dylan's, their fingers linking like connecting puzzle pieces.

"It's okay. I think I understand."

"You can come with, next time." Dylan looks a little more relaxed; his shoulders aren't so stiff, and the tight lines of his face have smoothed out. "To the group."

"Only if you want me to." Dylan uses the sleeves of his shirt to pat his cheeks dry one last time, grimacing at the paint that smears onto the fabric.

"I do." Landon turns Dylan's face toward his and kisses him. He thinks about their first kiss, years ago, sitting on the tiny bed in Landon's dorm room, both of them nervous and a little giddy. A winter storm raged outside, snow so thick it was impossible to see out the window, and Dylan showed up with a bag of jelly-beans, a smuggled bottle of peppermint schnapps and the movie *Gremlins*. They'd both been a little bit buzzed by the end, and inched closer and closer during the movie until their shoulders were touching and their knees were knocking together. They could hear other students in the hall, stomping snow from their boots, but Landon barely noticed. He remembers how his pulse started racing in his throat, his fingers itching to reach forward, something always stopping him—fear, nerves, the undeniable humiliation of rejection—until Dylan looked over at him and chewed his lip for a moment before the words "Fuck it" slipped from his lips and he leaned forward, capturing Landon in a kiss that tasted like cinnamon jelly beans.

It wasn't a perfect kiss, not by any means, but there was no one else he wanted to kiss, ever again. Dylan's lips were enough;

and he would be lucky to be granted a lifetime just to explore them, to get to know every part of the man who turned his heart into a quivering mess, who made him feel prepared to take on whatever life had to offer, if only Dylan was always at his side.

And even though whatever life had to offer had come to include things Landon could never have prepared for, he realizes now that it's still true. Things might seem terrible more days than not, might hurt so much it's hard to see a reason to keep trying, to keep going when everything seems so set on pulling him back, but with Dylan… it's worth it. Somehow he knows, every fiber of his broken soul knows, that despite the bad days still to come, he wants to try. He wants Dylan to keep trying. Whatever they have to do.

"I love you," Landon says, hoping that somehow Dylan understands everything contained in those words, everything that can't possibly be said. Dylan kisses Landon back and lingers with their foreheads touching, eyes fluttering closed. Dylan takes a deep breath, any remaining tension melts from his shoulders, and after a moment he slumps back against the couch.

Dylan looks up at Landon through long eyelashes. "I'm sorry I ruined your day."

"I don't care about the day. You come first."

Dylan squeezes his hand. "I love it when you talk dirty," he says, a smile pulling at his lips. Landon pulls back, aghast.

"Dylan Nayar, did you just make a sex joke during our very emotional conversation?"

"I think I did." Dylan gives a real, full laugh, his eyes crinkling in the corners. Landon puts on a mock-offended look and then chuckles and shakes his head.

"I take it back." Landon nestles in beside Dylan. "Wedding's off."

"Oh no," Dylan whines. He wraps his arm around Landon, pulling him close. "Whatever am I going to tell my mom?"

Landon shifts to look up at Dylan, the angle a little awkward from where his head rests against Dylan's shoulder. "First you talk about sex, and now your mom. I'm getting mixed... um, mixed messages."

Dylan laughs again and runs a hand down Landon's arm.

"I just like to keep you guessing."

"Apparently," Landon murmurs. Exhaustion is sinking into his bones, and he can't imagine how tired Dylan must be. His head is starting to throb, a faint ache that foreshadows something more, and he winces, pressing farther into Dylan's shoulder.

Dylan runs his fingers through Landon's hair. "You okay?"

"Maybe fireworks weren't the best idea." Landon's eyes close against his will. Dylan kisses the top of his head and then pulls Landon to his feet despite his groan of protest.

"I guess we both still have things to work on," Landon says, after Dylan guides him into the bathroom and helps him wash the smudged face paint off his cheeks. Dylan pauses, a damp washcloth clutched in his hand, a thoughtful look crossing his face.

"We'll get there."

The words echo in Landon's head even as the ache grows, as he changes into pajamas and slips under the covers. Dylan slides in beside him.

We'll get there.

He knows they will. It might be hard, it might take forever, a roller coaster of ups and downs, but somehow, deep inside, he knows.

They'll get there.

Chapter 12

"I thought all support groups met in stuffy church basements."

Dylan looks at the library in front of him. He thinks it's pretty much the opposite of stuffy, with sleek glass windows, smooth brick walls.

"You've been watching too many movies." Landon takes Dylan's offered hand and hauls himself out of the car. Dylan's hand rests on Landon's back as Landon settles his crutches into the grooves of his palm and finds his balance.

"Hey now, half of them I only watched because you wanted to." Dylan adjusts his bag over his shoulder. Landon pauses and then nods.

"Fair enough."

Dylan feels a little nervous and lets Landon take the lead. Landon looks so comfortable, walking across the parking lot; it's rare to see Landon actually looking confident going into a public space. He looks good, Dylan thinks, having donned clothes other than sweats, with his hair freshly trimmed and a strength in his step that wasn't there before.

"Hey," Dylan says, just as Landon reaches the front door. Landon stops, turns around and tilts his head. A bird chirps a lonely rhythm, and a small family makes their way past them and into the library.

Dylan shoves his hands into his pockets. "Do you want to go on a date, after this?"

"A *date* date?" Landon asks with a smile

"Yeah." Dylan doesn't understand the anxious flutter in his chest that comes from asking his own fiancé out on a date. "A date date."

"That sounds great great." Landon bumps his shoulder against Dylan's.

"Why do I like you?" Dylan asks with a laugh, shaking his head.

"My stellar good looks?"

"That must be it." Dylan nudges back. Landon laughs, his eyes bright and cheeks pink.

"Watch…" Landon starts, the word catching in his throat. His Adam's apple bobs, and Dylan can see him collecting his thoughts, but it doesn't seem to bother him. "Watch yourself."

Dylan smiles and squints up at the sun. "We'll be late."

Landon looks at him, a thoughtful look on his face, and then he turns and hits the button to open the door.

They make their way to a meeting room in the back of the library. It's larger than Dylan expected, with a circle of comfortable-looking chairs surrounding a few brightly-colored coffee tables topped with pitchers of juice and stacks of paper cups.

There are already half a dozen or so people in various chairs, and the light chatter of friendly conversation fills the air.

"Landon!" Dylan turns to see a tiny Asian woman stepping toward them.

"Ruby," Landon greets her, and Dylan knows this must be the woman he talked to on the phone.

"So glad to see you this week," Ruby says. Her smile is wide, her hair is cut into a neat bob around her face. "I hope you've been feeling better?"

Landon nods and she envelops him in a quick hug. "Much better."

"Good." Dylan can tell she really means it. Her attention turns to him, and she raises her eyebrows as she gives him the once-over. "Is this who I think it is?"

"I'm Dylan." Dylan holds out a hand. Ruby takes it in a strong grip and gives it a shake.

"It's so nice to meet you, Dylan." Ruby smiles brightly. "We've heard a lot about you."

She turns to wink at Landon, and his cheeks turn deep pink.

"Should I be nervous?" Dylan asks, returning her smile.

Ruby laughs. "Nonsense." She glances over at the chairs. "Please, have a seat. We'll start soon."

Landon thanks her and they make their way to the chairs. Landon hears, "Welcome back!" from several members of the group, and others wave. Dylan sits on the edge of a chair beside the one Landon chooses and surveys the room. He's not sure what he was expecting, but it all just seems so... normal. As if this is nothing more than a book club gathering or a group of friends catching up on current events.

He can tell that Landon is looking at him, and Landon mouths "Relax" when Dylan glances at him. Dylan tries; he sinks back into the chair, crosses his legs and stares at the dark fabric of his jeans. This seems like the best option. He can feel the curious stares the others are shooting at him, a newcomer amongst friends.

"Shall we get started?" Ruby asks, stepping to a chair near the front of the room and clasping her hands. The room goes quiet and her white teeth shine; Dylan gets the feeling that she's the kind of person who could smile at anything. "Since we have a few new bodies in our midst," she glances at Dylan and a timid girl a few seats away, "how about we start with introductions?"

It goes quickly, and Dylan tries to keep up. Ruby starts first, introducing herself and giving a brief explanation of her brain injury, the result of a car accident fifteen years ago. The dark-skinned boy to her left who looks barely over eighteen is next.

"Andre," he says. "Brain tumor just over a year ago."

Richard. Stroke.

Penny. Severe concussion during a basketball tournament.

Lauren. Two tours in Afghanistan.

August. Hemorrhage and thin blood.

Landon. Hate crime. "This is my fiancé, Dylan."

Dylan. Awkward smile, words that don't make their way past a nervous tongue.

Liam. Go-cart accident.

Katrina. Liam's wife. They hold hands tightly between their chairs.

Emilia. The timid girl. She whispers an explanation about an ex-boyfriend and an accident; her tangled red hair falls into her eyes.

Something about Emilia draws Dylan's attention: the way she hunches into her chair; how her clumsy hands push her hair behind her ears; and the way her eyes flit around the room, never focusing on one thing for long. He looks at her and sees echoes of Landon, Landon just home from the hospital, nervous and tired and struggling, barely scraping by. He thinks of Landon now, sitting tall beside him, talking to people, going places, doing things they never thought he could do again, and wishes he could tell her how much better it can get, even if it seems impossible. He wants to tell her to not squash the tiny flame of hope, that no matter how small it seems right now, someday it will get bigger and brighter and everything else will stay in the shadows.

"Change," Ruby says, and Dylan's attention snaps back to her. "Not so easy to accept sometimes, but an unavoidable part of our lives."

She looks around the room.

"As many of you know, my husband and I are in the process of remodeling our house. And as you might expect, we've run into some issues with our contractor and a few structural problems we didn't realize we had. We've had to change some plans, step back and reevaluate what we really want, and it made me realize how easy it can be to become so set on something that you stop seeing all the other paths out there. You walk the same road through the forest every day, and then one day there's a giant brick wall blocking your way. It can be frightening. But sometimes the brick wall can open our eyes to the other paths around us. To roads less traveled, as it were."

A few chuckles sound around the room.

"I don't think we can ever eliminate the fear these walls give us, but we can learn to accept them. We can learn to accept the obstacles life throws at us, to step into the unknown and forge new paths, to find new ways to do things we've always done a certain way. I think this is something we forget—I know I did during our remodel—and I know we've all had to deal with change in pretty big ways. Since we all deal with change differently, would anyone like to offer any advice or tips on what you do to handle change?"

The group is silent as thoughtful looks cross faces.

"I guess the hardest part for me was all the little things." Lauren is the first one to speak, and Dylan shifts to look at her. With her short dark hair and muscular arms that strain the fabric of her T-shirt, she looks as though she could easily take him down if he were to say the wrong thing. It's only upon a closer look that Dylan can see the trembling of her fingertips. "It wasn't even the big changes, it was the stupid things like forgetting if I washed my hair and using up all my shampoo in a week, or leaving the house and forgetting where I was going and wandering around for hours. It was all that little stuff that reminded me I was different now."

There are a few nods, some murmured words of agreement.

"But I guess I just learned ways to get around the little stuff," Lauren continues. "I would leave the lid open on my shampoo so I would know I washed my hair, and I started writing everything I was doing on sticky notes so I wouldn't forget." She shrugs. "In Afghanistan, we had to learn to adapt to our situations. I just did the same thing here."

Dylan looks over at Landon; his brow is furrowed in that way it gets when he's trying to concentrate, trying to commit things to memory.

"That's a very good point, Lauren," Ruby says, smiling at her. "It's not always the big obstacles that are the hardest. Sometimes the road is blocked by smaller hurdles that are difficult to cross, but not impossible."

Beside him, Landon shifts, his hand slides across the chair arms, palm open. Dylan threads their fingers together.

"I, um," Landon starts. He clears his throat. All eyes turn to him, and from the slightly surprised expressions, Dylan guesses that Landon doesn't speak up very often. "I had to learn to, uh, stop comparing myself to who I was... before. That I can't do the things I used to, and... I would get so *mad* that I couldn't do things, but... but now that I'm learning to accept my lim-limitations, it's easier to deal with things. With change."

Landon's cheeks have turned pink.

"I agree with Landon," says August, whose wheelchair is tucked between Lauren and Landon. "It's easy to get stuck comparing yourself to your old self, instead of finding new ways to adapt to things."

"I think that's something *we* forget to be aware of, also," says Katrina, the only other person in the room without a brain injury. "Spouses and family and friends, we can forget that our loved one might not react to things like they used to, or that they might need to do something differently than they did before. It's easy to see the person we love and expect the same things from before their injury."

Dylan looks down at their clasped hands and thinks of all the times he's said something and expected Landon to react a certain way, all the times Landon has broken down in tears over things that barely used to bother him and the times he remains stoic about things that used to upset him. Dylan thinks about his own expectations, the mixed view he has of the Landon from *before* and the Landon of *now*, the two bleeding together until he's never quite sure of the right thing to say or do, or what it is that Landon actually needs.

And maybe that's the problem, the idea of two separate Landons: a before and an after. Because sitting here in this room, surrounded by others who understand, Dylan just sees *Landon* next to him, the Landon he's always known: skin and sinew and bone, muscles strong enough to carry him through, shaggy hair and long fingers that wrap around Dylan's. This is all and undeniably Landon. A Landon who's had to change, to adapt and do what he has to do in order to get by, but still, irrevocably, the Landon he fell in love with.

Dylan closes his eyes and imagines the giant wall in the road they'd been traveling *before*, and all the smaller walls blocking the winding paths they've had to take since: all the unknowns, the setbacks and jumps forward; the fear and the hope; the hurdles they've jumped over, crawled under, knocked down and defeated since that fateful night in the alley.

He opens his eyes and sees Landon looking at him with concern. "I'm okay," he mouths, his lips pulling into a smile. Ruby is saying something about strength and support systems, but Dylan doesn't pay attention, not yet. Instead he curls their fingers a little tighter and thinks that even the most fractured lives come together again, somehow.

The group goes on for another half-hour, and while Landon doesn't speak again, he listens attentively to everyone, nodding in agreement and encouragement. Emilia doesn't speak either, and Dylan finds himself watching her, wondering what walls and hurdles she's facing and wishing that there was something he could do to help, to lift the weight from her shoulders, if only a little. Just so she can breathe. He hopes she has someone to do that for her.

The group dissolves into laughter when August recounts his encounter with a little girl who saw his chair and thought he was a robot, and even Dylan chuckles at the image. The meeting breaks after that, ending with Ruby's smile and warning that next week's group might involve markers and eighties music.

"Dylan," a voice says when Dylan stands, and he turns to sees Katrina coming toward him. "I'm sorry if this is a little forward of me, but I wanted to say how happy I am to see you here. I know how hard it can be to be in our situation, and I just wanted to let you know, if you ever need to talk to someone, I understand."

She has the gentle smile of someone who talks to people for a living; her clothes are professional and her hair is perfectly straightened. And yet there's a strained look in her eyes that only comes from years of heartache and her face is lined as if she's seen too much too young.

"Thank you," Dylan says. "I appreciate it."

Katrina pulls a small pad of paper from her purse and scribbles down her number. She tears off the sheet and hands it to Dylan.

"It's great to come to these meetings, but I know our experiences are a little different," she says. Dylan thinks she looks sad. Worn. "Please, feel free to call me."

"Thank you again." Dylan carefully places the paper in his pocket. Katrina nods and clutches her purse. Dylan wonders if this was really an act of kindness, or if she just wants someone to talk to. He knows how lonely it can get when no one really understands.

"My husband and I were going to get lunch at the sandwich shop down the street. Would you and Landon care to join?" Katrina asks, and Dylan wants to say yes, they'd love to, but right now he just wants to spend time with his fiancé. Just them.

"We'd love to, really, but we had sort of planned a date. A date date." Dylan looks back to see if Landon picked up on his joke, only to frown when he realizes that Landon is no longer behind him. It only takes Dylan a second to spot him near the doorway, leaning on his crutches and saying something to Emilia. Her hair looks even more tangled from this angle, and she tugs her sweater around her, but Landon makes a wild gesture and Dylan thinks he can see her smiling shyly.

"You're very lucky," Katrina says, and Dylan returns his attention to the woman in front of him. "You're both very lucky."

"We are." Dylan turns back to look at Landon. Landon must sense him watching, because he glances their way and gives Dylan a tiny wave. Emilia's eyes flicker up at him before looking back at the floor, but the hint of a smile stays on her lips.

"Maybe next time?" Dylan suggests, remembering that he's actually having a conversation with someone. "Lunch, I mean."

"I'll hold you to it," Katrina says, and turns back to her husband. Dylan watches her at his side, her hand instinctually moving to his back, supportive and strong. It's nice, Dylan has to admit, knowing there's someone who understands his side of things, who knows what he's going through, who can listen and relate. Someone to remind him that he's not alone.

He touches the number in his pocket, and makes his way across the room to Landon's side.

Regina Spektor plays in the background of the small cupcake shop, the walls are a vibrant teal, and the small tables are a pale shade of lavender. The chair is comfortable, and Landon rests his crutches against the wall and settles into it.

"Tiramisu?" Dylan raises an eyebrow at the cupcake sitting on the porcelain plate in front of Landon. "You know they had a jelly bean cupcake."

"I know," Landon says, swiping a finger through the frosting. "I don't... I don't think I like jelly beans. Anymore."

Dylan looks down at his own cupcake: red velvet, piled high with creamy white frosting.

"What?"

"Nothing," Dylan says, looking back up at Landon, his eyebrows drawn together in concern. "Things are just different now."

"They are," Landon says slowly, thoughtfully. "But that's not always a bad thing, is it?"

Dylan is silent, running a finger over a chip in table.

"No, I suppose it's not."

Landon smiles, holds his fork between delicate fingers, breaks off a portion of the cupcake and takes a careful bite. He's getting so much better, Dylan notes: his movements are increasingly steady, his hands sure, his grip strong. It's amazing, he thinks, how far his fiancé has come since his days in a hospital bed, barely able to say his own name.

"So..." Landon licks a remnant of frosting from his lip. "What should we, uh... we talk about on our date date?"

Dylan takes a bite of his cupcake, the rich red velvet melting in his mouth. His eyes flutter closed, and he can't help the moan that escapes him; then his eyes snap open in embarrassment.

Landon is staring at his lips but quickly looks away, a blush rising in his cheeks.

"What did you say to Emilia?" Dylan asks, trying to turn the attention away from his indecent display. "Back at the support group."

"Oh, I, um, just wanted to tell her that group can be… scary at first, but," Landon pauses, face creasing as he tries to find the right words, "but I hope she comes back."

"That was very considerate of you."

Landon gives a sad smile. "Thanks." There's more to what Landon said, to what he's feeling and thinking now, but Dylan doesn't want to push; he knows there are some things Landon's not ready to share, some things that are just for him.

They eat their cupcakes in silence, watching the occasional customer bustle in and out of the bakery, listening to the sounds of employees laughing in the kitchen.

"Why won't you have sex with me?" The words are sudden, unexpected. Dylan blinks in surprise, his cupcake forgotten. Landon isn't looking at him, but staring down at the napkin he's quickly working on shredding instead.

"What?" Dylan hopes that somehow he misheard.

"Why won't you have sex with me?" Landon repeats, the words still soft, but distinctly enunciated.

"I…" Dylan glances over at the elderly couple eating their own pastries a few tables away and a mother with her daughter at the counter. "Why are you asking this here?"

Why are you asking this at all?

Landon looks up at him, an almost despondent look on his face.

"Why does it matter where we are?"

"Lan—" Dylan starts, lowers his voice. "We're in public. Let's talk about this at home."

Landon sits back in his chair, crossing his arms over his chest. "Are you ashamed?"

"What? No!" Dylan says, mind whirling with this sudden change in Landon's demeanor. He knows Landon's prone to outbursts now, his moods can change as quickly as the Minnesota weather, he's been living through it for almost an entire year, but he wasn't expecting *this*. Not when things were going so well today.

"This just isn't the appropriate place for this conversation." Dylan nods toward the elderly couple.

"Since when have we cared what others thought?" Landon challenges.

Dylan feels something rising in him, hot and angry and so close to snapping. "Since we were attacked for it," Dylan says, louder than he intends. The elderly couple looks over at them, frowning. "Since we were cornered and beaten until you nearly *died*, just for being ourselves."

Landon's face grows hard; the muscles in his face shift as he clenches his jaw.

"Landon, please. Not here."

Why doesn't Landon understand? The world isn't safe anymore, not for people like them. Others are okay with them existing, but only in theory, and the moment there's any physical evidence, it's over. And maybe next time it will be over for real. For good. And though logically Dylan knows that they're probably safe here, that nothing bad is going to happen in the corner of a cupcake shop, it doesn't stop the panic from crawling back in, sinking its claws back into where it's found a home for so long. "Please. Let's just go home."

Landon looks at the table, picks up the napkin and resumes its destruction, this time angrily.

"Do you not..." he starts, and despite the fire in his eyes, his voice sounds defeated. "Do you still want to marry me?"

Dylan gapes, sure he looks like a fish out of water. The idea of him no longer wanting to marry Landon is so completely ridiculous that he can't fathom why Landon would say such a thing. The sting starts, once the words take hold, burning like alcohol over a wound—how could Landon think that after all this, after *everything*, Dylan would just walk away, would call everything off?

"What are you even saying?" Dylan swipes a hand through his hair in frustration and tries to gather his thoughts. "Of course I want to marry you."

"Then tell me why." Landon looks straight into Dylan's eyes. "Why we haven't had sex since *before*. Am I not..." The words catch in his throat, frustration flashes across his face and he crumples the napkin in his palm.

"Landon, *please*. At home."

"Fine." Landon throws his napkin back on the table, and Dylan can't help but think this whole thing seems... off, so unlike Landon, even now.

"Landon..." Dylan rests a hand over Landon's clenched fist, the knot of anxiety pulling tighter. "Is everything okay?"

"Let's just go." Landon reaches for his crutches. "I just... have a headache."

"Do you need your migraine stuff?" Dylan asks, already reaching for it, but Landon shakes his head, the annoyance on his face replaced by a wince of discomfort as he pushes to his feet.

"You wanted to go," Landon says, more softly than Dylan expects him to; his face grows paler the longer he stands there. Dylan leaves the half-eaten cupcakes on their plates, murmurs a soft "All right," and starts toward the exit. He can hear Landon's footsteps behind him until they stop, halfway across the shop.

"Dylan…" The name is uttered too quietly, and Dylan spins around to see Landon, his skin ashy and shining with a film of sweat, crutches trembling in his grip. His eyes are unfocused, pupils too dilated, and Dylan can't move fast enough: Landon's body is turning to liquid, a tidal wave crashing to the floor.

Dylan is by his side before he realizes he's moving, a steady stream of "No, no, no," escaping his lips. There's a cut on Landon's temple, and Dylan is pretty sure he smacked his head on a chair on his way down. Panic rises so hot inside of him, he's sure he's going to be sick. But he holds it together—he has to, as people rush to his side: the employee working the counter, another from the kitchen, a young woman who was browsing cupcakes.

"What happened?"

"Is he okay?"

"Should I call an ambulance?"

Too many questions asked too quickly and Dylan tunes them out. He rests a hand on Landon's shoulder, the other automatically reaching to feel the pulse in Landon's wrist. It's there, slow but steady, and Dylan lets out a breath he didn't realize he was holding.

"Landon?" He reaches to touch Landon's cheek, the skin clammy under his fingers. Landon's eyes slip halfway open at the touch; a stuttered groan rises in his throat.

"We should put him in the recovery position," the employee from the desk says, and Dylan can only nod. He lets her help roll Landon onto his side, shrugs off his jacket and bundles it into a makeshift pillow. Landon blinks, but his eyes are weighted, heavy.

"You're okay." Dylan uses the sleeve of his shirt to wipe the blood from Landon's temple. "You're going to be okay."

He's not sure whom he's trying to convince.

Landon shifts, grimacing in discomfort, and Dylan runs a soothing hand along his arm.

"What happened?" one of the bystanders asks, and Dylan doesn't know how to answer. The whole scene has played out like one of his nightmares, and he has no idea *why*, Landon was fine, happy and laughing just a few hours ago, and now…

All Dylan can do is shake his head, think of the paths through the forest and wonder when the brick wall became so high. When did the demon start clutching at him once more, claws shredding everything he has left?

"An ambulance is on its way," the employee says, kneeling beside them. She has blue in her hair and a kind look on her face, and she makes Dylan think of Janessa's attitude and the way she always knows how to help, how to make them feel better. He wishes she were here now, wishes anyone were here who could take over and help Landon while Dylan fights the panic threatening to take over.

"Don't…" Landon murmurs. He tries to push himself up with weak arms, but Dylan stops him. "'M okay."

No one believes it, not with the way he can barely keep his eyes open and the sickly hue to his skin.

"Rest." Dylan blots the cut on Landon's face once more, and this time Landon flinches, his breath catching. "I'm sorry."

I'm sorry this is happening to you. I'm sorry this is all my fault. I'm sorry I'm not good enough to help you. I'm sorry.

Landon's hand lifts, his fingers climbing until they find Dylan's, and Dylan automatically curls them together and holds on as tightly as he can.

And then, like a fast-forwarded movie, noise and activity bursts around them. Paramedics arrive in starched blue uniforms and Dylan is being pushed aside, questions thrown at him too quickly while Landon is pulled away to have his vitals taken and lights shined in his eyes. It takes a moment for Dylan's brain to catch up with the situation; a dazed feeling washes over him, rooting him to the spot, before he realizes he needs to give the paramedics information so they can help Landon.

He's my fiancé.

He fell and hit his head.

No, that's not normal.

He has a traumatic brain injury.

Yes, he takes medication.

No, I don't know.

I don't know.

I don't know.

And then they're moving. An oxygen mask covers Landon's face, and he's on the gurney and being loaded into the ambulance. His eyes flutter open and closed, searching for something, for someone.

"I'll be there," Dylan says, the words sounding weak even to him, and he hopes Landon can hear them. The paramedics tell him where they're going and then the doors close and they're gone, leaving Dylan in dust and defeat.

CHAPTER 13

The couch is unforgiving, the cushions lumpy under his back, *his legs bent in order to fit. Dylan shifts, pulls the comforter back over his shoulders and readjusts the pillow under his head. He pictures Landon alone in the bedroom, and wonders if he's still mad. He could go in, could whisper apologies, could shower Landon with kisses and try and make everything right again. But he's not sure Landon would want to hear it, and he's not sure he deserves it right now. Landon will forgive him when he's ready.*

Dylan forces his eyes to stay shut and tries to find a comfortable position. He dozes, drops in and out of sleep. The milky light from the moon slips across the floor as the night drags on. The couch dips next to him, startling him out of the light sleep he'd managed, and Dylan blinks open blurry eyes to see Landon beside him.

"Scoot over." Landon's voice is rough, and there are dark shadows under his eyes. Dylan pushes himself into the back of the couch until Landon can crawl in beside him, his back pressed flush with Dylan's chest, and drag the blankets up around them.

271

"Couldn't sleep," Landon says once they're situated, his fingers finding Dylan's, pulling Dylan's arm around him.

"Me either."

"Fighting is the worst. Let's not do this again." Landon squeezes Dylan's fingers, and Dylan bites his lip and feels the traitorous prick of tears.

"Lan… I'm sorry." Landon is still. "I should have asked you before I accepted. I wasn't—I just wasn't thinking."

Landon kisses Dylan's knuckles.

"I'm not mad. I thought I was, but I think I'm more disappointed that you would make such a big decision without me. And that I'm not going to see my fiancé for six weeks."

"I'm so sorry." Dylan's voice cracks and he squeezes his eyes shut, embarrassed and frustrated with himself.

"Hey." Landon shifts, the couch bouncing, and then there's a gentle touch to his cheek and Dylan opens his eyes to see Landon looking back at him. "It's okay."

"I keep screwing up."

"And what… I don't?" Landon laughs and kisses him gently. "We're both figuring this out. We're bound to screw up sometimes. It would be weird if we didn't."

"You're right," Dylan says with a sigh, bringing a hand up to wipe away a shameful tear. "Since when did you become a wise old man?"

Landon shoves him playfully. "Better watch yourself, or this couch is going to be your friend."

Dylan laughs, the knot in his stomach unraveling.

"It's not so bad. Only a few lumps."

Landon makes a face and wiggles closer to Dylan.

"A night out here and my back would agree with your wise old man comment."

Landon pushes himself into a sitting position and tugs Dylan up by his hand; the blanket slips onto the floor.

"Just promise to include me in big decisions in the future?"

Dylan gives a sharp nod. "I promise."

Landon smiles and leans in for another kiss, and this one lingers. "Come to bed?"

"Okay." Dylan lets Landon guide him into the bedroom.

The chair is hard, and one of its legs is shorter than the others, causing it to tip with the slightest movement. Dylan gives up sitting and paces around the waiting room, feeling as though he's about to explode with every step. Combust. Burst into flames. Something dramatic and deadly will happen, something that will take him away from here, from the waiting that never ends, from the creature that gnaws on his exposed nerves, wrapping its tail around his lungs and squeezing.

He calls his mom.

His hands shake and he almost drops the phone, has to lean against the wall to steady himself.

"Dylan?" Adele's voice is honey through the phone, warm and calm.

"Mom." He kicks a small table, and a glossy magazine with creased pages slips to the ground.

"What's going on?"

"I can't fucking do this again." Tears build in his eyes, but he doesn't let them fall. Instead he looks up at the tiled ceiling and sucks in a breath. "I can't…"

273

The waiting room mocks him. He moves to the hall.

"Dylan, what happened?" His mother has moved past her worried voice into the one that demands answers, that doesn't allow for wasted time.

"Landon fainted." Dylan is almost surprised at how easily the words come out. "At the cupcake shop. He hit his head and someone called an ambulance and now he's getting an MRI and I'm stuck in this stupid waiting room, and… I can't do this. Not again."

It rises up, hot acid burning through his veins: pure, unadulterated panic.

Somehow he ends up on the floor with his head between his knees. Adele's voice is a distant echo on the phone.

"Dylan, honey. You need to stop and breathe."

I'm trying. Every breath burns, makes his lungs ache, but he tries. In and out. In and out.

"This isn't last time," Adele says, once Dylan has started breathing in something resembling a normal rhythm. "Okay? Landon's going to be okay. He hit his head and they're just doing the tests they need to do. It's not like last time."

Someone in pale green scrubs walks by, glancing down at him before hurrying on. Dylan lets his head fall back against the wall.

"I couldn't do anything," Dylan says, after a moment. "He fell and I just… I froze. I didn't know what to do."

"But he got help. He's getting help right now, you did nothing wrong."

"I feel…" Dylan rubs a hand painfully into his eyes. "I feel like I keep failing him."

"Sweetheart," Adele says softly. "You've both been through so much, no one blames you for being lost sometimes. You've done so much for Landon, you've been with him through all of this. You are not failing him."

Knowing there is nothing either of them could say that will erase the ache inside him, Dylan doesn't respond.

"I can be there in half an hour," Adele says, after the silence stretches on just a moment too long.

"No." Dylan shakes his head. "You don't have to come. I... I'll call you when I get to see him. I can do this."

"Okay. But call as soon as you can, okay? And if you need me, I can be there right away."

"Thank you." Dylan lets the phone fall into his lap. He sits in silence for a moment before he stands, brushes the lint from his pants and makes his way back into the waiting room. He feels jittery, as if a thousand bees are buzzing under his skin, and he walks circles around the room with the phone clutched in his hand, eyes darting toward the door every few seconds, waiting for someone, anyone to come in with good news and an assurance that everything is going to be okay.

Fifteen minutes pass. Twenty.

A nurse steps into the room, and Dylan is by her side in an instant, sure he looks desperate.

"Landon's done with his MRI," she says, a gentle smile on her face. "We've admitted him for observation, just for the night. I can take you to his room."

"Please." Dylan tries not to sound too eager. The nurse motions for him to follow and leads him down a hall of the general medicine floor to a tiny room near the end of the unit.

Landon is sleeping under a pile of thin hospital blankets. There are dark shadows under his eyes and a bruise on his jaw from where he hit the floor. The nurse assures Dylan that the doctor will be in soon, as soon as they've had time to review the results of the MRI; but Landon will probably sleep for a while after his stressful day. Dylan thanks her, drags a chair to the side of Landon's bed and tries to ignore how familiar this feels. A painful lump forms in his throat when he spots two small stitches in the cut on Landon's temple, and the IV threaded into the back of his hand. But his face is relaxed, his lips are parted, and Dylan smiles; Landon has always denied that he sleeps with his mouth open, but Dylan thinks it's cute, endearing.

He waits. It seems he's spent the past year waiting: waiting for doctors, for therapists, for good news and bad news. Waiting for their lives to piece themselves back together.

The door creaks as it opens, and a doctor with short dark hair and a stethoscope around her neck steps inside.

"You must be Landon's fiancé," the doctor says with a smile, crossing the room to shake Dylan's hand. "I'm Doctor Matera."

Dylan finds himself relaxing; something in the doctor's demeanor puts him at ease. *Doctors don't smile like that if there's something wrong.*

"How is he?"

"As you know, we did an MRI, due to Landon's history of a brain injury, and it did show a minor concussion from the fall. Normally this is something someone could recover from with a little rest, but because of Landon's history, we'd like to keep him overnight, just to keep an eye on him."

"Why did he faint?" Dylan looks at Landon and remembers the fear he felt watching Landon collapse to the floor.

"It's hard to say, exactly. His labs indicate some mild dehydration, and he came in with low blood pressure; it could have been a combination of those factors. We'll be giving him some

IV fluids overnight, and provided everything goes well, I think you should be okay to go home tomorrow."

Dylan nods.

"I understand Landon's made a pretty spectacular recovery from his brain injury." Dr. Matera says softly. Dylan lets himself smile.

"Yeah, he's been amazing."

"Landon is very strong. The concussion might set him back a little, but I have a feeling he's going to do just fine."

"Thank you." Dylan says.

She leaves with the assurance that she'll be back in the morning, and tells Dylan to let the nursing staff know if there's anything they need.

Then they're alone again, and Dylan kisses Landon's cheek, mutters "I'm sorry" and tries not to cry.

There's an ache in his back and a crick in his neck when he wakes, and it takes a moment for Dylan to remember why he fell asleep in a chair. Then he sees the ugly tan walls, the IV pole and the starched hospital blankets.

He looks up and hazel eyes meet his, tired but aware.

"Hey," Dylan says softly, resting a hand on Landon's arm. "How do you feel?"

Landon wets his lips before speaking. "Like I have a hangover." The words are rough and slightly slurred, and Dylan scrunches his face in concern.

"I can imagine," he says, brushing a strand of hair from Landon's forehead. "Do you need any pain medicine?"

Landon shakes his head, squeezes his eyes shut.

"I…" he starts, and clears his throat. "I'm sorry."

"About what?"

"For yelling at you." Landon opens his eyes and catches Dylan's gaze. "I knew you were uncomfortable, and I… I kept going."

"It's okay," Dylan says. He bites his lip in thought. "I'm not ashamed of you, you know that, right?"

Landon smiles, his head falling back against the pillows.

"I know."

"Good." Dylan holds Landon's hand, runs a thumb over his knuckles.

"So…" Landon picks at a small hole in the blanket with his other hand. "Square one, huh?"

Dylan thinks back to the last time Landon was in the hospital and then when he came home—how lost they felt, how unsure everything was, hope only a tiny flicker in a guarded heart.

"No." The claws inside him release for the first time since Landon fell. "Not square one."

Landon looks at him with curiosity.

"We've got to be at least at square twenty by now."

"Square twenty-seven," Landon offers with a twitching smile.

"Definitely twenty-seven," Dylan says seriously. "And you know what twenty-eight is?"

Landon raises an eyebrow in question.

"Sex." Dylan lowers his voice and takes an exaggerated look around the room, as if checking that they're alone. "Lots of sex."

A laugh bursts out of Landon, his eyes crinkling at the corners.

"I love you."

Dylan tips forward in the chair and leans over the bed to gently kiss Landon's lips.

"I love you, too."

* * *

They let Landon go home early the next afternoon, with a handful of mild painkillers and instructions to take it easy. The ride is mostly silent, with Landon staring out the window, lost in a buzz of pain meds and his own thoughts. He's not sure why, but he has the unshakable feeling that everything is about to change. Something is different, and things can't go on the way they have been, not after this.

But maybe that's not such a bad thing. Maybe change is okay. Maybe the path they have to take is different from anything they expected, always changing, and maybe they'll never know exactly where they're going to end up. If there's one thing Landon has learned, it's that everything can change in the blink of an eye, in the span of seconds, in a measured breath. For so long he's resisted, fought back and lashed out and pushed away, but despite the anger and frustration, he's still *here*, still stuck in this body he doesn't understand, in this life with choices always just out of his reach.

He's not sure what they put in these pain meds, but for the first time, Landon feels free, almost normal, like he's just Landon again: Landon, who is getting married; Landon, who works with kids; Landon, who loves candy so sweet it burns his tongue; Landon, who can't sing but does anyway, who loves his fiancé and won't stop asking for a dog, even though he knows Dylan is a cat person at heart.

Landon, whose heart still beats just as it always has.

He's beginning to realize that he's not just defined by what's happened to him in the past, but by who he is now, by what he does in the future and by the choices he still has to make. A new door has opened, leading to choices and futures and experiences he has yet to live, and it's exhilarating.

The world didn't stop because of some hateful idiots; it just paused and waited for him to catch up again. These last few months, he's never really considered the future in a broad sense. Day by day, week by week, he's been trying to scrape by. Go to therapy, make it through this migraine, navigate a schedule of medications and appointments and survive long, drawn-out hours. There have been frustrations that never leave him alone, a desperate clinging to the past, a refusal to let go, and recently he's been so focused on the present that the idea of a future has just been unfathomable.

But now, despite the concussion, the throb in his head and the aches from his fall, Landon feels the weight of his injury lessen and the iron grip of a stagnant life leave him. He's not Landon the Victim, or Landon the Brain Injury. He's just Landon, with a past full of good and bad, highs and lows, and a future so vast and inviting it makes his toes curl with excitement. Because more than anything, he wants to *live*, to navigate the future that was almost taken away from him, to discover everything the world has to offer with Dylan by his side, hand in hand. He's made it through, despite the impossible odds, despite the world trying to crush him into nothing more than a memory, and he's determined not to waste it. Not anymore.

He looks over at Dylan, at the way his long fingers grip the steering wheel, at his dark hair unruly from sleeping in a hospital chair, at his eyes shadowed with exhaustion.

"You okay?" Dylan asks when he notices Landon's gaze, glancing away from the road to look at him with concern.

"I'm fine." Landon rests his hand on the middle console, and Dylan takes it without hesitation. "It's going to be okay, you know."

Dylan's knuckles tighten on the steering wheel, and the hand in Landon's twitches.

"We'll get there," Dylan agrees, and although Landon can tell the hope in his eyes is cautious, at least it's there. They pull into the driveway. Dylan shifts into park and pauses before turning off the engine.

"It's not..." He bites his lip and avoids Landon's eyes. "It's not that I don't want to have sex with you. I've just... I've been so scared of doing the right thing or the wrong thing, and I didn't want to push you into anything. I didn't know what you were ready for, or what *I* was ready for, and I should have talked to you, I know I should have, but..." Dylan shrugs, eyes still downcast. "I was scared."

Landon looks out the window at their house, at the oak tree in the front yard, and the ugly lawn ornament Lana got them, knowing they'd be too nice to take it down.

"I shouldn't have yelled at you." Landon glances over at Dylan and finds him looking back. "At the cupcake shop. I shouldn't have gotten mad. I'm sorry."

"It's okay," Dylan says, and Landon believes him. "We'll work on it together."

Landon nods, and Dylan leans across the console to press a quick kiss to Landon's cheek. Landon is still wrestling with his seat belt when Dylan opens the passenger door.

"I, uh..." Embarrassment creeps into Landon's cheeks. "The chair?"

"Screw the chair," Dylan says. He leans down and slides one arm under Landon's knees and one across his back before lifting him out of the car with a groan, bridal style. Landon laughs and instantly wraps his arms around Dylan's neck, clinging to him as Dylan carries him inside.

"This might be my favorite mode of transportation," Landon says, as Dylan lowers him gently onto their bed.

"I need to start lifting weights." Dylan flops onto the bed. Landon gives him a playful slap on the shoulder before rolling over and nestling into his pillows with a sigh.

"You know, I managed to hold off the masses for today, but tomorrow everyone wants to come see you." Dylan runs a finger across Landon's arm.

"Lots of time for sleep between then and now," Landon mumbles into the pillow, but something about those words make him feel warm, like a crackling fireplace on a cold winter night. They aren't doing this alone; they have their parents, and Lana, Janessa, Tate, even Logan, to help them and support them, to walk with them through the forest, offering backup and encouragement, even if they take the wrong path or meet a wall too high to scale.

"They didn't win." Landon rolls over to look at Dylan beside him. "We did."

Dylan reaches for Landon's hand. "We did."

No matter how much hate is in the world, no matter how many people want to bring them down, they will triumph as long as they still have each other.

"Thanks for still wanting to marry me." Landon tangles their fingers together.

"Thanks for putting up with me." Dylan squeezes back.

"Anytime," Landon says, already feeling sleep pull at his eyes.

He feels Dylan's lips on his own, the kiss soft and lingering.

And they sleep, hand in hand, side by side.

Together.

Epilogue

"Come on, we're going to be late."

"It's my own birthday party," Landon protests, sitting at the bench to slip on his shoes. "Doesn't it start when *I* arrive?"

"Try explaining that to Lana and Janessa." Dylan holds his hand out to Landon and tugs him back to his feet. "They've been slaving over this party."

"Valid point," Landon gives in with a nod, and allows Dylan to lead him out to the car. A giddy feeling rises in his stomach, a flutter of butterflies; his blood feels carbonated. "Isn't this supposed to be a surprise party?"

Dylan slides into the driver's seat with a sheepish look on his face. "Yes, so if you value my life at all, please act surprised."

Landon laughs. "I can be a great, um… a great actor."

Dylan looks at Landon with a smile. "Well, you definitely put on a great performance last night."

His cheeks growing hot, Landon slaps Dylan's shoulder, and Dylan bursts out laughing.

"A one-time performance, if you keep that up."

Dylan pouts. "What if I promise I have something special planned for you tonight?"

"Hmmm…" Landon puts a finger to his chin, pretending to consider. "You may be able to sway me."

"Good." Dylan winks. He stops at a red light. Landon lets his head fall back against the headrest.

"You know what my favorite birthday was?"

"Please don't say the food fight." Dylan wrinkles his nose and Landon laughs.

"How did you know?"

"Because you bring it up every birthday."

"Admit it, it was fun."

"It was messy."

Landon can't argue with that, even though he knows Dylan only pretends to protest.

"I suppose you're right," Landon gives in.

"I'm always right."

Landon delivers another slap to Dylan's arm, and Dylan protests, "Hey, I'm driving!" Landon smiles the rest of the way to Lana's apartment.

He acts sufficiently surprised at the balloons and streamers and accepts embraces from his mom and dad, from Adele and Sam, Lana, Janessa and Tate.

"Happy Birthday, little big bro," Lana says, patting his head. Landon brushes her away just in time to see Janessa take Tate's hand, whose cheeks are bright red as he flashes Landon a thumbs-up.

"What's this no-crutches business, you stud?" Janessa asks, dragging Tate across the room with her.

"Been practicing," Landon shrugs, as if it's no big deal, as if he hasn't put in hours of practice, as if he doesn't have the carpet-burned knees to prove it.

"Gotta learn to jive for the wedding, right?" Lana asks, nudging Landon in the ribs with her elbow. He almost loses his balance, grabs onto a chair for support and glares at her. "Sorry," she mouths, gives a chaste kiss to his cheek.

"Actually, speaking of weddings—" Dylan starts, but he's cut off by the door swinging open with a loud bang and Logan bursting through. His face is red and his chest is heaving, and he's holding a large duffle bag that he sets gently onto the floor.

"I'm sorry I'm late," Logan pants, wiping his brow. Landon can feel his mind go blank, his surprise at seeing Logan squashing any thoughts he might have had. And then he's wrapped in Logan's arms, a disbelieving laugh making its way loose.

"Logan… what…?"

Logan releases him, and Landon is surprised to note Logan's haircut: it's too short to be pulled back into a ponytail now.

"You didn't think I'd miss your birthday party, did you?"

Landon glances at Dylan, who is kneeling next to the duffle bag, and he can swear he sees the bag move.

"Well, yeah, actually." He hasn't seen Logan since Christmas, when they flew out to New York for a week-long getaway.

"I'm offended, brother." Logan puts his hand to his chest, and Landon is about to respond when a noise captures his attention, causing his head to swivel toward the duffle bag.

"Did that just… bark?" Landon asks, taking a step away from Logan. Dylan looks up from the bag, a wide smile on his face, and Landon's heart starts to slam against his ribcage.

"Why don't you open it?" Lana says from behind him. Landon kneels beside Dylan, hesitating for a moment as he reaches for the bag until Dylan nudges him forward. His hands are shaking, and it takes him two tries to grab the zipper, which is only partly closed. Something inside the bag nudges the fabric, hitting his legs.

"Oh my God." The words slip from his mouth in a shaky breath, emotions building inside him like a whirlwind as the flap of the bag falls open and a little golden head sticks out. "Oh my God."

The puppy blinks against the brightness of the room, its tongue lolling out of its mouth as it looks around.

"Landon, meet your fur baby," Dylan says, reaching to lift the puppy out of the bag when Landon stays frozen. A cry-laugh sound escapes Landon when the puppy is set on his lap and it sniffs Landon's shirt, its tail wagging excitedly.

"Fur baby," Landon repeats, running a hand through the puppy's soft fur.

"She's a golden retriever, about four months old, we think," Dylan explains, reaching forward to scratch behind her ears. She licks his hand. "Someone found a litter abandoned in their backyard and brought them to the shelter."

Landon stares at Dylan for a moment, still working to understand what's happening. The puppy's paws are too big, and she trips over herself trying to jump from Landon's lap, falling and rolling onto her back.

"Landon?" Dylan voice is tinged with worry. "Is this okay?"

"Oh my God," Landon whispers, beginning to sound like a broken record. "You…"

The puppy wiggles on her back, jumps back onto her feet and slobbers on Landon's hand. Landon's eyes blur with tears, and he's not sure he has any control of his emotions right now.

"You got me a dog?"

Dylan nods, a cautious smile on his face, and reaches forward to wipe a tear from Landon's cheek.

"I know how much you've wanted one, and I thought… maybe she could help you? Help both of us." Dylan shrugs nervously. "Besides, she's really cute."

Landon laughs and kisses Dylan with more force than he meant, nearly knocking him backwards.

"I take it you're happy then?"

Behind them someone cheers, another person claps and Landon hears the sound of someone sniffing and blowing her nose.

"Very." Landon's voice is still soft with disbelief, and he feels a tug on the hem of his pants; the puppy is pulling at him playfully. "Does she have a name?"

"Whatever you want to name her," Dylan responds, a hand resting on Landon's back as he picks up the puppy once more. Landon considers the puppy, her wide brown eyes, her white-gold fur and her short tail, that keeps wagging frantically.

"Jelly Bean," he announces after a moment, the puppy cocking her head to look at him curiously.

Dylan laughs. "Jelly Bean. I like it."

Landon looks over at Dylan with a soft smile on his face. Janessa kneels beside them and scratches the puppy under her chin.

"Hey, little Beanie."

Jelly Bean licks her hand before the sound of Adele in the kitchen draws her attention and she pads across the apartment, tripping once on her too-large feet.

"So what do you say," Janessa says, bumping her shoulder against Landon's. "Best birthday ever?"

"I don't know..." Landon starts, winking at Dylan, who shoves his shoulder playfully. "Definitely."

The rest of the evening is filled with food and cake. Logan regales everyone with stories of Jay-Jay in New York while playing with Jelly Bean with a toy made from one of Lana's old socks. Landon stays beside Dylan. He can feel the warm press of his engagement ring.

"What was it you were saying about a wedding earlier?" Helen cuts in, when the sun has dipped low and Lana has illuminated her apartment with string lights and candles.

"Oh." Dylan tightens his grip on Landon's and pulls his gaze from where Jelly Bean has curled up under the coffee table, clearly exhausted from all the attention. "We decided to set a date. Next July. The twenty-fourth."

They share a look amid the congratulations and excitement, and Dylan leans forward to press a deep kiss on Landon's lips.

"That's the day—" Helen starts, and Landon nods, digging his thumb into the couch cushion beside his leg.

"We want to take it back." He looks back up, imploring them all to understand, to not question their choice. "Turn it into something good."

Lana smiles at them, bends forward from where she's sitting cross-legged on the floor and squeezes Landon's knee.

"I think that's great."

"Thank you," Dylan whispers, placing a hand on top of hers. A lump forms in Landon's throat, the emotions of the day piling on, somehow both heavy and happy, and Dylan must sense it because he pulls Landon to his feet, yawns dramatically and insists they head back. The next few minutes are filled with more hugs, kisses on cheeks, a few wayward tears. Jelly Bean wakes up with the noise and starts sniffing around on the carpet as if on a very important mission.

Landon slips on his coat and shoes and is waiting by the door as Dylan fishes out his keys, accepting the dog leash pressed into his hand, when Lana's voice sounds from the back of the living room.

"Landon… your dog just peed on my carpet."

And he can't help it, more laughter shakes loose. Amid a flurry of people with paper towels and cleaning supplies, with an ashamed-looking puppy pressed into his arms, he realizes.

He's truly lucky.

Acknowledgments

First I want to thank the entire team at Interlude Press: Annie, Lex, Candy, Becky and everyone else who contributed to making my dream come true. You believed in me and this story and gave me the opportunity to achieve something I never thought possible, and for that I will forever be grateful. Thank you to CB for her amazing artwork. I feel so honored to have her beautiful art on the cover of my book.

A huge thank you to Sandy Hall, who has been there for me since the original version of this story was just a baby. You've encouraged me, provided me with so many writing resources and dealt with my excessive use of commas.

Courtney Lux, my fellow IP author and late night texter. Thank you for providing valuable information from your grad school studies, and keeping me sane with promises of future wine and balcony writing dates.

Thank you to Chelsea Wilson for the hours upon hours we've spent writing together and keeping many coffee shops in business. One day, I will start a story with "three men burst in guns blazing."

Of course, to Mary, my amazing mother, who has always encouraged me to follow my passion, no matter how crazy it might seem. You've instilled in me a love and appreciation of literature and art, and I wouldn't be who I was today without you.

To fandom, and everyone who has encouraged me in the wild world that is the Internet. This story wouldn't even exist without all of you, and I am hugely grateful to every single person who has read my stories and encouraged me to write more. You guys rock.

And last, but certainly not least, to Caroline. You are my light. Thank you.

About the Author

Becca Burton penned her first Nancy Drew fan fiction at the age of nine and has been an avid writer ever since. Currently working as a NICU (Neonatal Intensive Care) nurse, Becca is a recent Oregon transplant from the Midwest. Becca has a weakness for coffee, the smell of old books, rainy days and her cat, Luna. *Something Like a Love Song* is her first novel.

Questions for Discussion

1. There were many things that could have prevented the boys from being beaten that night. What things could have changed to eliminate the attack before it began?

2. The idea of culpability comes up over and over in the story. Who or what do you believe was really at fault for the attack on Landon and Dylan?

3. Landon and Dylan's attackers were never brought to justice. How would it have made a difference to the story if they had been?

4. Both Landon and Dylan had to grieve what was lost in the attack. How did they each mourn in different ways?

5. Nietszche said "What does not kill me makes me stronger." How does this maxim apply to Landon and Dylan's experience?

6. There were places in the story where Dylan was overwhelmed and ready to give up. What kept him going? Where was the turning point for him, beyond which he knew he could be what Landon needed him to be?

7. Was Landon's parents' divorce related to his injuries? Why or why not?

8. Why was Dylan so hesitant to seek help when he was experiencing such significant flashbacks and signs of anxiety/PTSD?

9. How is Landon and Dylan's relationship with each other changed by going through this experience together?

10. It has been said that "It takes a village to raise a child." In this book, it took a village to help Landon and Dylan heal. Describe the role each of the people in their lives had in helping the men heal and move on from their traumatic experience.

11. What do you think will happen next in Landon and Dylan's story? What does their future look like?

—AC HOLLOWAY

Also from interlude press™

Sweet by Alysia Constantine

Alone and lonely since the death of his partner, a West Village pastry chef gradually reclaims his life through an unconventional courtship with an unfulfilled accountant that involves magical food, online flirtation, and a dog named Andy. *Sweet* is also the story of how we tell love stories. The narrator is on to you, Reader, and wants to give you a love story that doesn't always fit the bill.

ISBN 978-1-941530-61-0 | Coming Feb 1016

Bitter Springs by Laura Stone

In 1870s Texas, Renaldo Valle Santos, the youngest son of a large and traditional family, has been sent to train with Henry "Hank" Burnett, a freed slave and talented mesteñero—or horse-catcher—so he may continue the family horse trade. *Bitter Springs* is a sweeping epic that takes themes from traditional Mexican literature and Old Westerns to tell the story of a man coming into his own and realizing his destiny lies in the wild open spaces with the man who loves him, far from expectations of society.

ISBN 978-1-941530-55-9

One **story** can change **everything**.
www.interlude**press**.com

Now available from

interlude press

™

Right Here Waiting by K.E. Belledonne

In 1942, Ben Williams had it all—a fulfilling job, adoring friends and the love of his life, Pete Montgomery. But World War II looms over them. When Pete follows his conscience and joins the Army Air Force as a bomber pilot, Ben must find the strength to stay behind without his lover, the dedication to stay true and the courage he never knew he'd need to discover his own place in the war effort.

ISBN 978-1-941530-22-1

The Luckiest by Mila McWarren

When memoirist Aaron Wilkinson gathers with his high school friends to marry off two of their own, he must spend a week with Nik, the boy who broke his heart.

As they settle into the Texas beach house for the nuptials, Nik is clear: he wants Aaron back. "He's coming hard, baby," a friend warns, setting the tone for a week of transition where Aaron and Nik must decide if they are playing for keeps.

ISBN 978-1-941530-39-9

Chef's Table by Lynn Charles

Chef Evan Stanford steadily climbed New York City's culinary ladder, but in his rise to the top, he forgot what got him there: the food and life lessons from a loving hometown neighbor. Patrick Sullivan is contented keeping the memory of his grandmother's Irish cooking alive through his work at a Brooklyn diner. But when Chef Stanford walks in for a meal, Patrick is swept up by his drive, forcing him to reconsider if a contented life is a fulfilled one.

ISBN 978-1-941530-17-7

Sotto Voce by Erin Finnegan

Wine critic Thomas Baldwin can make or break careers with his column for Taste Magazine. But when his publisher orders him to spend a year profiling rising stars of California's wine country and organizing a competition between the big name wineries of Napa and the smaller artisan wineries of Sonoma, his world gets turned upside-down by an enigmatic young winemaker who puts art before business.

ISBN 978-1-941530-15-3

One **story** can change **everything**.

www.interlude**press**.com

interlude **press**

One Story Can Change Everything.

interludepress.com

Twitter: @interludepress   * * *   Facebook: Interlude Press
Google+: +interludepress   * * *   Pinterest: interludepress
Instagram: InterludePress